INTRODUCTION
TO INFAMY

The gentleman who came up behind Serena in the garden was deeply in his cups and quite out of control.

His hands went to her hips, and Serena felt his warmth seeping through the thin silk of her gown. The tenor of her response alarmed her, perhaps more than the stranger's touch. She shivered.

"Not 'fraid of me, are you?" he drawled.

"Of course not," she replied contemptuously. "I need to go inside to fetch my shawl. So just let me go, will you."

"Cold, are you? Why did you not say so?" To Serena's dismay, the implacable hands drew her hips tightly into the curve of the stranger's body and settled them there. "That better?" And then, before she had time to absorb the horror of her situation, his mouth had captured hers.

"Still cold?" he asked after a moment. She felt the ripple of his chest muscles against her as his hands moved over her back.

How Serena wished she could say she was.

An Unsuitable Match

by

Patricia Oliver

A SIGNET BOOK

SIGNET
Published by the Penguin Group
Penguin Books USA Inc., 375 Hudson Street,
New York, New York 10014, U.S.A.
Penguin Books Ltd, 27 Wrights Lane,
London W8 5TZ, England
Penguin Books Australia Ltd, Ringwood,
Victoria, Australia
Penguin Books Canada Ltd, 10 Alcorn Avenue,
Toronto, Ontario, Canada M4V 3B2
Penguin Books (N.Z.) Ltd, 182–190 Wairau Road,
Auckland 10, New Zealand

Penguin Books Ltd, Registered Offices:
Harmondsworth, Middlesex, England

First published by Signet, an imprint of Dutton Signet,
a division of Penguin Books USA Inc.

First Printing, March, 1997
10 9 8 7 6 5 4 3 2 1

 REGISTERED TRADEMARK—MARCA REGISTRADA

Printed in the United States of America

PROLOGUE

The Invitation

Yorkshire, August 1816

"Serena!"

The lifting cry floated over the rolling meadow, riding the warm breath of the late summer breeze, and bounced lazily between the sunlit Yorkshire hills in ever-diminishing echoes of the childish voice.

Opening one eye, Serena watched the powdery yellow wings of a butterfly flutter nervously as their owner probed the hidden depths of a golden buttercup six inches from her nose. She sighed deeply, breathing the sun-warmed sweetness of the grass deeply into her lungs and expelling it slowly, loath to break the trancelike communion between her lethargic prone form and the couch of crushed grasses and summer flowers. How she wished she might close her eyes again and slip back into her daydream, denying the intrusion of her sister's call.

"Serena!"

Pressing her ear close to the earth, Serena caught the faint tattoo of racing hooves. Cecily had evidently given poor old Rufus his head in spite of their father's off-repeated instructions to ride sedately rather than race around the neighborhood like hoydens. Her sister was disinclined to pay serious heed to Sir Henry Millbanks's strictures on the proper behavior expected of young ladies of gentle birth, and Serena could not blame her. A vivacious fifteen-year-old chit had little use for ladylike airs and graces when the wild Yorkshire moors lay just beyond the boundary of her father's land, waiting to be explored. Their father thought differently, of course. Ever since Serena had turned sixteen, Sir Henry seemed to grow more repressive with each passing year, causing her to look back nostalgically at that time, seven years ago, when Lady Millbanks was alive and Millbanks Hall had been a place of joy and laughter.

Serena sighed again, glorying in the sensuous pressure of

the warm earth against her knees, her thighs and breasts, and beneath her cheek. She closed her eyes to indulge her fantasies for the few precious moments left before Cecily would shatter her make-believe world with her childish prattle. But the magic was already fading, obliterated by the insistent pounding of the approaching pony's hooves. The music of the imaginary orchestra diminished, and the smile of the fair-haired gentleman who held her snugly in his arms grew fainter as did the touch of his hand on her waist. As the sound of her sister's intrusion grew steadily louder, Serena's daydream evaporated completely, leaving her with a vague sense of longing which she could not name.

Abruptly, she sat up and brushed the dry grass from her hair. She would have to stop reading those deliciously romantical novels in which the most unlikely heroines overcame—with immense suffering and enormous fortitude—a seemingly endless series of impossible obstacles to win the devotion of dark, brooding noblemen with intense black eyes.

Serena laughed out loud. She was being ridiculous again, she thought. She had never—in all her twenty-three years—met a dark brooding nobleman with intense black eyes. And if she did, she thought with a flicker of amusement at her own silliness, he would no doubt prove to be odiously bad-tempered and full of self-consequence. Certainly, Brian Westlock had never smiled at her in just that way. He had never smiled at her at all that she could remember, Serena admitted with uncompromising honesty. And furthermore, Brian was fair—gloriously fair, with eyes the color of larkspurs.

Serena pushed the elusive, unattainable Brian Westlock firmly out of her mind and sat watching her sister, fair pigtails bouncing wildly behind her, race up the incline and pull Rufus to a slithering, puffing halt scant inches from Serena's bare toes.

"So, here you are," Cecily remarked unnecessarily, slipping off her pony and flinging herself down beside her sister.

"As you see," Serena answered dryly. Her eyes swept the damp roan flanks and withers of her sister's pony. "Why are you riding without a saddle again, Cecy?" she demanded. "You know that Papa has forbidden it."

"He has forbidden everything!" Cecily exclaimed petulantly. "Everything that's fun, at any rate. Mama would never have made me sit for hours over that stupid embroidery. Or put up with Mr. Mincewort's lectures on the correct fingering for Scarlatti's sonatinas. I *hate* Scarlatti, and the devil fly away with his sonatinas."

"Cecily!" Serena exclaimed severely, although privately she found the pale, simpering music master's sermons more than sufficient justification for Cecy's outrage. "That is no way for a young lady to speak. And I am quite sure that Mama would have wanted you to be a lady, dear. Papa is right, you know; ladies should learn how to embroider and play the pianoforte—"

"Fiddle!" Cecily stared at her sister accusingly. "Surely you don't believe all that blather, Serena? You're as bad as old Higgy, always on about things that don't interest me in the least. Who cares whether Charles the First was beheaded when he was thirty-nine or forty? The real issue is that he was beheaded at all."

"*Forty*-nine," Serena amended automatically, reluctantly pulling on her scuffed half-boots. "And you must not call poor Miss Higgenbotham by that dreadful nickname, Cecy," she added, wondering what her old governess had done to inspire her little sister's wrath.

"*You* always did," Cecily shot back, a mutinous gleam in her blue eyes. She smiled impishly when Serena could find no convincing rebuttal for this argument. "Deny it if you dare, Serena," she challenged gleefully.

Serena shrugged. "You will never find a gentleman mad enough to marry you if you can neither embroider nor play the pianoforte," she pointed out without conviction. Cecily already showed signs of being a radiant beauty, and Serena doubted very much that in a few years' time any gentleman with eyes in his head would quibble at her lack of ladylike skills.

"Pooh!" Cecily snorted. "That's the biggest whisker I've heard all day. Why, only look at Priscilla Winston. Prissy can't sing or play to save her life, yet Brian Westlock is besotted over the silly chit." She glanced meaningfully at her sister and lowered her voice. "I never told you this, Serena, but at Lady Huntington's public day last month, I saw him kissing her in the hot house. She didn't seem to mind a bit, although I've always thought it must be rather horrid to be kissed on the lips by some stranger."

Serena jumped to her feet and strode over to where her own horse, Jason, was tied to a gorse bush. "Brian Westlock is hardly a stranger," she said shortly, conscious of a searing ache in the pit of her stomach. "Prissy has known him all her

life." She lifted the saddle flap to tighten the girth, hoping that
Cecy had not noticed her sudden agitation at hearing of
Brian's perversity.

"So have we," her sister pointed out, obviously unwilling to
drop the subject. "And he has never shown any sign of wishing to kiss *me*." She paused briefly. "Has he ever kissed *you*,
Serena?" she asked innocently.

"No, he has not," Serena answered flatly. And he never will,
she thought with a pang of regret. She was not Priscilla Winston, empty-headed, self-centered, and spoiled beyond belief,
but blessed with an enchanting face, a mass of golden ringlets,
eyes the color of pansies. And wealthy parents who doted on
her. At seventeen, Priscilla was the acknowledged Belle of the
neighborhood.

Cecily was silent as Serena mounted and turned the gelding's head towards home. Then she scrambled onto Rufus's
back and urged him alongside her sister's mount. "Well," she
remarked with maddening nonchalance, "Prissy won't be so
full of herself when she hears that you are going to London
next month. There must be hundreds of gentlemen there who
will kiss you, Serena. That cat can keep Brian—"

"London?" Serena stared at her sister curiously and recognized the smug expression on her impish face. "Where did you
get that cork-brained notion, Cecy? You know that Papa cannot afford to give me a come-out this year either, even during
the Little Season. He told me so."

"I know what he told *you*, Serena," Cecily murmured complaisantly. "But he told *me* to fetch you immediately. He wants
to see you in his study before tea. The post brought a letter
from Aunt Hester today, and it contained the most astonishing
good news."

"Why didn't you say so at once?" Serena demanded crossly,
then reined in her temper. Cecy could be annoyingly perverse
when she chose. "What did the letter say?"

Cecily would only smile mysteriously. "I am sure Papa will
wish to tell you himself," she replied with mock primness.
"All I can say is that it will make Prissy positively green with
envy."

With that provocative statement and a mischievous glance
from under long lashes, Cecily gave Rufus his head and flew
off down the slope, her long pigtails whipping out behind her
and her delighted laughter floating back over her shoulder.

Serena followed at a more prosaic pace, her thoughts leaping erratically between the satisfaction of watching Miss Priscilla Winston's perfect face turn a bilious green and a sudden wrenching ache at the thought of having to leave her beloved moors.

"You will do as I say, and that's the end of it, missy."

Sir Henry's voice, naturally rough-edged and sharp, had become increasingly loud as the argument with his elder daughter progressed. The baronet's ruddy, weathered face flushed an angry red as he sat behind his desk and regarded Serena with growing annoyance. "The devil take it, Serena," he said petulantly. "I thought you would welcome the chance to visit the Metropolis for a few months. Acquire a bit of town bronze and get yourself a husband, lass. You may never have another chance, you know. If it had not been for your aunt's invitation, I could not have given you a Season to get yourself riveted to some grand gentleman."

"But I do not want to get myself *riveted,* Papa." Serena tried to keep her voice from revealing her growing distress, but it was heavy going. Rarely had she seen her father more determined to have his way. If Aunt Hester's invitation had been for Cecily, she thought without bitterness, Sir Henry might have been persuaded to turn it down. Although the baronet would have denied it strenuously, Cecily had ever been his favorite, and the minx had a way of cajoling him into a good humor that Serena had never mastered.

She preferred to assume that men were rational creatures who could be swayed by reasonable arguments, but of late her faith in logic had received a crippling blow. Did Brian Westlock not *see,* for example, that Prissy Winston was a scheming, heartless hussy who was determined to lead him down the aisle on the strength of her fluttering eyelashes and positively indecent low décolletage? Serena remembered how she had looked forward to Brian's return from Oxford, confident that, having absorbed the best learning England could offer, he would immediately see through Prissy's duplicity and recognize her own sterling qualities. But he had done neither of these rational things. If anything, Brian behaved more foolishly than ever, and Serena was forced to spend her entire summer watching him become ever more infatuated with a silly chit who delighted in recounting his every tender word to anyone who would listen.

And now her father's obtuseness over Aunt Hester's invita-

tion to spend the Little Season with her in London went ever
further to confirm what Serena had begun to suspect these past
few months—men had no sense where females were concerned. If her Papa had any at all, he would see that a few
months in London would not—by some act of magic—procure
a wealthy husband for his plain daughter. More than likely,
Serena thought ruefully, such a visit would make her more
miserable than she was now. She would be the ugly duckling
among the swans. Even her violet eyes—her best and perhaps
only remarkable feature—would not save her from the humiliation of being regarded as a country nobody. Now if Cecily
were to go, London might well sit up and take notice.

"It is high time you gave some serious thought to getting
yourself settled, my girl." She heard her father's voice harden
perceptibly and braced herself for the taunts she knew would
soon be hurled at her.

"Or are you still languishing over Westlock's boy?" he
sneered, leaning back in his chair and glaring at her from beneath threatening brows. He gave a harsh crack of laughter
that cut through to Serena's heart and made her wince. "More
fool you, child, if you think that puppy will spare one glance
for you when he is being handed that shameless Winston
hussy on a silver platter. Along with fifty thousand pounds."
His lips curled in disgust as Serena's eyes widened.

"Fifty thousand . . ." Serena repeated, her breath catching in
her throat.

Sir Henry grinned sardonically. "Yes, my girl. Your precious Miss Winston comes with fifty thousand pounds of
dowry. Now do you understand why Westlock is so eager to
let himself be leg-shackled? You never stood a chance, my
dear, believe me," he said bluntly. "The Westlocks need that
kind of fortune to get them out of the hole the old viscount dug
them into before he stuck his spoon in the wall last year.
Young Brian will live under the cat's paw for the rest of his
life, of course, but that's a small price to pay."

Serena clasped her hands until she felt the nails dig into her
palms. She did not believe a word of it. How could it not be
love on Brian's part? she thought miserably. For all her faults,
Prissy was stunningly beautiful. Somehow, Serena could bear
it with more fortitude if Brian's motives were romantically irrational rather than coldly mercenary. She could even forgive
him for being irrational, if his feelings were truly engaged, although it irked her to see him make a cake of himself over a

brainless chit. And if Brian offered for Prissy—perhaps already had offered for her—how could she live next door to him for the rest of her life and watch him . . . Serena shuddered. She raised her eyes to meet her father's and was startled to catch a hint of softness in his gaze.

" 'Tis the way of the world, child," he said ponderously. "That is why I insist that you go to London with your aunt. She does not move in the very best circles, it is true, but she is related by marriage to the Dowager Countess of Mansfield, which should count for something."

"I have no dowry, Papa. And nothing to wear. I will not go to be laughed at." She spoke calmly, but her heart wanted to shriek out at the unfairness of the world. Why hadn't she been born with Prissy's golden curls and fifty thousand pounds of dowry?

Sir Henry smiled wryly. "That is true, of course, and I cannot remedy your lack of dowry. But as for clothes, my dear, I have already sent for Mrs. Tobin from the village, and tomorrow I will send you both in the carriage up to Malton to purchase whatever you need to make up some new gowns."

Her father looked so pleased with himself that Serena could not find the heart to point out that Malton—a small farming town eight miles to the north—could hardly be expected to provide the selection of silks and satins required to rig out a female on her way to London to mingle with the *ton.* So she said nothing. Indeed, she thought morosely, what was there to say? Sir Henry had made up his mind, and it would be useless to argue that he was putting his blunt on the wrong horse if he expected his country-bred daughter to overcome the handicaps she would carry with her to London.

But then, her Papa had a special knack for putting his money on the wrong horse, Serena reflected later as she sat before her dresser, watching Annie—the abigail she shared with a reluctant Cecily—brush out her auburn curls with her usual vigor. And if the money was to be spent, it was up to her to see that it was not wasted, she decided abruptly. At least she could benefit from her stay in the Metropolis by visiting the Tower, the libraries, and the museums. She would come back bristling with knowledge and full of tales of her experiences which might edify her rag-mannered sister and help to while away the tedious evenings at Millbanks Hall for the rest of her life.

Serena laughed aloud at her own mawkishness. It was not like her to feel sorry for herself, she thought, clasping her mother's gold locket round her neck and brushing down the folds of her only silk evening gown. Annie glanced at her oddly, and Serena realized that she was grinning at her own reflection in the beveled glass.

"Cook says as 'ow ye'll be going up to Lunnun soon to find a 'usband, Miss Serena," Annie said suddenly, breaking her normal stolid silence. "I wish ye luck, missy, that I do."

Touched by the old abigail's obvious sincerity, Serena gave Annie's plump arm a squeeze and made her way downstairs. A stay in London with her aunt might not be so bad after all, she mused. It was clearer now than ever before that Brian would never be hers, and it was high time she admitted the painful fact. And did she really wish to stay here at home and watch her White Knight fawning over Prissy Winston? Serena shuddered at the thought. Papa was right; there was no real future for her here in Barton Hill, Yorkshire.

Suddenly the visit to London did not seem so disastrous at all. Of course, the thought of being *riveted*—as Papa had so crudely put it—was out of the question, but it might be amusing to discover for herself if those dark, brooding heroes with intense black eyes really existed. Her favorite romantical authors obviously believed they did.

For the first time since her argument with Sir Henry that afternoon, Serena felt a glimmer of pleasure at the idea of going to London. If such mysterious, sensuous men existed at all, wouldn't they be in London?

Serena smiled as she swept into the drawing room to join her father for a small glass of sherry. Where else *could* such devastating men be? she thought, amused at her own whimsy. *If* they existed.

If they existed, she would find them, Serena told herself firmly, accepting the delicate glass from Sir Henry with a smile. And her trip to London might not be wasted after all.

CHAPTER ONE

The Hawk

London, October 1816

"Oh, Serena! I do believe that is the new Duchess of Ridgeway. The one in the blue silk over there, talking to that dreadful fright in the purple turban. Isn't she beautiful! The duchess, I mean."

Serena turned her disinterested gaze toward the potted palms clustered at the far end of Lady Berkford's ballroom. After a month in London, she had grown weary of the malicious gossip that seemed to be the only acceptable conversation in the polite world. But the young duchess, whom her Cousin Melissa had pointed out so enthusiastically, had caused more scandal in the past month than most females could dream of in a year. She was the absolute darling of the *ton*, having recently brought the aging Duke of Ridgeway up to scratch and causing a duel between the wayward scions of two illustrious families, and was rumored to have one of London's premier rakes dangling at her lovely fingertips.

"If we can believe everything we hear, Her Grace is a trollop," Serena remarked acerbically. "Which is highly unlikely, of course. No female could be as perverse as the Tabbies make Honoria Littleton out to be."

Serena paused to examine the beautifully proportioned young duchess, who had evidently stopped on her way across the ballroom to exchange greetings with the ponderous matron in purple. She was indeed beautiful, everything that Serena knew she herself was not. From the top of her golden curls, piled modishly in a crown on her delicate head, to the tip of her expensive stain slipper peeking from beneath her glittering blue silk ballgown, the duchess radiated the kind of sensuous femininity that could be counted upon to attract the eye of every man in the room. Several of them were even now converging on her as though mesmerized by her throaty laughter,

which carried lightly across the room to where Serena and her
cousin sat beside Lady Thornton among the dowagers.

With a sigh, Serena turned to her cousin, whose blue eyes
were riveted on the duchess in silent adoration. "Yes, she is indeed an Incomparable, Melissa," she said softly, wondering
what it might be like to possess that kind of radiant beauty.

"And she is married to a duke," Melissa murmured breath-
lessly. "How romantic!"

The sight of her cousin's wistful face impelled Serena to
throw a damper on Melissa's childish illusions. "The duke is
fifty if he's a day" she remarked caustically. "As old as her
Papa, I daresay. I hardly think that can be in any way romantic, Melly. Just think on it for a moment. No doubt a man that
age will have a paunch and probably snores, too. My own
Papa does, and he is about the same age. I find that rather revolting myself. Definitely not romantic."

"How horrid you are, Serena." Melissa giggled, putting her
hand quickly to her mouth to avoid her mother's censure. "Actually, I was thinking of the *other* one, the rake who is reputed
to have stolen the duchess's heart away. No one knows quite
who he is, though. There are so many rakes in London, I never
would have credited it. And all so dashing." She sighed
gustily. "I wish Mama would allow one of them to dance with
me. Just once. Then I could go back to Norfolk and put Letty
Crompton's nose out of joint. She had her come-out last Season, you know, and never received a single offer. Her father
was furious."

Serena laughed. She could sympathize wholeheartedly with
her cousin. Several of London's better-known rakes had been
pointed out to her by her Aunt Hester, who appeared to know
all of them and could recite their more nefarious exploits in
minute detail. Lady Thornton had strictly forbidden either of
her charges to waste so much as a glance on these dangerous,
dashing gentlemen, much less dance with them. Of course, this
warning was quite superfluous in her case, Serena thought ruefully. In the month she had been in London, she had danced
only twice. The first time was with a gentleman of such advanced years and ponderous girth that she had quite expected
him to capsize in the middle of a lively cotillion. Her second
partner had been a bashful, blushing youth whose feet had tangled painfully at every step and who had—after repeated attempts to master the intricacies of the country dance—fled in

panic, leaving Serena to make her way back to her aunt on her own.

These reminiscences were abruptly interrupted by Melissa's excited tugging at her shawl. "Oh, look over there, Serena, do!" she breathed, gazing toward the entrance, an expression of open admiration on her pretty face. "The man in black who just came in. The one with—"

"I see him," Serena cut in sharply. Indeed, who could miss him, a tall, rangy figure of a man, standing in the doorway surveying the couples on the floor through a ridiculously ornate quizzing glass as though they were somewhat less than human. How extraordinarily rude, Serena thought, repressing a shudder of disgust. Even at that distance, she could tell that this broad-shouldered, arrogant man was another of London's rakes, out on his nightly prowl, no doubt. The notion that such men were received by most of London's leading hostesses was incomprehensible to her. Why invite the rogues at all if they were definitely off limits to decent females?

"What about him?" she inquired crossly, although she could well imagine what had caught her romantic cousin's eye. "And don't stare, Melly," she hissed. "People will think you know the wretch."

"I wish I did," the irrepressible Melissa responded shyly. "Isn't he magnificent!"

Serena glanced a second time toward the man in black and had to admit—grudgingly to be sure—that the rogue did have a certain flair. His snowy cravat, tied in an monstrous but undoubtedly fashionable creation, emphasized the deep tan of his rugged face, and his black pantaloons clung so snugly to his long legs that they left nothing, or almost nothing—Serena realized with a jolt of embarrassment—to the imagination. But before she could tear her eyes away from this shameless exhibition of male depravity, Serena saw the black figure waver slightly and put out a hand to steady himself against the door jamb.

She turned to her bedazzled cousin and fixed her with a jaundiced stare. "He's disguised," she said scathingly. "And don't stare, Melissa. The man is obviously a rogue of the first water."

"He is staring at the duchess," Melissa whispered in shocked tones. "Do you suppose that—"

"I suppose nothing of the sort, Miss Thornton," Serena cut in sharply. "And I suggest you spend your time on the eligible

gentlemen present tonight, instead of ogling rakes and cast-
aways." Even as she spoke, however, Serena found her gaze
wandering to the radiant young duchess, and she was not surprised to note that the Duke of Ridgeway's lady slanted a deliciously wicked glance in the direction of the gentleman in
black.

Suddenly tired of the hypocrisy of it all, Serena got abruptly
to her feet. "I am thirsty, Aunt," she explained as Lady Thornton threw her an inquiring glance. "May I bring you a glass of
punch?"

Her aunt eyed her speculatively. Then, evidently deciding
that her niece was in no immediate danger from any of the
gentlemen present, most of whom were either twirling around
the dance floor in a newfangled waltz or clustered around the
Duchess of Ridgeway, she nodded majestically, the scarlet
plumes in her turban dipping alarmingly.

Serena made her way toward the dining room where refreshments had been laid out—enough to feed the household at
Millbanks Hall for a month, she thought cynically. She had
read her aunt's mind like a book, and what she saw there had
only confirmed her own impression—reached during the second week of her London stay—that she was not going to *take*.
Her new gowns were unfashionably severe, her bonnets were
definitely gauche, her manners were unbecomingly forward—
according to Aunt Hester—and nobody, not even one of her
aunt's bosom bows, had noticed that her eyes were her best
feature. Even her skill at the pianoforte, which was considerable, had not won so much as a glimmer of approval from anybody.

Serena was quite ready to go home. She missed the fresh
country air, the songs of her favorite birds, the wild rides on
Jason across the open moor, the unquestioning adoration of
her dog Jollyboy—she could still hear his high-pitched wail as
she drove off that morning over a month ago. And of course,
she missed Cecily, pest that she often was. Even Sir Henry had
acquired, in her present nostalgic state, an aura of kindness he
so rarely exhibited to either of his daughters.

She poured herself a large glass of punch and drank
thirstily. None of the rich food tempted her, and since she was
reluctant to return to the stuffy ballroom, she wandered over
and opened the French doors to let in some fresh air. Beyond
the small balcony outside, Serena saw shallow steps leading

down to a shadowy stone-paved garden enclosed by brick walls. The silvery sound of running water intrigued her, and she stepped out onto the balcony and made her way down to a small fountain, half hidden behind a bank of shrubs. The sight delighted her, and impulsively she sat down on the edge of the pond and trailed her hand in the water. After several minutes, a gentle nibbling at her fingers told her that Lady Berkford's secret pond contained friendly fish, and she leaned forward to see if she could catch a glimpse of them in the dusk.

"Where are you, pretty fellow?" she murmured softly, her nose within inches of the water.

"I am here," an amused voice answered from the shadows behind her.

Serena nearly jumped out of her skin and, given her precarious position, would have fallen facedown into the pond had not two strong hands grasped her waist and lifted her easily to her feet. She stood for a long moment, her body trembling uncontrollably and her heart pounding with fright. Then she turned slowly to gaze up at the man whose ill-timed jest had brought her so close to disaster.

He was standing with his back to the solitary lamp on the balcony above, so Serena could not see his face clearly, but she sensed that he found the whole incident amusing. "Well?" he drawled in a slightly slurred voice. "Are you not going to thank this White Knight for saving you from an unscheduled bath, demoiselle?"

An alarm went off in Serena's head. The brute was thoroughly disguised, she realized, suddenly conscious of the man's large hands resting lightly on her hips. She went rigid with indignation and a tinge of fear touched her heart.

"Release me, sir," she commanded in what she hoped was her most frigid tone. "If you had not so thoughtlessly frightened me with your reprehensible conduct, I would not have been placed in the position of needing your assistance. And furthermore—"

"Hold on there, love," the mysterious gentleman interrupted, swaying quite noticeably on his feet. "I do not quite follow you. I did save you from falling in the pond, did I not?"

Serena glared up at her savior—or her captor, she was not quite sure which. "Never mind that now," she snapped. "Release me immediately."

"Release you?" The gentleman swayed again, his hands tightening on Serena's hips, much to her dismay.

"Yes," she replied icily. "Release me. Take your filthy hands off me, in other words."

"Cannot do that," he mumbled soddenly.

"Why ever not?" Serena was beginning to believe she had stepped into a nightmare. "Take your hands off my . . . off me." She trembled at how close she had come to naming that part of herself which his hands seemed incapable of releasing. "Or I shall scream," she added belligerently.

"Cannot do it, lass. I shall fall flat on my face."

To her horror, the man's hands took an even firmer grip on her hips and Serena felt the warmth of him seeping through the thin silk. It was not entirely unpleasant, but the size of his hands spanning her hips and holding her firmly made her feel vaguely decadent. The tenor of her thoughts alarmed her, perhaps more than the stranger's touch. She shivered.

"Not 'fraid of me, are you lass?"

"Of course not," she replied contemptuously. "I need to go inside to fetch my shawl," she added with a flash of brilliance. "So just let me go, will you?"

"Cold, are you, love? Why did you not say so?" To Serena's dismay the implacable hands drew her hips tightly into the curve of the stranger's body and settled them there. "That better, sweet?" the man murmured, his mouth suddenly warm on her rigid neck. And then, before she had time to absorb the horror of her situation, his mouth had captured hers roughly, and a hot tongue assaulted her clamped lips with teasing insistence.

The smell of brandy was overpowering, and Serena wrenched her mouth away, gasping for breath. The stranger's mouth trailed over her face and one hand climbed her back to press her against his chest. To escape the brandy-tainted taste of his questing mouth, Serena buried her face in the frothy cravat, and as she did so, a frisson of disgust shook her. The man who held her captive and seemed determined to take every conceivable advantage of her could be no other than the stranger in black with the quizzing glass.

Serena shuddered.

"Still cold, lass?" came the muffled voice from the curve of her neck. The pressure of the stranger's arms increased as he enfolded her slight form more closely, almost lifting her off the ground. Serena tried to remain rigid, but there was no gainsaying the implacable force of those arms, and before she could rally her defenses, she found herself pressed flat against the obnoxious stranger. No, not flat, she thought, her mind ever punctilious, even under stress. There was nothing flat about this rogue. He was all corded muscle and hard sinew. She could feel the ripple of his chest muscles against her breasts as his hands moved over her back.

The seductive warmth of them began to lull her senses, and her initial revulsion and fright began to drain away, replaced by an emotion Serena could not name. Was it possible that she was actually *enjoying* this . . . this frankly erotic embrace with a total stranger? she wondered, her mind appalled at the notion of her own unsuspected weakness. No wonder Aunt Hester had warned her never to allow a gentleman the least hint of license, because one false step could ruin a young lady forever.

Serena wondered fuzzily if Aunt Hester might consider her present situation a false step. The question was undoubtedly rhetorical, she realized, feeling the insidious warmth of the stranger's thighs against her hips, which snuggled into the curve of him as though they belonged there. None of her romantic daydreaming had prepared her for the sensuous abandon she felt at this moment, which seemed to have robbed her of all common sense.

The vision of Aunt Hester's horrified reaction if she so much as suspected that her niece had allowed a rake—and a bosky one at that—to hold her in this undoubtedly sinful way caused Serena to regain a modicum of sanity. She must get out of this coil and back inside before her aunt become suspicious and came looking for her. Serena's blood curdled at the thought of the picture she would present to Lady Thornton's astonished gaze.

"Please," she murmured against the gentleman's cravat, hoping she sounded pathetic enough to touch some cord of decency in the rogue. She pretended to tremble and was relieved when the iron grip relaxed slightly.

"What is it, m'lovely?" The stranger's voice was husky, and he swayed so noticeably that Serena thought they might both land on the stone paving of the courtyard. The fear of what might happen to her if this rogue got her down on the ground gave Serena the extra strength she needed to wrench herself out of his loosened grasp. As she turned to flee, however, she felt a large hand clamp down on her shoulder.

"Not so fast, m'lovely," the stranger mumbled, twirling her effortlessly round to face him again. "The night is still young, m'dear." He leered at her, and Serena could now see something of his face in the weak lamplight. The lean, handsome features were slack with a surfeit of drink, and his eyes squinted so badly that Serena could not even guess at their color. She had been right; it was indeed the rake with the quizzing glass.

"I can think of a hundred delightful things we might do together, sweetheart." He swayed against her with a groan, of pain now, rather than passion. "The devil fly away with this damned head of mine," he muttered, raising a hand to brush back the dark hair that had fallen over his broad forehead.

This momentary lapse of attention was all Serena needed. She twisted away and ran for the steps. But once again she was not swift enough to escape the long reach of the stranger.

"Do not play coy with me, wench," he growled, jerking her roughly back into his arms and bending his head menacingly down toward her.

His intentions were unmistakable, and Serena reacted instinctively. She swung her fist up in a tight hook, just as Jeremy, her father's stable boy, had taught her when she was fifteen, and planted a neat facer on her assailant's aristocratic nose. Her fingers felt as though they were broken beyond repair, but she had the unholy satisfaction of seeing the stranger reel back, stagger on the uneven paving, and come to rest on the seat of his elegant black pantaloons in the wide stone container of one of Lady Berkford's exotic potted palms.

After an initial grunt of pain, the stranger sat for a moment cradling his nose in one hand then, quite unexpectedly, gave a moan of pure agony and leaned over to cast up his accounts among the yellow chrysanthemums in a large, cherub-encrusted pot nearby.

Serena gaped at him in fascinated horror, arrested in her flight by the pathetic angle of the broad shoulders, hunched over the unfortunate chrysanthemums. The shoulders heaved, and another heart-wrenching groan escaped the stranger. He fumbled ineffectually at his cravat, cursing weakly.

"Sweet Jesus," he moaned, "I'm as weak as a damned cat." His shoulders heaved again, and Serena could bear the sight of his suffering no longer. Her desire to escape forgotten, she stepped up to the hunched figure and put a hand on his shoulder. The stranger glanced up at her and then clasped his head in renewed agony. "Damn you, wench," he growled in a weak voice. "You've broken my nose."

"You asked for it," Serena replied shortly. "Do you have a handkerchief?"

He motioned vaguely to his coat pocket and after a short search, Serena pulled out a pristine lawn handkerchief. She took it over to the small pond and immersed it in the cool water. As she was wringing it out, she heard further unmistakable sounds of distress from the stranger.

"The devil fly away with inferior brandy," she heard the stranger croak as she came back to stand beside him.

"Nonsense," she replied tartly. "It was undoubtedly your own fault for drinking too much of it. Now hold still," she added, lifting his face up with one hand while mopping up the traces of his debacle with the damp cloth. "You should be grateful you did not cast up your accounts in the middle of the ballroom. That would have given the Tabbies fodder for the next sennight at least."

"I was perfectly all right until you hit me, wench," the stranger muttered. "Lord, I feel rotten."

Serena laughed mirthlessly. "You deceive yourself, sir," she snapped. "You were castaway when you arrived."

"So? You were watching me, were you, you artful baggage?" His smug confidence in his own attraction stung Serena, causing her to answer unwisely.

"Everybody was gawking at the spectacle you made of yourself," she replied sharply. "It was nothing to be proud of, let me tell you."

She rinsed out the handkerchief and returned to his side. He was looking a little less peaked by now, but his nose was still bleeding. "I hope I did break your nose for you," Serena could not resist saying. "Perhaps it will remind you to behave like a gentleman next time rather than a lout. If you are one, that is, which I sincerely doubt."

"A gentleman or a lout?" he murmured, smiling for the first time since Serena had hit him.

"A gentleman, of course," she answered. "Although I have my doubts that you know the meaning of the word."

"Are you always such a virago? No wonder you were out here by yourself, my dear. Men cannot abide a nagging female, you know."

"It is lucky for you that I was," Serena shot back. "Not many of your fine ladies would stoop to help a disgusting creature like you."

"Yes," he murmured, amusement in his voice now. "I was indeed lucky to find you out here alone."

Serena blushed at the implication of these words and gave his face a final pass with the damp cloth, pushing the dark curls back from his wide forehead. "Can you stand?"

"Of course I can stand, wench." The stranger lurched to his feet, teetered there for a moment, and then sat down heavily against the palm tree. "Well, perhaps not quite yet. Give me a few minutes, m'dear."

"Get up," Serena commanded abruptly.

The stranger looked up at her and grinned weakly. "You are a regular harridan, love," he said. "But for you, I am willing to attempt the impossible." He staggered to his feet again, and Serena automatically put out a hand to steady him. Before she realized how it had happened, the stranger's arm was draped across her shoulders, and he was leaning heavily on her. "Ah, this is more the thing, love. Where are you taking me?"

Serena's patience was wearing rather thin. "First of all, we will get up these steps," she said firmly. "Do you think you can?"

"Of course, love. With your help, naturally." He seemed to think the whole scene rather amusing, but Serena was breathing heavily by the time she had pushed and pulled his unsteady bulk up the shallow steps to the French doors.

Once they reached the narrow balcony, it suddenly occurred to Serena that she could not very well drag the inebriated gentleman into Lady Berkford's dining room. To be caught in such a compromising situation with a notorious rake—she had no doubt that the stranger's reputation was at best unsavory— would catapult her into a scandal of major proportions, and Serena was reluctant to subject her aunt to public ridicule.

She paused and glanced up at the stranger, only to find that he was grinning at her as though the whole affair was a huge joke. Resolutely, she pushed him back against the balustrade.

"Stay here for a moment, while I fetch help," she ordered softly, pushing his chest again to assure herself that he was firmly wedged against the stone wall. "And don't fall down," she added. "Do you think you can do that without making a mull of things?"

The stranger started to laugh, but Serena quickly clamped a hand over his mouth. "Have your wits gone begging?" she hissed crossly. "Do you want to be discovered out here in this disgusting state?"

Serena could feel his lips twitch beneath her hand, and the feeling was so disturbing that she snatched it away and glared up at him. He was indeed grinning widely, and Serena had the primitive urge to smack his face for him. In the light filtering out from the dining room, she noticed that his eyes were much lighter than she had imagined, and at the moment had a devilish glint in them.

"It would seem to me, m'dear, that *you* are the one who is afraid to be caught out here alone with me." His voice was still slurred and as he spoke, he rocked forward and ran his knuckles lightly down her cheek. Serena slapped his hand away, stepping back out of range.

"You had best not tax your sodden brains with too much speculation, sir," she said acidly. "Concentrate on staying upright until I can bring a footman. Or two," she added, glancing at the stranger's big frame.

"You *will* come back again, won't you?" he said unexpectedly.

Serena stared at him in astonishment. "Whatever for?" she demanded bluntly. "Your conduct has been highly reprehensible, sir. In fact, you have nothing to recommend you at all that I can see."

"I am feeling devilishly unwell again," he groaned, running a shaking hand over his face and closing his eyes.

Serena noticed that the stranger's face was indeed very pale, and his nose was bleeding again. Against her better judgment, she felt sorry for the wretch. "Here," she said in softer tones, holding out his damp handkerchief which she still held in one hand. "Wipe your nose; it is bleeding."

When he made no move to take it, Serena stepped closer and reached up to place the cool cloth gently on his overheated forehead. Then she gingerly mopped the blood that ran sluggishly down his face.

"Oh, you have blood on your neckcloth!" she exclaimed. "It is quite ruined, I am afraid. You might as well loosen it and be comfortable." Without waiting for his consent, Serena worked the now wilted cravat loose with her fingers. "There," she added, when the extravagant knot was quite unrecognizable. "Does that feel better?"

It didn't occur to Serena until she glanced up and found the stranger staring at her with an odd glitter in his eyes that the liberties she had taken with his clothing were of an uncomfortably intimate nature. She dropped her hands and turned away, embarrassed for the first time during that nightmarish evening.

"I shall summon assistance," she murmured stiffly.

"At least tell me your name, m'dear."

"There is no need for you to know my name," Serena responded sharply, suddenly distressed at the notion that this rake might bandy her name around London as another of his conquests.

"Well, at least allow me to introduce myself—"

"I am not the least interested in who you are, sir," Serena countered.

"Hawkhurst," the stranger continued, quite as though she had not spoken. "Guy Hawkhurst. At your service, ma'am." He tried to sketch a bow but staggered and would have fallen on his face had not Serena quickly placed her hands on his chest and pushed him upright again.

"*Do* stand still," she hissed, exasperated at the man's obtuseness. "I shall be back immediately." She had no intention of returning, of course, so she could not resist glancing over her shoulder as she stepped into the dining room. To see if he was still standing, she told herself.

Guy Hawkhurst, if that was indeed his name, gave her a lecherous wink and grinned crookedly.

It was not until later, when Serena was making her way back to the ballroom with Aunt Hester's glass of punch grasped in one trembling hand, that she noticed that she still held the stranger's damp handkerchief in the other.

CHAPTER TWO

Gentleman Caller

The day after Lady Berkford's ball, Guy Hawkhurst, the fifth Duke of Wolverton, opened one jaundiced eye as the hall clock downstairs struck twelve and wondered why he was still abed instead of riding in the Park as was his wont each morning. Then he raised his head and the racking pain brought it all back to him. He groaned and subsided onto the pillow. He had done it again, he thought disgustedly. The evening had started innocently enough with dinner at White's in the company of his cronies Lords Gresham and Monroyal, and Colonel Laughton. Then they had joined several other members at the card tables, and the night had slipped away from him. All he remembered was winning an embarrassing sum from old Lord Grifford, who had been subsisting on his luck at cards for the past fifteen years or so. And he remembered the drinking. He had come home in his cups again.

Hawk rubbed a hand over his face as if to brush away this disagreeable memory, but an excruciating pain made him catch his breath and sit up, an action which intensified the throbbing in his head. Gingerly, he touched his nose. It seemed to be larger than usual and definitely tender to the touch. Had he got into a fight last night? he wondered. Tentatively, he felt the areas around both eyes and sighed with relief when he found no sign of damage. Luckily, whoever had punched his nose had not darkened his daylights as well. That would have been most inconvenient, he thought wryly, since he was engaged to escort his mother and sisters to the opera tonight.

Abruptly, he swung his legs out of bed and reached for the bellpull to ring for Slowe. He was in desperate need of one of his old batman's vile concoctions this morning. Once *again*, he thought disgustedly. Hawk wondered idly how many mornings in the past three years—three years that had seemed to stretch out interminably after Derek's death at Vittoria during the final months of General Wellesley's campaign in Spain—

he had woken with a head as cavernous and noisy as a ball-room during a riotous country dance.

Ballroom? At some point after leaving White's last night, he had been in a ballroom, hadn't he? He was almost certain that he had kept an assignation with some wench or other. The devil of it was, he had no recollection who that wench might have been or even which of the many London hostesses he had honored with his presence. Honored was perhaps not the right word, he thought cynically, depending on whether or not he had made a cake of himself at yet another affair.

"Top of the mornin' to ye, Major!" a cheery voice abruptly shattered the duke's melancholy musing and caused him to wince. The door had swung open energetically to reveal the bulky figure of ex-Sergeant Robin Slowe, late of the 18th Hus-sars and more recently elevated to the austere heights of gen-tleman's gentleman to His Grace, the Duke of Wolverton.

Hawk glared at his valet's battle-scarred face. "We are no longer in the army, Slowe," he said belligerently. "How many times have I to remind you of that fact?"

"Right ye are, Major," came the cheerful reply. "Yer bath will be ready in a jiffy, sir."

Hawk groaned and touched his nose again.

"Feeling poorly this morning, are we?" Slowe remarked as though he were thoroughly accustomed to his master waking up in acute pain. Which of course he was, Hawk thought dis-gustedly.

"I have the devil of a head, Slowe," he muttered. "Get me one of your foul draughts, will you? And Slowe," he added as the valet turned smartly about to leave the room.

"Yes, sir?"

"Where did I go last night?"

The question did not seem to phase the valet in the slightest, Hawk noted cynically. "Engaged to dine with the Marquess of Monroyal, ye were, sir. At White's, I believe."

"Yes, yes, I know that. Was I going anywhere afterward?"

The ungainly batman raised a huge hand to his face and coughed discreetly. "There was some mention of Honoria Lit-tleton, m'lord," he answered impassively. "The chit who leg-shackled—that is to say," he hastened to correct himself, "the young Duchess of Ridgeway, sir."

Honoria? Hawk grimaced. How in Hades had he managed to get himself tangled up with that hot little chit again? She had thrown herself quite openly at his head when he had come back from Spain three years ago to assume Derek's title.

Derek's title, he mused. Even three years after his twin's death, the title still felt too uncomfortably like Derek's. Hawk still occasionally flinched when an acquaintance addressed him as Wolverton. His friends all called him Hawkhurst, thank God, and in their company he could forget for a while the corroding guilt he carried in his soul. And the drink helped, too, of course. Brandy, women, and wild wagers at the card table that he couldn't seem to lose. And more money than he knew what to do with. Derek's money, or at least the fortune that should have been his brother's—had he lived to enjoy it.

Hawk shook his head brusquely to banish these morbid thoughts and instantly regretted it. He groaned and buried his face in his hands, careful to avoid touching his aching nose.

"Where was I supposed to meet Ridgeway's lovely bride?" he asked, an edge of cynicism in his tone.

"That I canna say, m'lord." Slowe replied. "Ye dinna confide in me, sir." The valet regarded him with a glimmer of sympathy, then remarked with evident relish, "But ye did seem to 'ave 'ad a regular dust-up with some one, m'lord. Yer cravat was fairly dripping blood, it was, when Murray finally got ye upstairs. A devil of a job we had, if I might say so, sir—"

"Blood on my cravat?" Hawk jerked upright, his eyes suddenly filled with a gleam of amusement. "Blood on my cravat, you say? Tell me, Slowe, is my nose broken by any chance?"

"No, sir. Bleeding like a stuck pig ye were, but no, broken." He examined his master with birdlike intensity, his brown eyes twinkling with humor. "Merely bent a little at the tip and swollen up like a billiard ball. A little cold water should fix that all right and tight, sir. But not broken, sir, not at all."

Blood on his cravat? Hawk thought, the haze of last night's activities beginning to lift. He dimly recalled a shadowy courtyard, a fountain, and a pair of really first-class ankles. He smiled to himself. And then he remembered the unexpected facer. What had he done to deserve such a furious reaction from the lady? he wondered, his smile broadening at the memory of a pair of violet eyes blazing up at him. Whatever it was, it must have been highly offensive. He racked his brain, but the fog still shrouded much of the night's activities after he had left White's.

"What a pity," he murmured, unable to remember more than the violet eyes and shapely ankles.

"I beg your pardon, m'lord?"

Hawk saw that his valet was regarding him with raised eyebrows.

"I said what a pity it isn't broken," he repeated, grinning widely now. "The wench will have to hit a deal harder next time."

Slowe gaped at him. "A lass did this to ye, m'lord?" he asked bluntly. "I never thought to see the day when a female would draw blood from Major Hawk himself. And that's a fact."

"No need to bruit it about, Sergeant," Hawk remarked, his humor vastly restored. "Now I need you to discover from the coachman where I went last night, and then . . ." He grinned at his ex-sergeant, a conspiratorial gleam in his gray eyes. "And then I want you to find out the name of a female who attended that ball, wherever it was."

Slowe's homely face assumed a martyred air. "And what does the wench look like, if I might inquire, m'lord?" he demanded in a long-suffering tone.

"She had violet eyes," the major replied softly, his mind reaching for more details about the odd female who had crossed his path so briefly yet vividly last night. "And she is definitely a lady, Slowe, although not of the first stare. Dressed in some prim, outmoded gown of lilac silk. At least I think it was lilac." It was beginning to come back to him now. "And a deuced sharp tongue, she had. About so high," he placed his open palm at the level of his cravat, had he been wearing one. "And . . ." Hawk paused. The memory of the chit's soft mouth and unexpectedly generous curves flooded back, but he did not suppose the servants would know anything of that. At least he hoped not.

"What about her phiz, gov'nor?"

For the life of him Hawk could not say what the mysterious female looked like. "With a tongue like that," he said firmly, "the wench is bound to be a bit of an antidote, but I owe her an apology. So find her for me, Slowe, and order the curricle for two o'clock, will you?"

Such was the efficiency of the duke's household and the valet's connection with the underground network of servants working in various noble houses in London that the major's request was not as difficult to fulfill as he might have imagined. By the time Hawk sauntered downstairs just before two o'clock and received his tall beaver and ivory-handled malacca cane from Murray, the Hawkhurst butler, the entire staff knew that the major had taken an inexplicable fancy to a very plain female by the name of Miss Serena Millbanks, presently residing with her aunt, Lady Thornton, at Number Seven Mount Street.

Lady Thornton's residence was unusually quiet the afternoon after Lady Berkford's ball, her ladyship having gone to pay calls on various of the dowagers she considered might conceivably be of assistance in furthering matrimonial plans for her darling Melissa. Miss Thornton had been only too glad to accompany her mother, for the evening before she had actually been in the same room as the notorious Duchess of Ridgeway and was eager to inform the world of her good fortune. And since neither of the ladies pressed their guest to accompany them, Miss Millbanks found herself free to pursue her own inclinations for a change.

Serena welcomed the time alone. London, she had soon discovered, offered little enough of the solitude she had enjoyed in Yorkshire. There were no moors to provide a refuge when she felt the need for meditation or an excursion into the imaginary world of her daydreams. And after the strange adventure in Lady Berkford's shadowy courtyard last night, she felt in dire need of a respite from her cousin's constant chatter and Aunt Hester's well-meant lectures. She had not recognized herself last night in the female who had dealt so brazenly with a total stranger. Her emotions had experienced a severe shock, and Serena was not at all sure—looking back from the safety of her bedchamber—that she had acted with her usual common sense.

So she had escaped to the music room—the only substitute available to her for the sunlit moors of home—and lost herself in her favorite compositions. She had even played two of Scarlatti's sonatinas, remembering, as her fingers flowed effortlessly over the keys in the soothing, intricate patterns, her little sister's frustration with poor Mr. Mincewort. It was true that the music master could be very tiresome with his insistence on perfection, but Serena had profited greatly from that same tiresome trait. She had been challenged to strive for that perfection, and when Mr. Mincewort had nodded his head in unspoken approval of a certain piece, Serena had felt amply rewarded for the time and effort she had put into her practice.

Her solitude was interrupted just after two o'clock by Simmons, her aunt's elderly butler, who tapped at the door to inform her that a gentleman had called and was asking for her.

"For *me?*" Serena repeated in surprise, her fingers poised above the silent keys. "Are you sure, Simmons? I should think it must be my cousin the gentleman means."

"No, miss," the butler insisted. "The gentleman expressly asked for Miss Millbanks. He has brought a lovely bunch of chrysanthemums for you. Big yellow ones, miss. He said they would remind you of him."

Serena felt her mouth go dry. This could not be happening to her, she thought, panic rising like a cold wave from the pit of her stomach. How had the rogue found out who she was and where she lived? She had imagined herself safe by refusing to give her name, but here he was, in this very house. She stared at the butler as if she could find a solution in his impassive face.

"Shall I tell him you are not receiving, miss?" Simmons suggested.

For some reason she did not examine too closely, Serena instantly rejected the idea of sending the stranger about his business. "What did he say his name was, Simmons?"

"Hawkhurst, miss," the butler replied after a tiny pause. "Mr. Guy Hawkhurst. I have put him in the Yellow Saloon, miss."

"When do you expect my aunt to return?"

"Not for another hour, yet, miss. Shall I send up a tea tray?"

"If you will, Simmons," she answered calmly. "And tell Mr. Hawkhurst I shall be along in a few moments."

As soon as the butler closed the door, Serena forced herself to continue the piece she had been playing. When she finished, she closed the pianoforte and glanced into the mirror above the hearth before making her way to the Yellow Saloon. It was pointless to imagine that she could improve her appearance even if her caller merited it, which she told herself unequivocally he did not.

He was standing before the fire, one arm on the mantel, his eyes on the dancing flames in the grate, and for a dreadful moment Serena thought he was disguised again. He turned as Serena closed the door behind her, and she felt his amused gaze upon her as she moved toward him across the Oriental carpet. She paused, wondering what she could say to a man who evidently had no conception of decency or good manners, who thought nothing of accosting young women in dark places and inflicting his disgusting attentions upon them, and who then could present himself in their drawing rooms as if nothing were amiss. She also wondered what madness had impelled her to receive him.

His eyes were a curiously light gray, she saw upon closer scrutiny, perhaps flecked with green—she could not be sure. His face was aristocratically lean, certainly too severe for classical beauty, but with more than enough animal magnetism to make up for any symmetrical deficiency. It was the face of a rake and libertine, Serena reflected, as she had had ample opportunity to discover for herself. The face of a dangerous man, one not to be trusted with impressionable chits who would be dazzled by the magnetism and disregard the danger. Luckily, she was forewarned, Serena though with a flash of cynicism, and therefore forearmed.

He had stood nonchalantly silent under her scrutiny, but now he made her a mock bow and drawled in a bored voice, "I trust I meet with your approval, Miss Millbanks?"

"Not at all, sir," she replied with matching dryness. "As a matter of fact, I do not approve of you at all."

He straightened at this, his smile turning into an easy grin as he advanced toward her. Divining his intent, Serena gestured impatiently. "There is no need for false civility, sir," she said, turning away to take a seat in one of the leather wing chairs near the fire. "And I must say that I am disappointed that you could not take a hint, Mr. Hawkhurst."

He went back to his position by the hearth and glanced down at her. Serena caught a gleam of speculation in the gray depths. "Hint, Miss Millbanks? I do not recollect any such hint."

"That does not surprise me," she answered tartly. "You were odiously foxed and quite disgustingly sick all over poor Lady Berkford's unfortunate flowers." She wrinkled her nose in distaste. "But even a man as disguised as you were last night, Mr. Hawkhurst, must have concluded—if he had any intelligence to speak of—that I had no desire to see you ever again. Frankly, I cannot imagine why you are here."

Serena had spoken calmly and without the rancor she had felt earlier, but she saw her visitor's lips tighten and his eyes turn flinty. She hoped that he would lose his temper, so that she could have the satisfaction of ordering him from the house, but after a moment, his lips curled into a cynical grin.

"I fancied I must have vastly exaggerated the acidity of your tongue, Miss Millbanks, but I see that I underestimated it instead," he said smoothly, his smile mocking. "I am here because I do recall causing you considerable inconvenience last night, my dear. I wish to apologize—"

"Inconvenience, indeed!" Serena hooted with laughter. "How odd that I recall something quite different, Mr. Hawkhurst. Something a good deal more contemptible, I am afraid. Your memory is faulty, my *dear* sir," she snapped sarcastically, her temper suddenly flaring at this blatant attempt to brush off the stranger's despicable conduct as a minor *faux pas*.

Any reply the visitor may have made was interrupted by Simmons, who entered at that moment with the tea tray, which he set down on a low table beside Serena's chair. He was followed by a footman carrying an immense bowl of yellow chrysanthemums. The sheer extravagance of the bouquet left Serena speechless and stoked the fire of her anger.

"Thank you, Simmons," she murmured. "Put the flowers on the oval table if you please." She waited until the servants had left the room before daring to look up at her visitor.

"You must have a very guilty conscience indeed to plunder half the flower shops in London," she remarked dryly. "Either that or you suspected the *inconvenience* you caused me might be greater than you remember."

"You are even more of a harridan than I recall, Miss Millbanks," he said softly, his gray eyes narrowing dangerously.

"I am glad to hear it, sir," Serena replied with certain relish.

"And I have been wondering about your nose," she added, changing the subject abruptly. "I see it is somewhat swollen. Is it broken, by any chance?" She smiled at him expectantly.

"Sorry to disappoint you, my dear virago," he drawled. "I seem to have emerged from our brief encounter with my nose intact." He smiled maliciously. "I trust you can say the same, my dear. Next time, you will have to hit me a little harder."

"You deceive yourself, Mr. Hawkhurst," Serena shot back. "There will be no next time. I cannot imagine meeting you again, and would not look forward to such an encounter, I assure you." She turned to the teapot and poured a cup of the dark liquid. "Will you take a cup of tea before you go, Mr. Hawkhurst?" she said sweetly, convinced that he would decline rudely. She had mistaken her man, however, for the gentleman strolled over and sat down on the yellow brocade settee, stretching his long legs out before him as though settling in for a lengthy visit.

"Delighted, Miss Millbanks," he drawled, a mocking smile on his well-shaped lips. "And I trust you are merely funning about there being no next time. I had hoped to persuade you to drive out with me in Hyde Park tomorrow afternoon if the weather is fine." He was staring at her with deliberate provocation, Serena saw, daring her to deny herself this unexpected treat. It was not every lady, even one blessed with a modicum of beauty—which Serena never claimed to have—who was invited to drive in the Park with a fashionable gentleman. Even if he were a rake of the first stare, Serena reminded herself. She could readily imagine her Cousin Melissa's reaction if she ever discovered that Serena had turned down just such a heaven-sent opportunity to display herself before the *ton*.

But two could play this game, Serena thought smugly, and smiled at the final barb she was about to throw. "Very condescending of you, I am sure," she replied gently. "But I never, *absolutely never,* drive out with a gentleman I hardly know." She gazed limpidly at him, noting with a jolt of apprehension that his eyes were crinkling at the corners and his mouth seemed unable to repress a grin.

"You do not know how glad I am to hear you say so, my dear," he said, his voice a smirk. "You see, I was under the impression that we know each other very well indeed."

Serena stared at him. The rogue remembered much more than he pretended. Much, much more, she thought with a tremor of alarm. As she watched, the gray eyes danced with secret amusement, and his mouth—a mouth she did indeed know very well and remembered all too vividly—quirked into a triumphant grin.

Serena lowered her gaze to the tea tray, wishing it were hemlock and not expensive China tea she had to offer him.

Major Hawkhurst was feeling very pleased with himself. His headache had vanished, and the throbbing of his nose had diminished to a dull ache that plagued him only when he laughed. And furthermore, he was thoroughly enjoying the discomfiture of the young lady sitting so primly, her back rigid with indignation, in the green leather chair beside the hearth in Lady Thornton's Yellow Saloon.

He had not expected to find the interview with Miss Serena Millbanks at all amusing, but he had been curious to see the shadowy nymph of last night's secluded courtyard again. His vague memory of the violet eyes and trim ankles had promised a diversion from the anguish which had weighed on him ever since returning from the Peninsula three years ago.

He had never known the meaning of boredom before he had arrived back in London, bringing his brother's body home in a sealed casket, to try to take up where Derek had left off. And of course, that had been an impossible task. Hawk had realized that as soon as he had taken Derek down to Hampshire and buried him next to their father and their brother who had died in infancy. Faced with the enormity of what was expected of him, of ever being worthy of stepping into Derek's shoes, Hawk had fled back to London and embarked on a life of dissipation and debauchery which at least kept his thoughts from straying back to that dreadful afternoon of his twin brother's death. At least, most of the time.

However, any hopes Hawk might have entertained of a dalliance with the mysterious Miss Millbanks evaporated when she came into the Yellow Saloon that afternoon. By no stretch of the imagination could she be called beautiful or even intriguing, and Hawk felt his expectations fizzle into disappointment. Except for her rather startling violet eyes, she was definitely unappetizing. Furthermore, Hawk noticed with a shudder, her taste in clothes—if her dowdy morning gown in dull green bombazine was any indication—bordered on the execrable. And her manners, he decided—as Miss Millbanks examined him with disconcerting frankness—left much to be desired. Her first words were equally unprepossessing and immediately put his back up.

So she didn't approve of him, did she? Hawk choked back an acerbic retort and held his temper in check with considerable difficulty while Miss Millbanks went on to label him a drunken brute she had no desire to set eyes upon ever again. Sweet Jesus, he thought to himself as he listened with mounting anger to her venomous litany, he must have comported himself with more than his usual license last night to provoke this barrage of insults. A flicker of apprehension struck him. Had he perhaps committed some gross indiscretion with the wench? he wondered. He did not usually prey upon plain females like Miss Millbanks, but it had been dark in the courtyard, and his memory stirred with faint recollections of a wonderfully supple body and a mouth of warm silk. Surely not belonging to the harridan sitting with him now, Hawk reasoned. A harridan who had the audacity to inquire—with a glimmer of unholy expectancy in her eyes, he noticed wryly—whether his nose was broken.

The blistering set-down that trembled on his lips died when the butler entered with the tea tray, accompanied by a footman with the flowers he had—in a moment of regrettable weakness—brought with him to lend credence to his apology. But instead of melting with gratitude at his thoughtfulness, as any right-minded chit would have done, Miss Millbanks had seen fit to accuse him of being guilty of some unidentified breach of conduct, and in the same breath offer him a cup of tea with such deceptive sweetness that, instead of storming out as he had intended, Hawk sat down and found himself—quite on the spur of the moment—inviting the rag-mannered chit to drive with him in the Park tomorrow.

Miss Millbanks had refused, of course, with a neatly worded rejection designed to deflate his audacity. But Hawk had expected that and was racking his wits for an unexceptionable ploy to force her to acknowledge the signal honor he had paid her, when the doors of the Yellow Saloon burst open and a shrill female in a monstrous bonnet—designed expressly, Hawk thought with a glimmer of amusement, to scare crows out of cornfields—sailed into the room.

Reluctantly, the Duke of Wolverton rose to his feet, knowing that his goose was cooked as far as preserving the little deception he had enjoyed playing on the innocent Miss Millbanks was concerned. The matron who bore down upon him, with hands fluttering nervously and face creased into a hundred wrinkles which no doubt she intended for a smile, had most certainly recognized him. For a moment Hawk wished he had sworn the butler to permanent complicity in maintaining his little charade of anonymity, but further reflection told him that such a scheme would be unwise. Sooner or later Miss Millbanks must be undeceived.

Hawk glanced at her briefly, half regretting the inevitable sheathing of that marvelously sharp tongue once she knew the illustrious identity of the gentleman she had so callously maligned for the past twenty minutes. Even the redoubtable Miss Millbanks would hardly dare be rude to a duke. His title shielded him from the barbs and pricks of real life, he thought bitterly, and in doing so took all the joy out of living. He wondered how Derek had stood the constant fawning of hangers-on, mushrooms, and hypocrites.

He turned back to the approaching matron and steeled himself for the avalanche of insincerity that was about to pour over his head.

"Oh, what a signal honor, Your Grace!" the matron exclaimed, sinking into a deep curtsy ill-befitting her stout form. "I must apologize for not being at home to receive you. I was visiting Lady Mansfield, the Dowager Countess, you know. Such a delightful creature . . ."

Hawk glanced at Miss Millbanks, who had risen to her feet at her aunt's appearance, and found her staring at him blankly, an expression of shock on her face. With a grimace of regret, he forced his attention back to Lady Thornton, who had not ceased chattering since her arrival.

"My daughter, Melissa, Your Grace," she was saying, drawing a starry-eyed young chit, obviously barely out of the schoolroom, forward for his notice. "Make your curtsy to His Grace, the Duke of Wolverton, my dear Melissa," she gushed. "Will you not sit down and join us for a cup of tea, Your Grace? I shall send for a fresh pot immediately. Melissa, my darling child, ring for Simmons if you please. We must have some fresh tea for His Grace."

The major cut ruthlessly through this fog of pointless civilities. "Miss Millbanks has been gracious enough to invite me to take tea with her, madam," he remarked with icy politeness. "I have spent a most entertaining half hour doing so," he added on impulse, feeling a sudden desire to rekindle the spark of battle in those violet eyes again.

Lady Thornton turned to stare at her niece as though she had only just noticed her presence, a piece of rudeness that made Hawk swear under his breath. "Serena? Oh, you should not have received His Grace alone, child. You will be thought terrible forward. I do hope you will take pity on the poor girl, Your Grace. She is recently come in from the wilds of Yorkshire, you know, and is not yet up to snuff on our London ways."

Hawk tried to catch Serena's eye, but she would not look at him. "I am quite certain that Miss Millbanks would never be guilty of the least impropriety, madam," he said with creditable sincerity, hoping that the enormity of such a whisker would tempt her to raise her eyes to acknowledge their private joke. When she did not, Hawk took a different tack.

"I am glad you have arrived in time for me to enlist your aid, my lady," he continued, before Lady Thornton could launch into another flood of tiresome pleasantries. "It seems that Miss Millbanks's modesty is such that she is unwilling to accept my invitation to drive in the Park without your express consent, Lady Thornton. I hope I can count on your support in persuading her that such an activity is unexceptionable?" He ended on a questioning note, and Lady Thornton could hardly refuse to agree with a personage of such elevated consequence as the Duke of Wolverton, Hawk thought cynically, watching the lady's face reflect her astonishment that a duke of the realm had actually shown interest in her countrified niece.

"I would rather not, if you do not mind, Aunt." Miss Millbanks's voice was subdued and held a note of pleading in it, but she could hardly have said anything more effective in persuading Lady Thornton to endorse the duke's invitation.

"Nonsense, child. You should be grateful that His Grace has singled you out for such an honor. Now, I will not hear another word, Serena. My niece is delighted to accept, Your Grace," Lady Thornton continued, turning to bestow a gracious smile on the duke. "It is only her natural modesty that prompts this missishness, you should know. But then modesty is so becoming in a young girl, do you not agree, Your Grace?"

"My sentiments exactly, madam," Hawk responded politely, stifling the urge to laugh. Modesty? If their first encounter had been any indication, the chit did not know the meaning of the word, he thought, wishing he could see some sign that Miss Millbanks was enjoying the irony of her aunt's ignorance as much as he was.

At no time in his rakish career had any female with a glimmer of discrimination dared to admit that she disapproved of him. Nor had any female of his acquaintance, which was extensive and eclectic, refused to drive out with him. Quite the contrary, in fact. As a member of the Four-in-Hand Club, Guy Hawkhurst had ever been plagued by young men anxious to learn the secret to feathering corners without overturning one's curricle, and by young women who aspired to be seen in the company of the young and very wealthy Duke of Wolverton. A feat considered by young ladies of marriageable age as a preparatory step in the frantic search for an eligible husband. In this respect, at least, Miss Millbanks was an original.

"Well, that is settled then," he murmured, eager to be on his way now that he had won the skirmish. "I shall call for you at four o'clock. If that is convenient, Miss Millbanks?" He addressed her deliberately, willing her again to raise her eyes.

For a long moment, Hawk thought she meant to ignore him, but finally Miss Millbanks did raise her eyes to stare at him. But there was nothing even vaguely resembling modesty or submissiveness in their violet depths. "Whatever you say. *Your Grace,*" she added, after a significant pause. She made him a perfunctory curtsy, but her mocking eyes never left his face.

Long after the front door of Number Seven Mount Street had closed behind him, Hawk wondered what excuse the redoubtable Miss Millbanks would come up with to avoid keeping her appointment with the Duke of Wolverton tomorrow afternoon.

CHAPTER THREE

The Ugly Duckling

After a night of unusually vivid dreams in which she found herself chased through the Park at dawn by a gray-eyed, inebriated satyrs, Serena was awakened by the sound of rain on her bedroom window. She lay immobile for a few moments, luxuriating in the sensual aftermath of her dreams. Where had the lascivious mythological beings sprung from? she wondered, amused at the odd direction her nighttime fantasies had taken. Usually they revolved around a tall, fair Adonis with the face of Brian Westlock, but a Brian whose gaze was full of passionate adoration and fixed—in the wonderfully irrational way of dreams—on Serena's face.

But last night she had dreamed of satyrs, of all things—quite possibly as a result of those decadent engravings she had peeped at during her visit to Hatchard's Book Shop two days ago. And their pursuit had been full of a joyous, sensual passion Serena had never—not even in her wildest dreams—associated with her fair-haired Brian. Not that he was hers at all, she reminded herself drowsily. He never would be. And in any case, she could not imagine Brian running through the Park—or anywhere else for that matter—in such a state of uninhibited arousal as those dream-satyrs had done. Chasing *her.* And the most disturbing part of the dream had been the knowledge that, sooner or later, she would be caught. She had *wanted* to be caught. Serena felt herself grow warm at the memory of her own wantonness. At the memory of those gray eyes so full of . . . so full of . . .

Gray eyes? Serena suddenly came fully awake as the memory of another pair of gray eyes—mocking, deceitful, decadent, and definitely lascivious eyes—returned to haunt her. She sat up and reached for her warm wrap. The carpet was cold against her bare feet, and when she pulled the thick blue curtains aside to let in the light, a draft of cold air made her shiver. And the rain. She had not dreamed it after all. The mild weather of the past two weeks had finally broken and the autumn rains had come.

Serena smiled thinly. Even a duke could hardly convince Aunt Hester that it was unexceptional for a young lady to drive around the Park in an open carriage in the rain, could he? She looked up at the sky, overcast and leaden, and smiled again. She was saved!

Back home in Yorkshire, Serena had enjoyed tramping about the countryside in the rain with her dog, Jollyboy. Everything changed with the autumn rains, she thought, wishing that Jollyboy were here to cheer her up with his boisterous romping. They were nothing like the rejuvenating rains of springtime, which helped to thaw out the frozen ground so the snowdrops could push their way up from their winter nesting places into a new cycle of life and beauty. Autumn rains had always seemed to Serena to be designed as an ending for that same cycle, to coax the last reluctant leaves from the trees and tamp them down in a thick carpet of reds and russets over an already somnolent earth. At home in Millbanks Hall the autumn rains would soon give way to snow, and snow meant that Christmas was not far away. Serena shivered again and this time it was not so much the chill air but the chill in her heart that affected her. She wondered if Cecily was remembering to take Jollyboy for his daily run on the moor.

"Ye'll catch yer death of cold, Miss Serena," her abigail scolded as she bustled into the room with her customary informality, a country trait much deplored by Lady Thornton. "Shame on you, child, standing there by the window with hardly anything on."

Serena ignored the scold. "I am so glad it is raining, Annie," she replied without turning. "It reminds me of home. Jollyboy must be chasing rabbits in the blackberry patch and getting his nose scratched." She paused, then added wistfully, "I wish he were here, Annie. I miss him."

"Come now, lass," the plump abigail chided. "Don't be moping yerself into a decline over that silly dog. He never had any sense to speak of, and what on earth would ye do with him in Lunnun?"

"He is wonderful company, Annie," Serena said mildly. "And he was a gift from Mama, remember. I'll always love him for that."

"God rest her sainted soul," the abigail murmured, reminding Serena that Lady Millbanks had been dearly loved by everyone on the estate. Without warning her throat tightened; she turned away from the rain-swept window and sat down at her dresser.

"Will you be wearing your new lilac cambric walking gown this afternoon, miss?" Annie asked. "It will be cold out in the Park, I reckon, and ye don't want to catch a chill."

Serena looked at her in surprise. "I am not going out at all today, Annie," she said. "It is raining, in case you have not noticed."

"The duke don't strike me as being the kind of gentleman to worry about a bit of rain, lass," the abigail replied with the casual certainty of servants who know everything there is to know about their betters. "And the lilac matches your eyes."

"I do not care what kind of man he is," Serena said impatiently. "And I shall refuse to go out in this weather. Even Aunt Hester will not ask it of me."

However, Serena was less certain of her aunt's strength of character than she might have liked. Would Lady Thornton indeed consider her niece's health more important than gratifying the whim of a duke of the realm, if His Grace should take it into his brandy-soaked head to present himself on her doorstep at four o'clock? Serena wondered. When four o'clock came and went, however, and the rain diminished not a jot, she began to feel confident that even a rake given to distempered starts—as Hawkhurst had proven himself to be—would be disinclined to ruin his exquisite boots by venturing out in such weather. With any luck, she thought, the rogue had forgotten all about her.

The arrival, at late-afternoon, of another monstrous bouquet of yellow chrysanthemums accompanied by a card inscribed with a curt "Hawk," severely undermined Serena's hope that she was rid of the stranger who had played such a deceitful trick on her. Guy Hawkhurst indeed! she thought disgustedly. Very likely that was his name, but he had made a fool of her by hiding his real identity. How was she to have known that the ungentlemanly stranger was a duke? And if she had? she wondered, her temper sparked again by the disturbing memory of the drunken stranger's embrace. Would she have curbed her unruly tongue? Would she have resisted the urge to exercise her pugilistic accomplishments upon his unwitting nose? Probably not, she had to admit. He had behaved most reprehensibly, and deserved to have his nose broken.

Serena gazed belligerently at the enormous yellow flowers

sitting in a crystal bowl on the pianoforte, telling herself that the blooms were innocent. She could not quite bring herself to call them beautiful. The urge to throw them out of the window was extremely irrational, she reasoned, and no doubt reflected her uncharitable urge to say something rude to the man who sent them.

She seemed inexplicably to be filled with violent, unlady-like urges, she thought, removing the offending flowers to a low table by the window. Quite possibly as a result of associating with violent ungentlemanly strangers in dark courtyards. Serena sat down and ran her fingers experimentally over the keys. She felt restless and unsettled. To calm her spirits she chose one of Scarlatti's sonatinas and was halfway through it when the door opened and Lady Thornton came into the music room.

"My dear Serena," she began as soon as she set foot inside the room, interrupting the sonatina in that unconscious manner of those who are either tone deaf or have little or no under-standing of music. "I am quite at a loss to know why the Duke of Wolverton has sent you another posy of flowers," she said. "Is there something you are not telling me, child?"

Serena wished her aunt would not refer to her as a child when she was quite patently on the shelf. At the moment she felt quite unlike her usual unruffled self, and it annoyed her to think that a rogue of Mr. Hawkhurst's reputation—she refused to think of him as a duke—could have such unsettling effects upon her. Aunt Hester's tone suggested that she was prepared to ferret out the truth of the matter, even if she had to invent it herself. Serena hoped she was equal to Lady Thornton's tena-cious curiosity.

She turned to smile at her aunt. "I suppose he felt badly about not keeping his engagement, Aunt, and sent the flowers to forestall my maidenly tantrums at being deprived of such a grand treat," she remarked serenely, conscious of another urge, this time to giggle.

"Oh, fiddle!" Lady Thornton exclaimed impatiently. "His Grace can hardly be blamed for the rain, can he?"

"Why not?" Serena inquired sweetly, amazed as she always was at her aunt's lack of humor. "I imagine dukes must have some sort of influence in such matters. He certainly acted as though his word was law when he was here yesterday."

"Now you are being ridiculous, child," her aunt scolded. "I

daresay the poor man is already regretting his rashness . . ."
Lady Thornton's voice trailed off uncertainly.

"What rashness do you mean, Aunt?" Serena inquired with
deceptive sweetness. She was all too familiar with her aunt's
unflattering opinion of her niece's countrified manners and
lack of polish, but Serena was feeling rather touchy this afternoon and quite unable to endure another petty tirade about her
unprepossessing appearance.

Lady Thornton cleared her throat ponderously, and Serena
steeled herself for the impending sermon. "I hear that the duke
is notorious for his practical jests and volatile moods, child,"
her aunt began. "He is also one of London's most de-
bauched—if I may be forgiven so strong a term—rakes and
care-for-nobodies. Addicted to drink, gambling, and—ahem—
a certain kind of female in the worst possible way. I find it
most unsettling that he has singled you out for his particular
attention, Serena. He is not a man to trifle with, you should
know, and I am uneasy that perhaps you have done something
foolish, child."

"Foolish?" Serena echoed with ill-disguised amusement.
"When have you known me to do anything foolish, Aunt?"
She grimaced inwardly at the notion of applying so innocuous
a label to what had transpired between Hawkhurst and herself
in that dark courtyard. Foolish, indeed? The word did not
begin to describe what the stranger had done to her. How
could it?

She herself could find no satisfactory explanation for the
way his hands on her hips had made her feel so weak and yet
so alive at the same time. Nor the sensations—utterly and
hopelessly decadent she was sure—that had spiraled through
her entire body as she felt his muscles ripple against her
breasts. No, she had no words to explain the overwhelming
urge to abandon herself to the sweet sensuality irradiating
from his tall frame. For one impossible moment she had even
wanted to return his kiss, Serena admitted with implacable
honesty. But the strong smell of brandy had almost choked
her. Saved her, perhaps, she thought ruefully, from disgracing
herself beyond repair. If only the stranger had not been in his
cups, Serena realized with sudden insight, she might have . . .
She brushed the notion aside with a faint smile, for whatever it
was, it was certainly not mere foolishness.

Serena suddenly realized that her aunt was regarding her
strangely and dutifully composed her features.

"I see nothing amusing in becoming the object of such un-flattering attentions, my dear Serena. The duke's intentions cannot possibly be honest, I should warn you. He must be at least twenty-nine or thirty, and has shown not the slightest sign of wishing to set up his nursery. I have it upon the most reliable authority that he has declared that he will drink himself into the ground before he will take a wife."

"A laudable ambition, to be sure," Serena could not resist remarking. "Let us hope, for the sake of all innocent females, that he will not tarry in accomplishing it."

Lady Thornton assumed a shocked expression. "You really must curb your tongue, Serena," she said. "No gentleman will offer for a female who bites his head off every time he opens his mouth."

"I am glad to hear it," Serena replied, remembering that a certain gentleman—but no, Hawkhurst was not a gentleman at all—had made a similar comment to her. "I wonder that you practically obliged me to accept an invitation from such a dangerous man, Aunt."

"It will do your consequence no harm to be seen in the company of the Duke of Wolverton, my dear," her aunt declared with what Serena considered an appalling lack of logic. "If His Grace can be induced to notice you and Melissa, your futures might well be assured."

Serena was about to point out, in her usual forthright manner, that the duke had not seemed to notice Cousin Melissa at all, but this acid comment was never uttered, for at that moment Simmons entered the music room to announce that Sir John Walker and Mr. Timothy Russell—two of Melissa's most conspicuous admirers—awaited the ladies in the drawing room.

After her aunt had left, Serena turned back to her sonatina with less than her usual enthusiasm. Was Mr. Hawkhurst the kind of man to enjoy a tramp in the rain? she wondered. There was no way she would ever know, of course, and she smiled at the foolish thought.

A week later, practical common sense had prevailed, and Serena had relegated all thoughts of the wayward Mr. Hawkhurst to the back of her mind. Well, almost all thoughts, she admitted with stringent honesty. An occasional memory of that fateful evening did intrude upon her quieter moments, of course. After all, the experience had been unique and deeply troubling. No man had ever brought her so close to the brink of disaster. Certainly not Brian Westlock, who seemed to have disappeared mysteriously from her dreams. But she was presumably safe from Mr. Hawkhurst, who had made no further attempt to see her; and no longer did the satyrs disturb her slumber with their indecorous rompings.

And after a week had passed with neither Hawkhurst nor satyrs to disturb her peace of mind, Serena concluded that the episode of the courtyard had been closed. She sensibly told herself that it was all for the best and threw herself—with what enthusiasm she could muster for playing the gooseberry—into steering her trusting cousin through the treacherous shoals of the *haut monde*.

It was only when Annie was helping her dress for an evening out with her cousin and Lady Thornton—as she was that evening—that Serena would pay any heed to the little voice within her that suggested the unthinkable. Hawkhurst might well be a threat to any decent female's reputation, but at least he had not bored her, she thought, as she had several times during the past week. In an extremely decadent and dangerous sort of way, he had actually been rather entertaining. Serena smiled at the perversity of this notion, as she allowed the abigail to slip the lilac silk gown over her head and pull it down around her hips. The gown reminded her of the evening she had encountered Hawkhurst on Lady Berkford's terrace. Every time she wore it—which was frequently, since she possessed so few gowns—the lilac silk conjured up sensations Serena would rather forget. No, she chided herself for this blatant dishonesty. She would do well to forget everything about that particular stranger and the unladylike emotions he had stirred in her that night, but she was honest enough to know that she would do nothing of the sort.

Would the duke attend the ball at Mansfield Court that evening? Serena wondered, picking up her gloves and cloak and making her way out onto the landing. A brief tremor of excitement touched her before her practical self concluded that it mattered little to a country mouse from Yorkshire, such as herself, whether the grand Mr. Hawkhurst deigned to grace the ball with his presence or not. He had presumably forgotten her existence, for no further invitations or yellow chrysanthemums had been forthcoming. Serena sighed and descended to the front drawing room to greet Sir John Walker, who was to be their escort that evening.

Lady Thornton was already there, ensconced in a wing chair by the fire, engaging the young baronet in a lengthy description of the sad crush the ladies had encountered several nights ago at the opera.

"Good evening, Sir John," Serena greeted him, smiling at the look of unconcealed eagerness on his youthful face. The baronet was one of Melissa's more assiduous admirers, and as the eldest son in a solid rather than prominent Sussex family, with a rumored ten thousand pounds a year, he figured high on Lady Thornton's list of prospective sons-in-law.

"Ah, there you are Serena," exclaimed her ladyship heartily. "Sir John tells me that Mr. Russell will join us at the ball, my dear. He is to escort his Mama and sister, it appears." She cast an ingratiating smile at the baronet. "Such a proper young man, your Mr. Russell. Our dear Serena is anxious to renew his acquaintance."

Serena grimaced but made no comment. Ever since Sir John had introduced his friend Timothy Russell to the ladies several days ago at a sparsely attended rout, her aunt had determined that the red-headed ex-officer would make her niece an excellent husband. Serena was equally determined that he would not. Russell was pleasant enough, she thought, and although his prospects were not nearly as attractive as the baronet's, his breeding and manners were unexceptionable. Serena's major objection—which she could not tell her aunt—was that Timothy Russell reminded her too nearly of Brian Westlock, and furthermore, his laughing blue eyes strayed too often to Melissa's face when he thought no one was watching.

Nevertheless, Serena's heart felt lighter than usual as she trod up the marble stairway at Mansfield Court later that evening at the thought that at least two presentable gentlemen would ask her to dance. As she was introduced to the gracious Dowager Countess and her darkly handsome son, the Earl of Mansfield, Serena wondered how her enterprising aunt had wangled invitations to the dowager's select gathering. Lady Thornton made much of her connection with the Mansfields—tenuous though it was—but Serena had seriously doubted that they would indeed receive a coveted invitation to the Mansfields' autumn ball based solely on the fact that her aunt's second cousin on her mother's side had, at the advanced age of thirty-five, married one of Lady Mansfield's Irish third cousins.

Such were the vagaries of the *beau monde,* Serena thought,

pleasantly surprised at the warm greeting she received from the young Countess of Mansfield. As they entered the brilliantly lighted ballroom, Serena felt a brief flash of envy—which she quickly suppressed—at the frankly doting gleam she had witnessed in the earl's eyes when they rested on his radiant countess. Clearly, the two were quite unfashionably in love and did not care who knew it. What would it feel like to be treasured by such a man? Serena wondered. The darkly taciturn earl reminded her of the satyrs who had so unexpectedly invaded her dreams a week ago, and Serena suddenly felt the odd certainty that the young countess's nights would never be spent alone in a cold bed as her own were destined to be.

Appalled at these indelicate, maudlin thoughts, Serena glanced at the group of matrons already established on the settees clustered at one end of the room for that purpose, and shuddered. Repressing a sigh, she seated herself among them beside her aunt and watched Sir John lead Melissa onto the floor to join a newly formed set for a country dance. Several minutes later she was relieved to notice the red-haired Mr. Russell dancing with an equally red-haired young lady in a vastly unbecoming pink muslin gown, who could be none other than his sister. Mr. Russell seemed to be paying little heed to his sister's lively chatter, however, for his eyes were fixed—rather wistfully, Serena thought—on the delicate figure of her Cousin Melissa, who was very much *à la mode* in her new yellow muslin.

When the set came to an end, Serena was amused to notice how smoothly Russell attached himself to Sir John and that both couples converged on the settee she occupied with her aunt.

"My dear Lady Thornton," Russell began, bending over to salute her aunt with commendable formality, "I am happy to see you in such looks this evening. I wonder if you would permit me to make my sister Elizabeth known to you and your charming daughter, ma'am?"

Lady Thornton, unaccustomed to such blatant flattery, was more than happy to accept Miss Elizabeth Russell's shy curtsy and gladly gave her permission to Melissa to accompany Timothy in the next dance. It was only after the young officer had borne away his prize, that Serena realized that she herself had been completely ignored. She caught Sir John's eye and the baronet blushed uncomfortably and requested the honor of leading her out for the cotillion just forming.

"I gather you have known the Russells for some time, Sir John?" she remarked pleasantly in an attempt to put the poor man at his ease.

"Yes, I certainly have, Miss Millbanks. Tim and I grew up within five miles of each other. But I must apologize for Tim's inexplicable rudeness just now. He could not have noticed you," he added, then blushed more deeply when Serena nearly choked on laughter. "Oh, my foolish tongue," he sighed. "Now I have to apologize all over again for my own unpardonable rudeness, Miss Millbanks. That's not what I meant at all, you see—"

"Do not tease yourself, Sir John," Serena reassured him. "I am invariably *not noticed,* you see, since I am always in my cousin's company, and she—as I'm sure you will agree—is beyond price." Which was nothing if not the truth, she reflected without rancor. And furthermore, she was more willing to be *not noticed* by Timothy Russell, who was so obviously smitten with Melissa. She smiled up at the baronet's flustered face.

"When you smile, you are not so bad yourself, Miss Millbanks," he stammered.

Seeing that the baronet had not perceived the incongruity of his backhanded compliment, Serena repressed the laughter that bubbled in her throat. "Thank you kindly, sir," she murmured demurely. "You are too good."

"Not a bit of it," he responded stoutly. "Nothing but the truth, ma'am, I can assure you."

He looked so relieved at brushing creditably over his *faux pas* that Serena did not have the heart to tease him further, and it was perhaps just as well, she thought ruefully, for Sir John's attention seemed to have wandered to the slight figure in pale yellow muslin dancing with his friend. Every time Melissa's tinkling laugh reached their ears, Serena saw her partner's jaw clench convulsively, and her heart went out to him. She knew all too well the anguish Sir John was experiencing. Her thoughts flew back to Yorkshire, and she remembered her own silent suffering when Brian had ignored her very existence in Priscilla's presence. Perhaps she was destined to fade permanently into the woodwork, she thought dispiritedly. A female who would eventually disappear entirely because nobody ever noticed her. The *not noticed* ape-leader, she mused, her fertile imagination expanding on the notion of becoming nominally invisible. What things might she not see and hear? she mused, resolutely shaking off her maudlin self-pity.

Not one to be long cast down by morbid thoughts, Serena set herself to draw out Miss Russell. She soon discovered a kindred spirit in the shy, young redhead.

"Are you enjoying your stay in London?" she inquired politely.

"Oh, yes," Elizabeth murmured gently, her eyes shining with excitement. "But I could wish that I were not so plain," she added with a refreshing honesty that delighted Serena. "I am very much afraid that red hair is not all the rage in London."

"I have often wished the same thing myself," Serena confessed.

"But I have long since decided that it does no good to repine over things we cannot change and have quite decided to enjoy myself regardless. Have you noticed, for example, how so many otherwise sensible females comport themselves as though luring an eligible gentleman to the altar were their ultimate ambition?"

Elizabeth looked at her in surprise. "Oh, but it is, is it not?" she asked innocently. "At least, my Mama always says so. And my Papa cannot afford another Season in London, that I do know. So if I do not receive an eligible offer before Christmas—which I seriously doubt will happen—I shall be in for a grand scold when my Mama takes us back to Sussex."

"Pray do not be cast down on that account, Miss Russell," Serena hastened to say, anxious to dispel the note of desperation she detected in the younger girl's voice. "I am in a similar quandary, you see. My Papa sent me to London to get myself riveted—as he put it. But so far I have not encountered anyone worth the effort. Quite frankly, I find London gentlemen vastly overrated. True, they are in general better turned out than the men in Yorkshire, but more than half of them seem to be rakes and libertines, and I have no wish to receive an offer from any of them."

By the end of that set, Serena and Miss Russell—who insisted upon being called Elizabeth—were on excellent terms and had quite decided that coming to London in search of a husband had been a dreadful waste of money. But after she had endured a lively country dance with Timothy Russell and a rather sedate waltz with Sir John, Serena felt the familiar fog of boredom descending upon her. Idly, she considered escaping to the dining room where refreshments had been laid out, but before she could pluck up the courage to do so, her attention was distracted by a commotion of raised voices and male laughter from the top of the stairs leading to the ballroom.

Even before the party of latecomers entered the room, Serena had recognized Hawkhurst's lazy drawl. The devil fly away with the man, she thought crossly, catching a glimpse of his tall figure through the twirling couples on the dance floor. As before, he was dressed in black, and yet again was regarding the guests through his ridiculous quizzing glass. He did appear sober, Serena had to admit, although she would not care to wager any great sum on it.

And he was not alone. Three equally attractive gentlemen had entered the ballroom in his wake and now clustered around the duke as he glanced about the room as if searching for someone. Well, he was in for a disappointment, Serena thought peevishly. The enchanting Duchess of Ridgeway was not among those present. For some obscure reason, the absence of the scintillating duchess gave her a glimmer of satisfaction. The rogue would have to seek out another victim for his odious attentions tonight, she reasoned as the group of elegant gentlemen moved across the room, throwing out casual greetings to various acquaintances and occasionally stopping to exchange pleasantries with friends.

"Why, there is His Grace the Duke of Wolverton," Lady Thornton exclaimed in a shrill whisper. "I wonder if he has seen us? Where is Melissa?" she asked suddenly, glancing around her with a frown. "Drat the child! Never at hand when I need her. Go and see if you can find her, Serena, and bring her to me instantly. No doubt the duke will wish to dance with her."

Serena did not need to be asked twice. Embarrassed at her aunt's presumption, she sprang to her feet and rushed with unseemly haste to the nearest exit. The doors to the refreshment room stood wide open and, after ascertaining that the only occupants were two portly gentlemen engaged in putting away a number of salmon patties, Serena scurried in and made a beeline for the punch bowl. She poured herself a generous potion and had raised it to her lips when an amused voice stopped her cold.

"Miss Millbanks, can it be that I find you drinking again? Shame on you, my dear girl. Believe me, it will be the death of you."

Serena stood perfectly still for several seconds, then she deliberately raised her glass and drank her punch, not in delicate sips as her aunt had told her time and again to do, but in defiant, hearty gulps as she did at home when no one was looking. Then she placed her empty glass carefully back on the table and turned around, her gaze instantly locking with a pair of gray eyes regarding her with sardonic amusement.

"You are a fine one to talk!" she said scathingly, her gaze deceptively bland. "Indeed, I am surprised—and a little disappointed—to find you still above ground, Mr. Hawkhurst. I had hoped to dance at your funeral."

CHAPTER FOUR

The Swan

As he stepped into Lady Mansfield's brilliantly lighted ballroom shortly after midnight that late October evening, Guy Hawkhurst felt a depressing sense of *déjà-vu* which caused him to utter a pithy expletive under his breath. Unfortunately, his muffled obscenity, meant for the ears of his three slightly foxed companions, was overheard by the tall, thin dowager in purple who had innocently entered the ballroom in their wake. Flustered out of her customary hauteur, the dowager threw a startled glance at the Duke of Wolverton and then stalked past him, her back ramrod-straight and thin lips pursed disdainfully.

Hawk laughed. He had not set out intentionally to shock the skinny matron in the purple gown and matching ostrich feathers bobbing and swaying in her ridiculous turban, but he obviously had done so.

"I say, old man," Robert Stilton, the Marquess of Monroyal murmured in his inimitable drawl. "Better watch what you are about, Hawk, or you'll have us all thrown out of here."

"Yes, indeed, Robert is right," cut in the fair-haired gentleman who was gazing after the departing dowager with a rueful expression on his handsome face. "That old Tabby is Lady Buxley, my lad, a bosom-bow of my mother's neighbor down in Hampshire. By the time this little incident gets back to Dalton Park, it will be me who uttered that quite reprehensible comment of yours, Hawk. I do not relish being called on the mat for your sins, old man."

Hawkhurst followed the stiff progress of the outraged dowager across the room with a faint smile. Then he turned to regard Tony Dalton with lazy amusement. "Happy to have Steele dispatch a letter to your mother first thing in the morning, Tony," he drawled, "Hate to have any of my peccadilloes laid at your door."

"Peccadilloes?" Dalton snorted. "I wonder if old Ridgeway

takes your exploits quite so lightly, Hawk? You have half the *ton* agog with your dalliance with the delectable Honoria, you know. Can't be too pleasant for Ridgeway, I imagine."

"Nobody asked him to get himself leg-shackled to a chit less than half his age," the marquess interrupted in a bored voice. "Asking for trouble, I would say. Besides, I have often wondered who was doing the pursuing, old Hawk here or the voracious new duchess."

"That appears to be a moot point tonight in any case," the fourth member of their party remarked quietly. "The lady don't seem to be here, so you are safe, Hawk. Unless you fancy a schoolroom miss in her first Season, that is?" he added with wry humor.

Hawk looked over his shoulder at the speaker and grinned. "Your wits have gone begging, Laughton," he quipped. "Do I look like a ravisher of innocents to you? Schoolroom chits are dangerous to a man's health, don't you know. Might end up as a tenant for life if you set your sights on one of those."

"I find all this talk of innocents a dead bore," Stilton cut in with a yawn. "Give me a female who knows the rules, like our sweet Chloe Huntington. I wonder if she is here tonight?" He scanned the room with hooded eyes.

"Hardly likely," Sir David Laughton remarked in his unruffled way. "If I remember rightly, Lady Huntington threw out some pretty serious lures for old Raven before *and* after he married Lady Mansfield. Caused a devil of a dust-up between them, I heard. Hardly likely that Raven's mother, who dotes on her daughter-in-law, would invite that cat Chloe to her ball."

"That must have happened while I was in Spain," Hawk-hurst murmured absentmindedly, and instantly cursed himself for bringing up a subject so painful to him. The specter of Derek, covered with blood, with one leg trapped beneath his dead horse rose in his mind's eye as it always did when he thought of Spain. God, he thought bitterly, how he wished he could relive that whole day, that ghastly battle, even that hour, or those final minutes which had changed his life forever, blighting it with guilt that still racked him.

"What the devil are we doing here anyway?" he muttered abruptly, lifting his quizzing glass to scan the room full of laughing, whirling couples. How could everyone be so happy, he thought, feeling one of his dark moods coming on. Derek was dead. And for all intents and purposes, he was dead, too,

Hawk admitted. Not one of the expensively gowned females in the room held the least attraction for him. At least not yet. He was not yet drunk enough to fall into bed with one of the elegant, experienced beauties who were even now surreptitiously slanting their lovely eyes in his direction. Some less surreptitiously than others, of course, but in the end it amounted to the same thing. An hour or two of mindless coupling, then home to his own bed, a pounding head the following morning, and a bitter taste in his mouth that was not entirely due to the brandy he had consumed.

"Raven invited us particularly, old man," Hawk heard Sir David Laughton's mellow voice murmur at his shoulder. "His delightful lady-wife aspires to reform us all, as I understand the matter."

The marquess gave a snort of derision. "I ain't ready to be reformed yet," he sneered. Robert always became more cynical when in his cups, Hawk thought, wishing he could so easily find an outlet for his own bitterness.

"What do you say we all go back to White's and—"

"Dammit Robert," Hawk interrupted the marquess angrily. "How can I think straight with you jawing us all to death?"

There was pregnant pause before the marquess spoke again. "Looking for a bout of fisticuffs, Hawk?" He spoke softly, but Hawk could detect the steel beneath the silk.

"I doubt Raven would thank us for causing a dust-up in the middle of his ballroom," Laughton interjected calmly. "I favor White's myself, unless Hawk has any more of that prime French brandy left."

The four men relaxed visibly, Hawk noted, and he smiled grimly. He favored the crowded ballroom with one last glance through his quizzing glass and was about to suggest that they repair to Wolverton Court to indulge in some serious drinking when he glimpsed a fleeting lilac shadow out of the corner of his eye.

"Aha!" he exclaimed, a sardonic smile curling his lips for the first time since arriving at Mansfield Court. "What have we here?" A sudden thought struck him and he turned to Lord Monroyal with a wide grin. "Would you say I was castaway, Robert?"

The marquess stared at him a moment, then a devilish glint appeared in his dark eyes. "Nothing to signify, old man," he drawled. "I doubt your faculties are in any way impaired," he added, with a lewd wink.

"Then follow me," Hawkhurst said, and abruptly turned to stride away down the hall parallel to the ballroom. He would have preferred to confront her alone, but it might be amusing to see how the starchy Miss Millbanks would react to being accosted by a phalanx of London's premier rakes.

She was standing by the punch bowl when he paused on the threshold of the dining room, her attention completely absorbed in pouring the pink liquid into a delicate crystal glass. By the time she raised it to her lips, Hawk had crossed the room behind her. When he spoke, twitting her gently about her drinking, his tone was cynical and amused.

For the longest moment, Miss Millbanks stood perfectly still, and Hawkhurst wondered briefly if she meant to snub him entirely. She was certainly capable of it, he had no doubt. Then she raised the punch and drank deeply, setting the glass down deliberately and turning in one smooth motion to stare him straight in the eyes.

Hawk stared back, wondering what was going on behind those marvelous violet eyes of hers. Without knowing quite why, he suddenly wished he had not teased her about drinking. The memory of their unfortunate meeting on that shadowy terrace must still rankle, and he had been so damnably foxed he had little recollection of exactly what he had done to arouse her ire. He had kissed her. That much he remembered. But what else had he done? Was Miss Millbanks still furious with him? he wondered.

Her first words left little doubt in his mind on that score.

No sooner were the taunting words spoken than Serena wished she might recall them. For even as she watched, petrified at her own temerity, the gray eyes turned a darker shade of pewter and the black brows lowered. She had done it again, she thought fleetingly; she had allowed her natural exuberance to betray her into an appalling social gaff. It was one thing to address the young men she had known in Yorkshire with a directness bordering on impertinence; she had done so for years and got away with it. But to do so with a London beau, a duke of the realm no less—even if he was a drunken rake and debaucher of innocents—was quite beyond the pale. Mr. Hawkhurst's set expression confirmed this suspicion.

It was then that Serena realized that they were not alone.

How she could have overlooked the presence of three other gentlemen looming around the duke, she was at a loss to understand, but overlook them she certainly had. But now one of them let out a crack of cynical laughter, followed by an amused chuckle that rumbled deep in his throat.

"Touché, old man," the gentleman drawled, in a voice that was both seductive and vaguely offensive. "It is not like you to disappoint a lady, Hawk. Losing your touch, perhaps?" he murmured, and the implications of his remark made Serena wish she could hide under the table.

"Shut up, Robert," Hawkhurst growled out of the corner of his mouth, his eyes never wavering from Serena's face.

"Dance at your funeral, Hawk?" a second, softer voice broke in. "What a novel idea. Wish I had thought of it myself."

"Yes, I could not agree more," the drawling voice continued. "When is this propitious event to take place?"

"Not before Christmas, I hope," the soft-spoken voice remarked. "That would put a damper on the holiday festivities, old chap. Cannot have that, you know. My mother would never forgive you."

Serena listened to the bantering exchange swirling about her, but she refused to drop her eyes as a gently bred female always did when confronted with a masculine stare. At least that was what Aunt Hester had insisted. What would be her aunt's advice to a lady who found herself the object of four pairs of masculine eyes? Serena wondered. The thought was so ludicrous that she was hard-pressed to keep from grinning.

Hawkhurst must have guessed at her thoughts, for suddenly his own lips twitched. "Am I to understand that you are wishing me in Jericho, Miss Millbanks?" he inquired with studied politeness.

Serena smiled sweetly at this. "Oh, no, indeed," she responded brightly without thinking. "I am afraid Jericho is much too close for comfort. I would much prefer to see you in . . ." Suddenly she paused in consternation and closed her eyes briefly. She had done it again. There was no hope for her at all. What gently bred female would dream of telling a duke to go to Hades? she wondered. It would serve her right if Hawkhurst and his friends turned on their heels and fled, disgusted at her rag-mannered display.

A burst of laughter caused her eyes to fly open. The gray eyes were still fixed on hers, although now they were full of amusement. Serena felt inexplicably relieved.

"In hell, I presume you mean, Miss Millbanks?" This new voice was deep and faintly amused, and Serena knew it must belong to the third of Hawkhurst's friends. "I could not agree with you more. And you will perhaps be glad to know that he is already halfway there."

"Yes, I know," Serena replied, thankful that her rudeness had not appeared too disastrous to at least one of the gentlemen.

"I say, Hawk," the man addressed as Robert drawled in a bored voice, "how much longer are you going to keep us standing about before you introduce us to this . . ." He paused so briefly that Serena hoped she had imagined the implied slight. "This *charming* young lady?" he finished, and any doubt Serena might have harbored that this particular gentleman was mocking her evaporated.

"I thought I told you to shut up, Robert?" Hawkhurst growled.

Serena was far from mollified by this half-hearted reprimand. Her chin went up and—for the first time since she had been accosted by Hawkhurst and the three strangers—Serena turned from the duke and looked directly into another pair of eyes. What she saw there made her heart quail. The dark gray eyes told her clearly that she was far beneath their owner's notice. She read all her inadequacies recorded there—her outmoded gown, her unremarkable face, her countrified gaucherie, her hoydenish manners. Serena knew that the brooding eyes, set in a face that was almost classical in its dark symmetry, saw into every nook and cranny of her soul. And that her body, as yet untainted by any man's gaze, was an open book to him. She felt suddenly violated—examined and found wanting by this unprincipled rogue. A surge of fury rose in her at this careless, arrogant invasion of her privacy, her femininity, her very essence. She raised her chin another inch and glared back at him.

"Unless your feet are rooted to the floor, sir, there is no reason for you to stand about here a moment longer," she said icily. "You may leave at any time you wish," she added, perversely gratified at the look of surprise that flashed in the gray eyes. "The sooner the better," she could not resist throwing in. "There is nothing stopping you. Certainly not good manners."

Serena was startled when Hawkhurst let out a crack of laughter. "Touché, Robert?" he purred, obviously enjoying his friend's discomfiture.

"Well done, Miss Millbanks," the soft-spoken gentleman

cut in with enthusiasm. "It is not everyone who can put Robert so neatly in his place. I applaud your intrepidity, ma'am."

"Miss Millbanks," the duke interrupted, an amused grin still on his face, "may I present to you three of the most notorious rakes in London?"

"Oh, I say!" exclaimed the fair-haired gentleman with the soft voice. "That's not fair, Hawk. Talk about the stove calling the kettle black."

Serena saw her chance to escape. "It is of no consequence, in any case," she said coldly. "I have no wish to meet any more rakes. So if you will excuse me . . ."

"Surely you cannot be so cruel, Miss Millbanks," the fair-haired gentleman immediately protested. "Anthony Dalton, at your service, ma'am," he added, clasping Serena's unresisting hand and raising it gracefully to his lips. "I had hoped to persuade you to grant me the next dance?" He ended on a questioning note, and Serena could not resist returning the smile in his dancing blue eyes.

"Cut line, Tony," Hawkhurst interrupted. "Miss Millbanks shows admirable good sense in not wishing to waste her time with four of London's most eligible bachelors. Am I not correct, my dear?"

Serena raised one delicate eyebrow in mock astonishment. "I am so glad we can agree on something, sir," she replied wryly. "But if this is the best London has to offer," she gestured vaguely at the four gentlemen still clustered around her, "then I believe it is high time I returned to Yorkshire. Would you not agree, Mr. Dalton?" She bestowed her most brilliant smile on the fair-haired gentleman, gauging him to be the least threatening of the four. "Perhaps I can prevail upon you to escort me back to my aunt, sir?"

"Delighted," Mr. Dalton replied quickly, offering his arm. "Perhaps I might change your mind about that dance, Miss Millbanks?"

"Not on your life, Tony," Hawkhurst intervened harshly. "The lady is promised to me for this waltz." He, too, presented his arm as though willing Serena to bow to his will. The orchestra was indeed warming up for a waltz, and the thought of dancing in such close intimacy with the duke set her stomach in a flutter. Memories of the stranger's arms around her on Lady Berkford's terrace caused her a moment of pure panic. Not that the vaguely decadent new dance allowed a lady to feel a gentleman's muscles ripple against her breasts, Serena thought, trying to overcome her momentary weakness. But the mere prospect of feeling Hawkhurst's hands on her again unnerved her, so her reaction was sharper than she had intended.

"I am promised to nobody, sir," she said bluntly.

"Good," the duke replied, a grin of triumph on his handsome face. "I am sure Mr. Nobody will be only too glad to give up his claim to me."

"As usual," Serena put in sharply, "you are entirely off the mark, sir. Nothing could induce me to dance with you."

"Would you care to place a small wager on it, Miss Millbanks?" His eyes held a faintly challenging gleam that Serena found hard to ignore.

The pause that followed was broken by a drawling voice, heavy with boredom. "My money is on Miss Millbanks, Hawk. A monkey says you will not get your waltz." He met Serena's surprised gaze with a bland face, but his eyes were mocking. "Robert Stilton, Marquess of Monroyal, at your service, my dear Miss Millbanks." He bowed with a flourish that matched the mockery in his eyes, bringing an angry flush to Serena's cheeks.

"No doubt you have heard what they say about a fool and his money, my lord?" she inquired with false sweetness.

Monroyal's faint smile vanished and his eyes became hooded. "I understood you to say that nothing would induce you to—"

Serena laughed outright, her pleasure at seeing this arrogant man at point non-plus overriding her natural caution. "Perhaps I should have said *almost* nothing," she said. Serena turned to the duke, who was regarding her with an odd expression in his gray eyes. Laying her hand on his arm, she grinned up at him as she would have grinned at Jeremy, her father's stable boy, when they had succeeded in besting Cecily at one of her own games.

"I believe our waltz is starting, sir."

As she allowed Hawkhurst to lead her onto the dance floor, Serena wondered fleetingly who would have the last laugh in the game she had unwittingly agreed to play with the notorious stranger and his outrageous friends.

Whatever else happened, Serena though—unwilling to speculate on what might be—one thing was perfectly clear at the outset. Miss Serena Millbanks would not find their company boring. Scandalous perhaps, but certainly not boring.

* * *

No sooner had she set foot on the dance floor and turned to face her partner than Serena began to regret her foolish desire to outwit the odious marquess. The crooked grin on Hawkhurst's face instantly warned her that he had read her thoughts, which had—quite of their own accord—flashed back to that evening they had first encountered each other on Lady Berkford's deserted terrace. She recalled it all too vividly, watching the same memories flicker in the duke's amused eyes. That intoxicated stranger was no longer a stranger, of course, and he was not noticeable disguised—although Serena caught a whiff of brandy on his breath as he placed a large hand on her waist and loomed over her, much as he had done that other evening.

"It is unseemly to smirk, sir," Serena said with some asperity, resorting—as she invariable did when flustered—to verbal fencing.

"I have every reason to do so, my dear Miss Millbanks," Hawkhurst replied smugly. "Thanks to you, I have just won five-hundred pounds."

"And if you delude yourself that I agreed to dance with you to help you win that absurd wager, you are grossly mistaken," she said coldly. "If that odious marquess had not smirked at me as he did and made such offensive insinuations, I would not be here, sir. It is nothing to me whether you win your silly wagers or not."

"Well, you should care, Miss Millbanks," came the drawling reply. "Half of it is yours, you know."

Serena's eyes flew to his face, and as soon as she saw that he was not teasing, her hackles rose. "Fiddlesticks!" she exclaimed crossly. "That is quite absurd. I want nothing to do with any wager."

So engrossed in this ridiculous argument had she become that Serena momentarily forgot they were in the middle of a crowded dance floor. It was as though they were back on Lady Berkford's terrace, she thought, the disturbing intimacy of Hawkhurst's hand on her waist recalling every nuance of the fright and pleasure she had experienced—quite unexpectedly and against her will, of course—in the arms of the inebriated stranger.

"Was your neckcloth quite ruined?" she demanded suddenly, glancing up at him from the pristine cravat several inches from her nose. The sight of it had brought to mind the indecorous way she had buried her face in the creation he had worn that dreadful night.

Hawkhurst grinned, again seeming to read her mind. "I have no idea. But I imagine that after you ruthlessly tore it from my neck, it must have suffered irreparable damage."

"I did not tear it . . ." she began hotly, before realizing that he was deliberately provoking her, and that her raised voice had attracted the curious stares of other couples.

"I wouldn't bruit it about that you undressed me, my dear," he whispered with a mocking grin. "The *haut monde* frowns upon such intimacies, even in country lasses from—"

"I did no such thing!" Serena retorted, her color high. She glanced nervously around and noticed several curious looks and no small number of hostile ones from the ladies. "And if you dare to make another improper remark," she hissed in a low voice, "I will land you another facer. And don't bother to wager that I would not do so."

"Here in the middle of the dance floor?" he taunted, gray eyes full of amusement. "Your reputation would be in tatters, my dear."

"So would yours."

He gave a bark of laughter that turned more heads in their direction. "It already is, my sweet innocent. Nothing you could do would make it any worse. And let me warn you, Miss Mill-banks, if you hit my poor nose again, I shall have to kiss you to even the score."

Serena stared at him in consternation. He was looking down at her through hooded eyes and his mouth curled up at one corner in a satanical leer. She was suddenly quite certain that he meant it, and a tremor of apprehension went through her as she considered the consequences. Lady Thornton would un-doubtedly send her back to Yorkshire post-haste, and her name would be mud among the *ton*, who would amuse themselves avidly for a week with her disgrace and then forget that Miss Millbanks had ever existed. The thought was rather lowering.

"You are foxed again, sir," she said scathingly, her voice cold with contempt.

"Not nearly enough, m'dear," came the unexpected reply. "Not yet, in any event.

Serena forgot her own anger at the hint of something deeper than mere bravado in Hawkhurst's voice. "Foxed enough for what?" she heard herself asking before she could quell her natural curiosity.

His gray eyes became remote, and Serena had the distinct impression that he had withdrawn into another world. No doubt a place of troubled memories, she thought, catching a flash of pain in his abstracted gaze. She felt a sudden well of compassion rise in her heart as she continued to stare into his blank eyes. The moment passed as quickly as it had come, and when he spoke, his voice mocked her.

"You would not want to know, my dear innocent," he drawled, his cynical grin suggesting depravities beyond her imagination.

"Something is troubling you," she said softly. "I can feel it. Perhaps you would feel better if—"

"Do not even think of it," Hawkhurst interrupted harshly. "There is nothing wrong with me that a case of French brandy and a willing . . ." He broke off abruptly, scowling down at her with hard, cold eyes.

The music stopped and Serena drew away from him. There was no mistaking what the duke had been about to say, and she knew that she should be outraged at such plain speaking. But all Serena could feel was pity that a man as young and attractive as Guy Hawkhurst could waste his life in such meaningless pursuits. With considerable difficulty, she reminded herself that it was nothing to her what he did with his life. She had more than enough to worry about concerning her own future.

"And wagers, Mr. Hawkhurst," she said frostily. "You forgot to mention the frivolous wagers you seem to find so entertaining." She glanced around and saw that Lady Thornton was seated nearby, smirking and gesturing in their direction. "Now if you will excuse me, I see my aunt beckoning." Without waiting for his reply, she whirled on her heel and strode over to her aunt, whose face took on a petulant expression when she realized that her niece did not have the infamous Duke of Wolverton in tow.

As she went, Serena felt the hard, gray eyes boring into her back.

After her uncomfortable waltz with Hawkhurst, Serena had expected to sink back into her usual role of wallpaper, sitting demurely beside her aunt and fetching refreshments for the elderly ladies who gathered to exchange crim-con stories about the more important guests.

But that evening proved to be vastly different, as Serena soon discovered.

The first to break the tranquil pattern of similar evenings spent watching her Cousin Melissa flirt with a bevy of young gentlemen was Mr. Dalton. This charming blond gentleman arrived almost before Serena could collect her breath from the waltz with Hawkhurst to beg Lady Thornton's permission to lead Serena out for the country dance then forming. Having ascertained—after a lengthy and convoluted discussion—that one of Mr. Dalton's maternal aunts was an old crony of hers from finishing school, Lady Thornton graciously granted her permission. But not before bringing her darling Melissa to Mr. Dalton's notice, as Serena had known she would. The fact that the dashing Mr. Dalton cast but a cursory glance in her cousin's direction before leading Serena onto the floor, afforded her a glow of satisfaction she immediately recognized as unworthy of her.

Nevertheless, the glow of happiness persisted throughout the set, entirely due—she admitted with scrupulous honesty—to the fact that Mr. Dalton's dancing blue eyes rarely wandered and his conversation was wholly focused on her. He was a sad tease and an accomplished flirt, as Serena told him frankly when—instead of returning to her aunt—Mr. Dalton led her into the dining room to procure a glass of lemonade.

"You malign me, Miss Millbanks," he protested, smiling with such devastating charm that Serena found herself wondering why some enterprising young lady had not snapped him up long ago. "And just when I thought I was impressing you with my upright, stalwart qualities, too. You have quite cast me into the doldrums, my dear. I swear I shall never recover unless you promise to drive in the Park with me tomorrow afternoon." His blue eyes twinkled at her so admiringly that for a delicious moment Serena was able to forget that she was plain Miss Millbanks from the wilds of Yorkshire.

"Shame on you, sir," she quipped, wishing for a wild moment that she had the requisite beauty and clothes and breeding to keep a gentleman like Anthony Dalton at her side indefinitely. "You are a sad rattle, I'm afraid, sir," she added, eyeing him over the rim of her glass. "It is a good thing I am not your average widgeon just out of the schoolroom. I am not taken in by your Banbury tales, you know."

"Do you mean to say that you are not thrown into transports at my flattering invitation, Miss Millbanks?" he countered in mock distress. "You wound me deeply to imply I am some frivolous Town Tulip who is all blather and no bottom."

"All blather and no bottom?" inquired a deep, amused voice from behind them. "What an appropriate description of your infamous self, Tony. You must know that he is not usually so honest in his assessment of his character, Miss Millbanks," Sir David Laughton murmured, directing his penetrating gaze at Serena. "How refreshing to know that you can be honest upon occasion, Tony."

"Run away and do your prosing to those in need of advice, David," Dalton replied easily. "Miss Millbanks and I have better things to do than listen to you, old man."

"As a matter of fact, I was about to rescue the lady from your insidious clutches, Tony," the baronet responded calmly. He turned to Serena and bowed. "Colonel Sir David Laughton, at your service, ma'am. May I hope you are free for the next dance, Miss Millbanks? A waltz, I believe."

"No, she's not," cut in a contentious voice from across the room. "All Miss Millbanks's waltzes are reserved for me."

Serena turned to watch as Hawkhurst came toward them. Although his step hardly faltered, she sensed immediately that he had been drinking again, and her temper flared at his impertinent assumption that she was at his beck and call.

"You are wrong again, sir," she said coldly. "And foxed, I might add. You are making a thoroughly disgusting spectacle of yourself."

Serena saw the flash of anger in his gray eyes as they bored into hers and felt a tremor of fear, which she quickly repressed.

"Do you know whom you are addressing, my dear Miss Hoyden?" Hawkhurst inquired in a soft, dangerous voice. "Guy Hawkhurst, the fifth Duke of Wolverton." He sketched her a mocking bow. "Protocol demands that you address me as Your Grace, unless I have given you the freedom of my name, which I disremember doing."

"Protocol be damned," Serena retorted, her anger overcoming her modesty. "You are nothing but a drunken reprobate, and I will address you any way I please." She glared back at him defiantly.

Dimly, through the haze of her fury, Serena heard Mr. Dalton's laconic voice. "Well said, Miss Millbanks. I couldn't agree more. But Hawk, old chap, you do pick the darnedest places to kick up a dust, you know. What say you and I—"

"Keep out of this, Dalton," Hawkhurst interrupted softly, his eyes never leaving Serena's face. "I intend to dance with Miss Hoyden here."

"Well, I have no intention of dancing with you," Serena declared stubbornly.

Hawkhurst opened his mouth to reply, but his words were cut short by a tinkling laugh from the doorway. "Hawk, darling, don't tell me you are in the middle of a vulgar brawl again," a melodious amused voice floated across the room.

A swift glance over the duke's shoulder caused Serena to wish herself back on her beloved moors. Her Grace, the Duchess of Ridgeway, was at her most seductive that evening in a clinging green satin undergown with a diaphanous gauze net spangled with glittering sequins. She was leaning—with shocking intimacy, Serena thought—on the arm of the urbane Marquess of Monroyal, and although her smile was radiant, her blue eyes were fixed on Serena with a malicious gleam.

Serena turned to Sir David Laughton and realized with something of a shock that he was the only man in the room not gaping at the scintillating apparition in the doorway. He was looking at her, and Serena widened her eyes in mute appeal. Sir David grinned, and offered his arm, whisking her out of the room just as the musicians struck up a waltz. Before she knew it, they were taking their places on the floor, safe from the duchess's venomous stare.

She breathed a sigh of relief, wondering why she did indeed feel so safe with the baronet. "Thank you, Sir David," she murmured. "Or perhaps I should say Sir Galahad. You saved me in the nick of time from the most terrible of dragons."

"Hawk?" he queried, one dark brow raised quizzically.

"Oh, no," she said blithely. "His Grace is not such a formidable monster as he seems to imagine he is," she added truthfully. "I am far more afraid of the duchess. She quite reduces me to the texture of a *blancmange*. I feel completely obliterated in her presence, as if I did not exist at all. I realize that is poor-spirited of me, but she is so . . . so . . ." Her voice trailed off, unable to find the words to describe the young duchess. "So like a swan to my ugly duckling; a true Incomparable, I suppose," she added. "Although that is hardly original of me to say so."

"Incomparable?" Sir David repeated. "Yes, I suppose she is if you judge by looks alone. But she is also greedy, self-centered, and incredibly vain. A very tiresome chit, in fact."

Serena grinned up at the colonel, noticing that his eyes were a dark, velvety brown, and that they crinkled when he smiled, as he was doing now. "I fear you are being rather harsh on the duchess," she murmured. "She is very young."

"Age has nothing to do with the matter," Sir David cut in. "Look at Hawk, for instance. He is often tiresome but tonight he seems to be exceptionally so." The brown eyes took on a quizzical expression. "He does not usually make such a cake of himself," he added.

"You are quite off the mark there," Serena contradicted him with considerable relish. She stopped abruptly, wondering why it was that she could not seem to control her runaway tongue. Sir David was regarding her with raised brows, unspoken questions—which Serena was quite sure he was too well-bred to ask—in his eyes.

"He was quite disgustingly foxed at Lady Berkford's ball over a week ago, and did indeed make a fool of himself," she explained. "You are an excellent dancer, Sir David," she added, hoping to change the subject.

The colonel ignored the diversionary tactic. "And what did he do to offend you, Miss Millbanks?" he inquired. His deep voice was compelling, and Serena could well imagine that his junior officers had jumped when he addressed them in such a tone.

"Well, he cast up his accounts on Lady Berkford's chrysan- themums, for one thing," she found herself saying rather de- fensively. "I can vouch for that because I was there."

"Not in the ballroom, I sincerely hope?"

"No, out on the terrace, thank goodness." Serena paused, suddenly aware that she had been led by an expert into giving away incriminating information about her own activities that evening. "But it was not entirely his fault. At least, that was what he said," she added in a rush, hoping to avoid having to confess the worst of her misconduct. "I provoked him, you see."

"I think I am beginning to," Sir David said laconically. "Just how did you provoke him, may I ask?"

Serena took a deep breath. "I knocked him down," she said defiantly. "I hit him on the nose, and he fell into the potted palm." Suddenly she could not repress a giggle. "He did look awfully funny. I think I rather surprised him."

"I wager you did, my dear Miss Millbanks." The colonel chuckled, his eyes crinkling again.

Serena felt a sudden affinity for the tall, serious baronet, quite as though she had known him forever instead of just a few hours. He could be trusted, of that she was certain. Before she considered what she was about, Serena found herself telling Sir David about her renewed threat to land the duke another facer, and of his strange comment on not yet being drunk enough.

"He would not tell me what he needed to be drunk enough for," she admitted. "But I rather fancy it must be something in his past. Don't you agree, Sir David?"

He looked down at her and smiled faintly, and Serena knew he had seen through her transparent curiosity. "I rather fancy it may well be," he responded quietly. "Perhaps he will tell you himself one of these days."

"I don't think so," Serena said. "After the revolting scene he put on for my benefit this evening, I hope I never see the man again."

As Sir David accompanied her back to her aunt, Serena reflected that—whatever his faults, and they were many—Hawkhurst had changed her life. Miss Hoyden, he had called her, and perhaps he was right. Could she ever return to being the bland Miss Millbanks again? she wondered. Did she even want to?

CHAPTER FIVE

The Wager

The hour was more advanced than usual when Serena came down to breakfast the next day. She had slept well and felt more like her old self than she had since her arrival in London more than a moth ago. All that was lacking she though ruefully, serving herself a healthy portion of coddled eggs, bacon, and fresh toast, was her usual gallop on the moors with Jollyboy in mad pursuit. But the stables in the mews behind the modest house her aunt had rented for the Little Season held nothing but the carriage horses, two overfed slugs that came with the old-fashioned barouche, the house, and small staff.

Serena sighed in resignation. She had the breakfast room to herself this morning, and the solitude was welcome after the unprecedented bustle of last night. It was difficult for her to believe that she—who had become accustomed to being invisible at such gatherings—had suddenly blossomed into the most sought-after partner at the Mansfields' ball. After her initial waltz with Hawkhurst, Serena had not been allowed to escape to her usual unobtrusive place once during the rest of the evening. The charming Mr. Dalton had claimed her twice, as had Sir David Laughton. Then so many other gentlemen had begged to stand up with her that Serena had had no time for either Sir John Walker or Mr. Russell, both of whom had eyed her with new respect after the Duke of Wolverton had singled her out.

Only Hawkhurst himself and the Marquess of Monroyal had not approached her again. She told herself that nothing had suited her better than to be ignored by these two unscrupulous rakes. The duke had stood up once with Honoria Littleton, but had been so unsteady on his feet in the lively country dance that the duchess had withdrawn from the set in disarray and gone to join her husband in the card room. The marquess had not once taken the floor, but Serena had felt his eyes upon her several times during the evening. His lean, aristocratic face was set in an expression of extreme boredom, and Serena had longed to ask him why he bothered to come to social gatherings at all if he did not enjoy them. His sole function—as far as Serena could determine—was to pick quarrels with Hawkhurst and accompany the duke when he made a rowdy exit at two in the morning.

Where had Hawkhurst gone after he left Mansfield Court? Serena wondered idly, slathering her toast with thick strawberry jam. He had certainly been foxed enough for whatever it was that drove him to seek this dubious solace. Had he progressed to the next cure, perhaps? And if so, who was the woman he had sought out? Had he cast up his accounts again? And if so, had the woman taken proper care of him?

Serena had no answers to these questions, which were—if truth be told—none of her concern. It was foolish to waste a perfectly good morning thinking about a man who was probably still in a drunken stupor, she told herself. Resolutely, she rang for a fresh pot of tea.

After a hearty breakfast, Serena went up to the music room to practice the two pieces she had agreed to perform at Mrs. Easton's musicale the following week. The thin November sun shining in through the tall windows conjured up memories of home, distracting her from practice. Was Cecily remembering to take Jason for his morning gallop? she wondered. Her madcap sister was a bruising rider, but too often prone to taking unnecessary risks. Like throwing poor Rufus at a fence that no pony should be obliged to refuse. She shuddered to think of the hedges the intrepid Cecily—without the watchful eye of her sister to restrain her—was taking on Jason.

These and other reminiscences finally drove her down to the library, where she buried herself in the latest issue of the *Weekly Dispatch,* a sporting magazine she had purchased surreptitiously two days ago and squirreled away behind the dusty volumes on the library shelves, the surest place to escape Lady Thornton's notice.

"Excuse me, miss." Her aunt's butler, appearing noiseless at the library door, made Serena jump.

"What is it, Simmons?"

"A gentleman to see you, miss." Serena heard the echo of disapproval in the butler's otherwise toneless voice. "I have put him in the Yellow Saloon, miss."

Serena glanced at the old-fashioned clock on the mantel. Two o'clock! She had been so intrigued by the article on the

Godolphin Arabian that she had forgotten to ring for her nuncheon. "Who is he, Simmons? Mr. Dalton?"

"No, miss. A French *marquis* by the sound of it," the butler volunteered with evident distaste. "Shall I inform the gentleman you are not at home, miss?"

Monroyal? Serena felt a pang of apprehension. He was the only marquess known to her, but certainly the last gentleman she would imagine had any reason to call on her.

"No, thank you, Simmons. I doubt his lordship will stay above a minute or two. Ask him to join me here, if you would."

A few moments later, the marquess himself confirmed her prediction. "I will not take up more than a minute of your time, Miss Millbanks," he said dryly, as soon as the obligatory greetings had been dispensed with. "In truth, I would not have inconvenienced you at all had not Hawk insisted that I bring this to you myself." He pulled a folded sheet of paper from his pocket and held it out to her.

Serena was so surprised at this speech that she forgot to guard her tongue. "Insisted?" she repeated foolishly. "You do not strike me as the kind of man who allows others to dictate to him, my lord," she blurted out, watching his dark eyebrows leap up in haughty disdain at her impertinence, and his gray eyes turn flinty.

"There are few who have Hawk's temerity," the marquess replied coldly.

Refusing to be put out by this chilly response, Serena grinned engagingly. "It would seem that you are the one who has been inconvenienced, my lord. How charming of you to run Hawk's errands for him," she purred, determined not to allow this arrogant rogue to intimidate her. "Won't you please sit down, my lord?" she added sweetly. "I shall ask Simmons to bring in the brandy. Or would you prefer a cup of tea?"

"No, thank you, Miss Millbanks," came the cool reply. "I cannot stay. I am merely here to deliver this bank draught for last night's wager." He tendered the folded paper again, but Serena drew back hastily.

"Wager?" she exclaimed. "I disremember making any wager with you, my lord. I do not have the temerity, I fear," she added daringly. "I am afraid Hawkhurst must have been hoaxing you. Very tiresome of him, of course, but no doubt you are accustomed to his vagaries by now."

The marquess laid the paper on the oval cherry-wood table

beside him. "I trust you will not take it amiss if I give you a piece of advice, my dear. I suggest that you stay clear of Hawkhurst. He is not the kind of man I imagine your mother has in mind for you." His languorous, slate-gray eyes raked her simple morning gown from ruffled collar to flounced hem, and his sensuous lips curled derisively. "And—much as it pains me to say it—you are not exactly in Hawk's style either, my dear."

Serena stared open-mouthed at this piece of effrontery. Then she stretched her lips in a thin smile. "Unfortunately, my mother is no longer here to guide me in such matters," she said in a tight voice. "She died seven years ago. But I thank you for your *fatherly* advice, my lord," she added stiffly. "And as for your friend Hawk, rest assured that he is quite safe from me. I find him most unsuitable indeed; for one thing, he is almost as rude as you are." All through this tirade, Serena fought to keep her temper under control, but toward the end her voice had risen and shook with fury.

She took a deep breath to steady herself, as the marquess stared at her, acute discomfort and anger chasing across his rigid face.

"Oblige me by taking your note and removing yourself from my sight before I become violent," she ordered in a clipped voice, pointing at the door with a trembling finger.

Before the marquess could make a move, the door opened and Simmons announced in his stiffest tones, "Mr. Anthony Dalton to see you, miss."

"Robert!" Dalton exclaimed, striding into the room. "What in Hades are *you* doing here?" He looked from his friend's rigid expression to Miss Millbanks's pale face expectantly. "Miss Millbanks, please forgive my outburst. It was unpardonably rude of me."

Serena regarded him coolly. "Fortunately for you, I am become increasingly immune to rudeness, sir," she replied acerbically before turning to the butler, who was an interested spectator to Mr. Dalton's incautious remarks. "Send up the tea tray if you will, Simmons," she said icily, then sat down on the green leather settee as though her legs could no longer sustain her. "And inform her ladyship that we have visitors."

"Her ladyship is not at home, miss," Simmons replied stiffly.

There was an uncomfortable pause after the door closed behind the butler, which Serena made no attempt to bridge. She sat, her hands resting limply in her lap, wishing she had not lost her temper and spoken as no lady of quality would dream of speaking to a gentleman.

Mr. Dalton regarded her uneasily, then addressed the marquess. "What have you done to put Miss Millbanks so out of curl, Robert?"

"I came—against my better judgment, I should add—to deliver a bank draught to the lady," the marquess replied shortly. "And got my head bitten off for my pains."

Serena snorted inelegantly. "I merely informed his lordship that I will not become embroiled in his foolish wagers. If he has more money than wit, and wishes to flaunt it in such a vulgar manner—"

"Damn it all, Tony," the marquess exploded. "It was only a small wager. Nothing to signify. You were there and saw the whole thing. I lost, and now I wish to pay up. That is if *Miss Hoyden* here will permit it." This last was spoken with such sarcasm that Serena's hackles rose.

"Your wagers are no concern of mine, my lord," she insisted tersely. "I refuse to be a part of such nonsense over a silly dance."

"Hawk insisted the winnings should go to Miss Millbanks," the marquess explained testily. "What would you have me do, Tony?"

Mr. Dalton regarded Serena speculatively. "If that is the case, I do not see that you have any choice but to accept Stilton's draught, Miss Millbanks," he said gently.

"No choice, indeed?" Serena snapped angrily. "Of course I have a choice, and I choose not to accept it. That is final," she added belligerently.

But accept it she did, although her reasons for succumbing did not bear close examination, she realized much later. Mr. Dalton proved to be as smooth as he was charming, and by the time Serena had served their tea—which even the sullen marquess had managed to swallow—he had produced any number of arguments which sounded all too reasonable to Serena's befuddled brain. But the one that finally changed her mind actually came from the marquess, who pointed out in barely concealed exasperation that by refusing to accept the winnings of last night's wager, Miss Millbanks only succeeded in helping Hawkhurst win a much larger one.

"Oh, indeed?" Serena's curiosity was instantly aroused. "How much larger?" she wanted to know.

The marquess smiled his thin, supercilious smile. "*Considerably* larger, Miss Millbanks."

"And who will benefit if I do accept?" she demanded.

"That I am not at liberty to say, my dear," the marquess countered adroitly. "But suffice it to say that Hawk seems to have unlimited confidence in your desire to thwart him." His gray eyes regarded her with amusement, and Serena was startled at the transformation a mere smile wrought to his saturnine expression. The rogue was definitely more attractive than she had thought, she mused, although the smile was more wolfish than she cared to see on a gentleman.

"Oh, he does, does he?" she murmured, a militant smile on her lips. "We shall see about that," she added, holding out her hand imperiously. "Give me the silly thing, and let us put an end to this foolishness. I daresay you will recuperate your loss forthwith, my lord?" she probed ingenuously.

"Who can say, Miss Millbanks?" he drawled in a bored voice. "Who can say? Now if you will excuse me, I cannot keep my cattle waiting any longer," he began, only to be interrupted by Mr. Dalton, who jumped to his feet.

"I saw that new team of yours downstairs, Robert. Prime-looking prads, of course, but I wouldn't mind wagering that the right leader is a confirmed limper."

"Oh, no you don't, Mr. Dalton," Serena interjected quickly. "No more wagers today if you please. Besides, I cannot believe that his lordship would knowingly drive a horse that was touched in the wind." She smiled sweetly at the marquess's surprised expression.

"Am I to understand that you are a judge of horseflesh, Miss Millbanks?" he inquired at his most supercilious.

Serena grinned. "I am accounted to be quite a fair one, sir," she replied, her spirits reviving miraculously at the mention of horses. "My father fancies himself rather an expert, and we have had some exceptional mounts in the stables at Millbanks Hall."

"In that case," the marquess responded laconically, "you may wish to place a small wager on whose team is more up to snuff, mine or Dalton's grays?"

Serena glanced at him sharply; the uncharitable thought that the marquess might wish to incite her into losing the money he had just paid her flickered through her mind. Like most men, including her own father, he probably had no faith in a woman's judgment regarding horseflesh. She smiled innocently at him. "I only bet on a sure thing, my lord. And I have yet to see either team."

"That can be soon remedied, Miss Millbanks," Dalton exclaimed, apparently much taken by the notion. And within an astonishingly short time, Serena found herself standing on the steps to her aunt's house, wrapped in her serviceable brown cloak against the November breeze.

"Those are mine," Dalton pointed out eagerly, indicating the four perfectly matched grays standing quietly under the supervision of a groom. "And those job horses," he gestured carelessly in the direction of the other team, "are Robert's. Now, which would you place your money on, Miss Millbanks?"

Serena stood for several minutes, running her eyes carefully over the horses. Mr. Dalton's grays were magnificent animals, well-muscled and broad-chested, and giving all the appearance of sixteen-mile-an-hour tits. The marquess's team of bays, on the other hand, were the flashiest she had ever seen, their glossy coats gleaming in the pale sunlight. They were indeed a sight to behold, and Serena was transported back to Yorkshire where she had first learned from Haskins, her father's head groom, how to tool a curricle and four down the narrow country lanes of her home.

"If it is flashiness you fancy," she said slowly, "then the bays win hands down. But appearances are often deceiving." She turned to meet the marquess's gray eyes, and smiled. "I prefer stamina and reliablity myself. I would not trust the bays getting past a flock of geese on a narrow lane without kicking up the devil of a dust." She stepped up to the right leader, who rolled his eyes and sidled nervously. Pulling off her glove, Serena put out a hand to touch the horse, but was interrupted by the marquess's groom, who looked at her askance.

"Wouldn't do that if I were you, miss. Solomon 'ere ain't too partial to females. And 'e bites," he added with evident relish.

"Solomon?" she repeated with an amused laugh. "A sad misnomer, I fear." Disregarding the groom's obvious reluctance to have her anywhere near his charges, Serena ran a soothing hand down the bay's neck and across his chest. The animal quieted down immediately as she spoke to him in an undertone. After a thorough examination of the marquess's team, during which the groom's hostility was replaced by grudging respect, Serena moved to inspect the grays. She could find nothing wrong with this team, which appeared to be in prime condition.

"Well, Miss Millbanks?" the marquess drawled when she finally stepped back to join the gentlemen. "What is your verdict?" His voice held a subtle note of mockery which Serena ignored.

"I fear Mr. Dalton may be correct," she replied. "Your right leader seems to be touched in the wind."

"I told ye so, m'lord," the groom cut in before his master could react to Serena's comment. "I always did say that fancy prad would turn out t'be a reg'lar puffer."

"Of course, I could not be absolutely sure unless I were to try out his paces, my lord. And I could be wrong, of course," Serena added politely, watching the marquess's predictable frown of annoyance.

Suddenly Lord Monroyal's frown deepened and he looked at her sharply. "Am I to understand that you are a whipster yourself, Miss Millbanks?"

"Whipster? No, my lord," she replied, forcing herself to ignore the implied insult. "I am my father's daughter, and he is Sir Henry Millbanks, known as *Horseman Harry* to his friends when he was somewhat younger."

"By Jove, Miss Millbanks," Mr. Dalton exclaimed in astonishment. "I never realized you were related to *that* Millbanks. I remember going to Newmarket with my father to see him race his curricle against Sir Giles Fairmont for some outrageous wager. Ten thousand pounds, I believe. He won, too, if I remember correctly?"

"Of course," Serena replied calmly. "Father always won in those days. He only started to lose after Mama died." She paused for a moment, memories of those happier days at Millbanks Hall washing over her. Then she glanced contemptuously at the marquess. "But to answer your question, my lord. No, I am no mere whipster."

"You may handle my team any time you wish, Miss Millbanks," Dalton said with one of his charming laughs. "In fact, please do so today. Welsh bred, they are, and you will find them as reliable as Monroyal's are skittish."

"Perhaps that would be wise, Miss Millbanks," the marquess drawled in a bored voice. "I doubt you could handle my bays, anyway. Too much spirit for a mere female, I'll wager. Tony's slugs are more your style. Safe and reliable, they surely are. No doubt my grandmother could handle them without coming to any harm."

Serena had been preparing to enter Mr. Dalton's vehicle, but at these mocking words, she turned to face Lord Monroyal, her eyes blazing.

"Lor' love us, guv'nor," the marquess's startled groom exclaimed. "Ye ain't goin' ter let no female 'andle the bays, now are ye, m'lord?" The open horror on the man's weather-beaten face made Serena smile in spite of her own outrage.

"No fear of that, Hobbs," the marquess remarked carelessly as he climbed into the curricle and gathered up the reins. "Not even Horseman Harry's daughter would dare take on a team like this." His words held like an unmistakable challenge, but his dark gray stare told Serena all too clearly that he still considered her a mere whipster. Something in the taunting voice stung her into action.

"Is that a wager, my lord?" she inquired with deceptive calmness.

Dalton's face mirrored the groom's horror. "You cannot be serious, Miss Millbanks? Robert is merely peeved that you preferred my team over his. Pay him no heed, I beg of you. Those bays are too hard-mouthed for a lady."

That remark was all Serena needed to cement her resolve to show these tedious gentlemen that she was her father's daughter. "Are you wagering against me, then, Mr. Dalton?" she inquired sweetly.

He stared at her aghast. "I cannot allow you to do this, Miss Millbanks," he said. "It would be most unseemly—"

"A thousand pounds says you cannot handle them," the marquess's taunting voice cut in.

"I haven't got a thousand pounds," she replied regretfully. "It will have to be five hundred."

"A thousand to your five hundred, then," the bored voice drawled.

"Miss Millbanks, I must insist—"

"I promise not to race them through the Park, Mr. Dalton," Serena interrupted gaily. "But I wish you would follow us, for I will need a ride back after we run these commoners into the ground."

Without waiting for the flabbergasted Mr. Dalton to assist her, Serena stepped up into the marquess's brightly painted curricle and put out her hands for the ribbons, her violet eyes dancing with excitement.

With a shrug of reluctant admiration, the Marquess of Monroyal relinquished his prize horses—for the first time in his life and against his better judgment—into the hands of a female.

Hawkhurst heard various versions of Miss Millbanks's feat when he returned to London after two days at his great-aunt's estate near Winsor. Lady Lexington, formerly Lady Elizabeth Hawkhurst, sister and daughter of dukes, was as autocratic and demanding in her seventies as she had been in her salad days as London's most feted Beauty. Her eccentricities were legion, and she still got away with them, Hawk mused ruefully as he made his way at a leisurely pace back to London along the Bath Road. Aunt Bess's preemptory summons had been awaiting him upon his return from the Mansfields' ball at a rather advanced hour in the morning.

Much against Sergeant Slowe's advice, Hawk had ridden out to Winsor without stopping to do more than change his rumpled evening clothes for buckskins and topboots and one of Weston's creations in blue wool tweed under his topcoat. Between them, his valet and butler had poured strong coffee down his gullet, which he had promptly and repeatedly thrown up. Enough had stayed down to render him more sober than he usually was after a night of debauchery, and he had counted on the cold morning air to restore him to a semblance of sobriety before he must face Aunt Bess's sharp eyes.

Arriving at Sutton House in time for a late breakfast, Hawk had not been surprised to find Lady Lexington enjoying a hearty repast in the breakfast room, in the company of her long-suffering company Miss Leticia Hedgerton, a spinster only a dozen or so years her ladyship's junior.

"I am glad to find you in such high gig, Aunt Bess," Hawk remarked with a smile as he bent to place a salute on her ladyship's remarkably smooth cheek. "I came *vent-à-terre* as soon as I got your message, *cherie*," he added glibly. "I thought I detected a note of urgency in your letter."

"Impudent puppy!" Lady Lexington snorted. "And don't simper at the rogue, Hedge," she snapped at her companion. Hawk felt her gimlet gaze fix mercilessly on his face and prepared himself for the chastising to come. He was not disappointed.

"You look as though you are at death's door, Guy," Lady Lexington said with characteristic frankness. "What the devil

ails you, boy? Sit down and let Holmes pour you some coffee." She gestured at the butler hovering in the background,
who immediately stepped forward to set a cup before the visitor. "Have you had any breakfast, lad? Fill up a plate for my
nephew, Holmes," she commanded without waiting for Hawk
to reply. "You look as lean as a wolf in midwinter, my boy.
Do they not feed you in London?"

Hawk grimaced at the generous helping of food the butler
placed before him, but he drank the coffee gratefully. "I assure
you that my cook takes very good care of me, *cherie,*" he
replied with one of his more charming smiles.

"That is a bouncer if ever I heard one," Lady Lexington
snorted. "But I did not bring you out here to discuss your do-
mestics, Guy. There is a matter of more importance I wish to
bring to your attention. Holmes," she broke off to address the
butler, "this tea is stone cold. Bring up a fresh pot, if you
please."

The conversation remained general until Lady Lexington
had satisfied herself that Hawk had eaten what she referred to
as a decent meal. But as soon as she was installed beside the
blazing fire in her private sitting room, where she spent a considerable part of her day when not out riding about her estate,
Hawk prepared himself to hear the real reason behind his
great-aunt's summons.

"I have received yet another sniveling letter from your
Mama," she began without further preamble. "She is under-
standably concerned about the future of the family. It is over
three years since you returned from Spain, my boy, and your
Mama is anxious to see you set up your nursery. What are you
now? Twenty-nine? She feels it is high time for you to assume
your responsibilities, Guy." She paused to gaze up at him with
her birdlike blue eyes.

Derek's eyes, he thought, wincing inwardly as he always
did when his great-aunt stared at him in just that way. Eyes
that reminded him far too acutely of his brother's anguished
gaze during those last few minutes of his life in that ferocious
attack under Lieutenant-General Sir Thomas Graham at Vittoria. Eyes that had begged for understanding, for forgiveness,
and for the relief from pain that Hawk had been unable to give.
It wrenched his very soul to remember, but he could not seem
to forget that most decisive of General Wellington's victories
in Spain in which his twin had lost his life. Only alcohol

seemed to blunt the edges of his cursed memory enough to provide brief respites from the torment of remembering.

"Well?" Lady Elizabeth's voice cut across Hawk's memories. "What have you to say for yourself, lad?"

"I am not ready for parson's mousetrap yet, Aunt Bess," he murmured, hoping that his answer would fit the question he had missed. He grinned ruefully down at her. "I see no reason to rush into this, do you, *cherie?* It's hard to think of tying myself down to a single female when there are so many . . . so many . . ." Hawk searched in vain for a suitable word that would not offend his aunt's ears.

"Willing hussies I think you mean, do you not, lad?" she suggested without the least sign of embarrassment. "Things are at a sad pass indeed when some of our most prominent matrons are reported to be no better than trollops. In my day these arrangements were conducted with a great deal more discretion. And what is this I hear about you and that chit old Ridgeway got himself leg-shackled to? More hair than wit that curst old rumstick, of course, and he deserves anything he gets, but I do not like to hear that the head of our family is sitting in the new duchess's pocket, Guy. Seems to me you are cutting too broad a swath with the married ladies, and not enough with the eligible lassies."

"You must know that most rumors are vastly exaggerated, *cherie,*" Hawk drawled, vaguely annoyed at the accuracy of the particular rumors that reached his aunt's ears. "There is plenty of time to think of marriage when I'm thirty-five or so."

"That is exactly the excuse your brother Derek gave us," Lady Lexington pointed out shortly. "But at least he spent his time managing the Wolverton estates when he was not out on the hunting field or in Manton's Shooting Gallery. I never heard of Derek's making a cake of himself rollicking through the boudoirs of half the married females in the realm."

Hawk stiffened. Even a veiled reference to his twin's monk-like existence caused Hawk to bristle defensively. "Derek died an honorable death fighting for his country," he replied curtly, a hard edge on his voice. "He would have married and produced an heir when the time came. Which it never did, of course," he added bitterly, wondering—as he often had since Derek's death—if his twin would not perhaps have passed the responsibility of providing a Wolverton heir to Hawk even had he survived the battle of Vittoria. "And I will do the same," he added harshly. "Eventually. But I won't be pushed, Aunt. I swear I'll go back to the army if Mama doesn't stop harping on the subject."

There was a pause after this revealing speech, during which Hawk could almost hear his aunt's unspoken question hanging in the air between them. He always hated it when his family faulted his brother for neglecting his ducal duties to follow his younger twin to Spain. Only Hawk thought he knew why Derek had done so, and he was not at all sure he truly understood Derek's motives.

Lady Lexington was the first to break the silence. "I think you would, lad," she said softly. "I think you would, at that. But I hope it will never come to that pass, Guy." She paused, and then added with a return to her normal tone, "Are you telling me that not a single young female making her come-out in these past three years had taken your fancy, lad? I find that hard to believe."

"Nary a one, *cherie*," Hawk answered with an ironic smile. "Except . . ." He paused, an odd thought crossing his mind.

"Except what?" demanded the dowager sharply.

Hawk laughed at his aunt's sudden curiosity. He had never considered the feisty Miss Millbanks in quite that light before, and the idea intrigued him before he brushed it aside. "She is ineligible, *cherie*," he said slowly, a wry smile twisting his lips. "An obscure baronet's daughter with a sharp tongue and violet eyes. From Yorkshire, I believe. I find her—what shall we say—amusing?"

"Bah!" her ladyship snorted. "I trust you do not intend to *amuse* yourself with an innocent, Guy? What is the chit's name?"

Hawk met Lady Lexington's shameless gaze and laughed. "I had not thought of it, *cherie*, but now that you mention it . . ." He let his voice trail off suggestively. Before his aunt could rebuke him for impertinence, Hawk added quickly, "Her name is Millbanks."

"Millbanks?" Lady Lexington's eyes took on a far-away look. "Millbanks? I've heard that name. From Yorkshire, you say? Ah, yes! Now I remember. *Horseman Harry*. She must be the daughter of Horseman Harry. A rare buck in his day, I warrant you, lad. Best all-around horseman in the country, or as near as makes no difference. I saw him race his curricle at Newmarket one summer. Lexington liked to wager on the races, and we attended quite regularly at one time." She paused, apparently caught up in the days of her youth. "Does she ride?"

Startled by the question, Hawk shook his head. "I couldn't say, Aunt, never having seen the lady on horseback."

"Well, I'm willing to wager that if the lass is truly Harry's daughter, she'll drive to an inch and take her fences with flair and style."

"You're on, *cherie*. Shall we say a monkey?"

Lady Lexington eyed her great-nephew speculatively. "You're a rascal, Guy," she said finally. "On one condition. You will bring the chit out here so that I can see Harry's daughter ride with my own eyes. Otherwise, the wager's off, my lad."

"Agreed." Hawk smiled at his aunt's dancing eyes, glad to have distracted her from the annoying subject of duty, and marriage, and the Wolverton estate. And Derek, he thought as he rode at a leisurely pace back to London late on the morning of the next day.

The question would be, he mused—the pleasant vision of a flashing pair of violet eyes filling his mind—how to cajole Miss Millbanks into accepting his aunt's invitation without arousing her formidable temper.

CHAPTER SIX

The Musicale

Mrs. Easton's musicale turned out to be very much like other such gatherings Serena had attended since her arrival in the Metropolis. Except definitely on a small scale, she mused, as she sat beside Lady Thornton and watched her cousin Melissa flirt with Sir John Walker, whose attentions were becoming increasingly marked.

There could be no more than fifty guests in attendance tonight, Serena thought, most of them venerable matrons and lesser luminaries of the social world who had not received invitations to the more coveted entertainments taking place that evening in the *haut monde*. Lady Thornton had not received any either, hence her gracious acceptance of her old friend Mary Easton's invitation to that lady's monthly musicale, and her promise that her niece would be pleased to play the pianoforte to entertain dear Mary's guests.

Serena had not minded being pressed into service without prior consultation. Her aunt was a simple, often thoughtless creature who rarely considered the convenience of others unless they were possessed of rank and fortune. She was blessed with a kind and generous heart, however, and Serena was glad of the chance to show her appreciation. She knew herself to be a very competent pianist and suffered none of the nervous palpitations the Snelling sisters had demonstrated when they took the stage to sing a duet of country songs accompanied by their devoted Mama on the piano.

The nervous sisters were followed by an earnest young violinist who played one of Beethoven's sonatas arranged for strings and two German lieder Serena did not recognize. She was agreeably surprised at the young man's proficiency and vowed to obtain the names of the lieder from him after her own performance, which was the next on the program.

Disregarding the scattered applause that greeted the exuberant Mrs. Easton's announcement of her performance, Serena moved easily to the instrument and immediately launched into the first of the two pieces she had prepared for the event. The opening bars of the sonatina—which had earned her one of Mr. Mincewort's rare nods of approval—carried her instantly back to Yorkshire. The rustlings and murmurings of the audience in Mrs. Easton's small, crowded drawing room faded into the background and the music transported her to her mother's cozy, slightly shabby morning room overlooking the flower beds and the tall stand of poplars in the distance. The recollection was so vivid that Serena could almost smell Lady Millbanks's roses and feel the warm summer breeze coming in the open window bringing with it the unmistakable scent of open fields and newly cut hay. Overcome with nostalgia, Serena could not resist adding a haunting Yorkshire melody to the formal pieces she had intended to play.

The audience reacted with unexpected approval and the hearty applause drew a radiant smile from Serena as she stepped down from the platform. Instead of returning to her seat beside her aunt, Serena moved to the back of the room where the young violinist—a Richard Towers, according to the program—stood by himself. She had barely introduced herself and complimented the violinist on his performance when she detected a familiar drawl from the entry hall explaining to Mrs. Easton's butler that the late arrivals were with Lady Thornton's party.

The lying, brazen-faced rogue! Serena fumed, feeling her heart lurch uncomfortably. What May-game was he playing now? She would wager the thousand pounds she had recently won from the marquess that His Grace, the Duke of Wolverton, had not received an invitation to Mrs. Easton's musicale. That poor lady—an enterprising widow who lived on the fringes of society, surviving on a small pension from her husband's estate—could hardly be on such terms with any duke. And if Mrs. Easton had had the temerity to send him one, she realized with mounting annoyance, he would undoubtedly have discarded it without giving it a second thought. The cream of the *ton* did not, Serena suspected, set foot in shabby drawing rooms such as Mrs. Easton's.

The lady's portly butler, fully conscious of the honor bestowed upon the hostess by the presence of such noble guests, ushered them into the crowded room and went in search of his mistress to inform her of her unexpected good fortune.

Serena tried to ignore the sudden hush that greeted the

duke's entrance and racked her brain for something intelligent to say to young Mr. Towers, but was hampered by that gentleman's inattentiveness. Like many of the other guests in the room, Mr. Towers was staring in fascination at the new arrivals. Without quite knowing how, Serena knew the duke was staring at her rigid back; she could almost visualize the mocking grin on his face. With a feeling of inevitability, Serena finally turned around and stared back at not one, but two pairs of gray eyes, one amused, the other mocking. Monroyal was with him, she noticed with a jolt. Two bored rakes on the prowl, she thought disgustedly, although why they had chosen Mrs. Easton's musicale, she could not imagine.

Without paying the slightest heed to anyone else in the room, Hawk came straight over to her, the marquess strolling in his wake with a supercilious sneer on his handsome face. Serena felt embarrassingly conspicuous as first one and then the other exquisitely clad gentleman bowed over her limp hand.

"My *dear* Miss Millbanks," Hawkhurst drawled, a wicked gleam in his pale gray eyes. "What a frosty welcome. One would almost believe that you are not overjoyed to see us. Robert did warn me you might not like it above half."

"What are you doing here?" Serena hissed under her breath, careful to keep the false smile pasted on her face as the music began again. "If you are foxed again, sir, and think to amuse yourself shocking Mrs. Easton and her guests with a display of your execrable manners, I warn you, I will not stand for it." She had no idea what she would do to prevent them from doing just as they pleased, but the absurdity of the threat did not deter her.

"Speaking of execrable manners, my dear Miss Millbanks," the marquess cut in softly, his sneer still in place, "you rather take the cake yourself."

Hawkhurst laughed and Serena saw that he was indeed halfway foxed. She glanced sharply at the marquess but could not tell from his bland expression whether he was in a similar condition. "I think I see your esteemed aunt bobbing and waving at us, Miss Millbanks," the duke remarked. "Perhaps we should go and pay our respects. What do you say, Robert?"

The marquess's reply was unequivocal. "I say the sooner we cut out of here the better, Hawk. The devil take it, man. You never told me this was to be a damned musicale."

"You have not yet explained your presence here," Serena

snapped, all too conscious of the curious stares of the other guests.

"We came to hear you play, my dear girl," Hawk answered nonchalantly, as though it was the most natural thing in the world.

"I fear you are too late, gentlemen," she replied frostily. "I have already played. And you also missed an inspiring performance by Mr. Towers here." She turned to introduce the young violinist, only to find that he was no longer at her side. "Oh, you have frightened him away," she said crossly. "Mr. Towers is a very talented violinist, and I think—"

"The devil fly away with him," Hawkhurst interrupted rudely. "Do you suppose we could get something to drink?"

"Oh, I am sure of it," Serena answered sweetly, knowing full well that Mrs. Easton never offered anything but a mild punch at her gatherings. She led them into the adjoining room where refreshments were laid out and could not resist grinning at the duke's wry face when he tasted the punch.

Hawkhurst glowered at her and then seemed to notice her plain lilac silk gown for the first time. He fumbled for his quizzing glass and gazed at her until her cheeks became flushed with a mixture of rage and mortification

"If you intend to catch yourself a husband, my dear girl, you will have to rig yourself out in something more fashionable than *that*. What do you think, Robert?"

The marquess raked her insolently with mocking eyes, and Serena felt her temper simmer. "I have seen rather more fetching gowns, Miss Millbanks," he drawled with commendable restraint. "Who knows? Perhaps rigged out in something a little less severe, you might yet snare an unwary blighter or two."

"You are odiously uncivil, gentlemen," she said bitingly. "I do not intent to waste money on finery since I am *not* in the market for a husband. Even if there were anyone suitable here in London, which there *definitely* is not," she could not help emphasizing. "I shall keep it for my old age, which, incidentally, is almost upon me." She tossed her head defiantly. "And there is absolutely nothing wrong with this gown," she added, cross at herself for caring what these two reprobates thought of her. "It is at least decent, which is more than I can say about some of the gowns I have seen in London."

"Yes, indeed," Hawkhurst agreed, with a deep-throated chuckle. "Altogether too decent if you ask me, my dear. And by the way," he continued, abruptly changing the subject, "if you do not wish to be considered deucedly fast, I should warn you not to be seen driving about town with Robert. His reputation leaves much to be desired, you know. And as for accepting wagers for madcap races, that is completely beyond the pale, Miss Millbanks. The *ton* frowns on such unbecoming behavior."

"Unbecoming b-behavior?" Serena spluttered indignantly. "And who are *you* to talk, sir? From the little I know about you, your behavior is anything but spotless."

"Touché, Hawk," the marquess murmured in his mocking voice.

"And furthermore, you are not my father, so I will thank you not to tell me what I can or cannot do. I shall drive with whom I please," Serena added with a petulance she immediately regretted as unworthy of her. How the duke had managed to upset her again, she could not understand, but she did know that he was not worth the turmoil this brangling caused in her emotions.

"Touché again, m'lad," the marquess repeated, his gray eyes no longer bored. "And allow me to add, Hawk, that Miss Millbanks behaved with utmost propriety and won the wager fair and square. I was forced to admit that—for a female—she drives to an inch."

Serena turned on him instantly, her eyes flashing. "And are you so poor-spirited, sir, that you cannot bring yourself to admit that a female can drive those bonesetters of yours as well as you do?" She glared at him for a moment, and then her lips relaxed into a mischievous grin. "Ah!" she remarked archly. "I see what ails you, my lord. You are still out of curl with me for winning the wager. I would not have thought it of you, sir."

"Ungrateful wench," Monroyal replied. "Next time do not expect me to defend your reputation."

"My reputation does not need any defense," she retorted, eliciting a crack of laughter from the duke. "Mr. Dalton and two grooms were present, you should know," she added, glaring at Hawkhurst. "And as for the next time," she added, turning back to the marquess, "there will be no next time. My gambling days are over."

Monroyal shrugged his elegant shoulders and glanced at his friend. "In that case, we may as well go back to White's, Hawk. Miss Millbanks is not interested in proving you wrong yet again, old man. Lady Lexington will lose by default, I suppose. But she can well afford to do so, after all."

Serena looked from one to the other, curious in spite of herself. "Who is Lady Lexington? And what is this wager you mention?"

Hawkhurst gave her a speculative stare. "Lady Lexington is my great-aunt," he said eventually. "Apparently she knew your father in his heyday and admired his horsemanship. Aunt Bess is horse-mad herself; always has been. She wagered that any daughter of Horseman Harry's was bound to be a fine horsewoman."

Serena gazed up at him, her lips tightening as an unpleasant thought crossed her mind. "And you wagered that I was nothing of the sort, I presume?" she snapped, her voice betraying her annoyance.

Hawkhurst grinned wickedly. "Why, as a matter of fact, I did, Miss Millbanks. Never seen you on a horse, so how could I know?"

"But you assumed—without any proof whatsoever—that I am unable to acquit myself on a horse?" She whirled on the marquess. "And you, sir?" she demanded. "Whose side are you on, if I may ask?"

He laughed, and once again Serena was startled at the transformation of his saturnine features. "Yours, of course, my dear. Need you ask? I have learned my lesson."

"Well, you must inform Lady Lexington that she has won her wager, if you please. I am accounted a fair horsewoman."

"An understatement, no doubt," the marquess countered. "But unfortunately, Lady Lexington insists upon seeing your disputed skills with her own eyes. Tell her, Hawk." He turned to gaze derisively at the guests who had been drawn into the refreshment room upon learning that a real live duke had stepped into their midst.

"That is correct, my dear—although I warned my aunt that she might lose the wager by default since you would in all probability refuse her invitation to visit Sutton House and try out her cattle. However, she does have an enviable assortment of prime goers in her stable. In fact—"

"Your aunt invited *me* to ride her horses?" Serena interrupted. "I don't believe a word of this Banbury tale. You are roasting me, sir. And I am not amused." Yet the thought of riding again made her nostalgic for Jason and the moors of Yorkshire.

"Oh, it is true enough, Miss Millbanks," Monroyal drawled. "But I would advise against accepting, of course. Lady Lexington has some bang-up bits of blood and bone in her stables and, being a bruising rider herself, would be a most demanding judge. No doubt she will expect you to ride Satan, and I would not wish that contrary brute on any female. Even *you*, my dear Miss Millbanks," he added with a slight depreciating smile.

Serena looked from one gentleman to the other suspiciously. She was certain there was a catch somewhere. "Why does your aunt care whether I ride well or not?" she inquired, wondering how this absurd wager had originated.

"My aunt is in her seventies and I fancy the excessive tranquility of Sutton House must chafe her lively mind. She also enjoys a wager occasionally. She won a packet on the curricle race your father had at Newmarket many years ago." He smiled with such unexpected charm that Serena's breath caught in her throat. "I imagine she would like to repeat the experience at my expense."

Then I shall certainly see to it that she does, Serena made up her mind instantly. "Where does Lady Lexington live?"

She knew she had stepped into a trap the moment the words were out of her mouth, but she disdained to draw back. The diabolical glitter in Hawkhurst's eyes told her so, as did the sly smile that flickered briefly on the marquess's sensuous lips.

Hawk had never imagined he would be quite so successful in persuading the prickly Miss Millbanks to agree to his great-aunt's wager. Monroyal had assured him that the best way to overcome the lady's frosty reserve was to challenge her, and had been willing to wager that if presented with the opportunity, she would be unable to resist the temptation to prove the duke in the wrong. The idea had so much appeal that Hawk had prevailed upon the marquess to forgo their planned card game at White's in order to put the notion to the test.

They had had little difficulty in running their quarry to ground. Lady Thornton's paunchy butler had proved most amenable to divulging the particular gathering the Thornton ladies had graced with their presence that evening, and had not demurred when Hawk slipped him a silver coin for his pains. Their appearance in Mrs. Easton's drawing room had astounded the other guests—an event Hawk had not anticipated, and which caused him a certain amount of bitter amusement.

"It appears we are to provide part of the entertainment this evening," he had murmured under his breath to Monroyal, as the two stood at the entrance of the stuffy room eyeing the assortment of befeathered, elderly matrons and stout gentlemen in old-fashioned knee breeches who had turned to stare in fascination at the two exquisites lounging in the doorway.

"There she is," the marquess had remarked tersely. "Talking to the young cub with the pale face."

Hawk had walked over immediately to confront Miss Millbanks, who had turned to glare at them belligerently. Her violet eyes had sparkled with annoyance and for a fleeting moment, Hawk had felt the urge to kiss her into acquiescence. But he was not far enough into his cups to undertake such a dangerous enterprise. He had teased her instead, and been secretly delighted at the becoming flush his words brought to her cheeks. But Monroyal had been right in his assessment of the chit's inability to resist anything that might put him in the wrong, and by the time they left, twenty minutes later, Miss Millbanks had promised to prove that he had made a grave mistake to bet against her.

Hawk had immediately dashed off a note to Lady Lexington, telling her to expect them in two days' time, but his anticipated enjoyment of Miss Millbanks's company was severely curtailed when Sir David Laughton pointed out to him the need to provide suitable female company for the young lady.

He had stared at Sir David in surprise. "Miss Millbanks does not strike me as the kind of female to cavil at such things," he argued. "Besides, you and Tony are coming, are you not? As is Robert. Any female with a grain of sense would jump at the opportunity to spend the day with four fashionable bucks." He grinned at the notion, but his friend had remained serious.

"I should have thought even you would have noticed by now that Miss Millbanks is hardly *any female,* Hawk. Having been raised in the country, she is far too trusting for her own good, I would say, and not at all up to snuff when it comes to men of your ilk, Hawk. Forgive me for being so blunt, old man," he added with a rueful smile, "but you are notoriously fickle and cavalier where the weaker sex is concerned."

Hawk instantly bristled, although he knew that Laughton spoke nothing but the truth. He really did not care to examine his relationships with the fairer sex too closely. In his heart of hearts, Hawk admitted, he secretly despised the endless procession of amorous females who threw themselves at his head, and studiously avoided the single chits angling for a husband. Those who were adept at the game of seduction, he often took to his bed, especially when he was in his cups, driven by an unspeakably dark need to prove himself again and again. He did not particularly care to have his sins—or his weakness—pointed out to him, however.

"They bore me," he said shortly, returning the colonel's gaze steadily. Besides being one his oldest friends, Colonel Laughton had been his commanding officer during the Peninsular campaign and had supported him during that terrible time of Derek's death. More than any of his other friends, David must have guessed at the truth behind the rumors about Derek's presence on the battlefield. They had never discussed it, of course, but from that day on, Laughton had quietly encouraged him to put that part of his life behind him and pick up where Derek had left off. Hawk had as yet lacked the courage to follow this advice.

He grinned cynically. "No need to bother your head about Miss Millbanks, Laughton," he said smoothly. "She is safe from me, and besides, she is quite unattainable, you know."

"That depends entirely on what you have in mind," the colonel said bluntly. "And I wonder if you have ever considered that *you* are unsuitable for Miss Millbanks, Hawk." Laughton grimaced at Hawk's blank stare. "No, I can see you have not. But I believe you should face that fact before you embroil her in activities that might damage her beyond repair."

Laughton's words had stayed with Hawk for some time after they parted, and in the end he had admitted—at least to himself—that his friend was right. The Duke of Wolverton—in his present rakehell mood—was indeed ineligible for plain Miss Millbanks from Yorkshire. And in that rare moment of introspection, Hawk also discovered in himself a hitherto unsuspected streak of lecherous intent toward the unsuspecting chit, a discovery he immediately suppressed as ridiculous. Had he not assured Laughton that Miss Millbanks was safe from him? he thought, reminding himself that the wench in question was unremarkable—except for those arresting violet eyes—and that her manners were almost as deplorable as her choice of gowns.

By all accounts, so unprepossessing a female should be perfectly safe from his advances—proper or otherwise—should she not? Then why did his thoughts so often stray to the brief and tempestuous interlude they had shared on Lady Berkford's shadowy terrace? He had come away from that first encounter with a bloody nose, nothing to recommend furthering his acquaintance with the lady, but the disturbing memory of her warm, pliant body pressing into his still haunted him. Or had he imagined it? he wondered. Had he been so foxed that evening that he had dreamed it all? In the cold light of day, during one of his few sober moments, it seemed improbable that a plain wench in an outmoded gown had turned to molten silk in his arms.

Two days later, Hawk had convinced himself that his inchoate infatuation with Miss Millbanks was a figment of his drunken imagination, and to prove that her country charms—such as they were—held no lure for him, he invited one of his former flirts, the voluptuous widow Mrs. Stella Waters, to accompany the party to Sutton House. To satisfy Sir David's sense of propriety, Hawk also invited his cousins, the young and vivacious Lady Sophia Hart and her husband Ned Greenley, Viscount Hart, who agreed to collect Miss Millbanks in their carriage.

When the party assembled at Wolverton Court just before noon that cool November morning, Hawk discovered to his chagrin that the attractive and very fashionable Mrs. Waters was accompanied by her brother, Captain George Waters, presently on leave from his regiment, who had also served under Colonel Laughton in the 18th Hussars.

He had been standing in the hall with Lady Hart and Miss Millbanks when Stella arrived with her brother, accompanied by yet another officer unknown to Hawk.

"We seem to have quite half of Wellington's army here today, Hawk," Lady Sophia remarked in her musical voice. "Now we can feel completely safe, Miss Millbanks, knowing we are surrounded by such a glorious escort. Ned will be quite impossibly jealous, poor thing." She cast a frankly flirtatious glance at her tall husband, who was already looking rather grim, Hawk noticed.

"I say, Hawk, what the devil is that Waters woman doing here?" the viscount said under his breath. "If I had known you meant to include her in your party, I would have left Sophy at home. Not good *ton*, old chap. Not the kind of woman you want to introduce to your wife."

Hawk let out a crack of laughter. "I do not have a wife, Ned, and besides, Stella is received everywhere, as you would know if you went out in society more," he teased his besotted cousin.

"And your lovely wife already knows Mrs. Waters, do you not, Sophy?"

"Yes, indeed," the viscountess assented. "She was one of Raven's flirts at one time, was she not, Ned darling?"

Her husband went very red in the face and glared at her. "You must learn to watch your tongue, Sophy," he remonstrated, glancing nervously at Miss Millbanks, who had missed nothing of the exchange, Hawk saw. "And your brother's former flirts are not an appropriate subject of conversation, let me tell you. He has put all that behind him, in any case, now that he is married to our dear Cassandra."

"Of course he has," the unflappable Lady Hart agreed quickly. "I merely wondered who is paying her gaming losses these days. It is not *you* by any chance, is it, Hawk?"

"Sophy!" the flustered viscount exclaimed sharply. "I will not countenance such hoydenish starts, do you hear me?"

Hawk recognized the gleam of mischief in Miss Millbanks's violet eyes and held his breath. "I am happy to hear that an earl's daughter can be as falsely accused as a baronet's, Lady Hart," she murmured, her gaze resting briefly on Hawk before settling on the fair-haired viscountess. "I often wonder what is left for the really wicked females if gentlemen waste all their insults on us poor innocents."

Before either gentleman could recover from this shattering remark, Lady Hart gave a delighted giggle and linked her arm through that of Miss Millbanks. "I can tell you all about that, my dear," she confessed gaily. "I am wise to the ways of rakes, you see, having been on familiar terms with any number of them. My father was the most famous rake of all England, before my mother tamed him, and my brother takes after him. He was the leader of the Seven Corinthians before he married Cassandra," she added. "A secret society of rakes and rogues, as far as I understand it. And Ned here was one, too, before he swore to reform for my sake. Is that not true, Ned dear?" She glanced lovingly at her husband, who stared at her in dismay throughout this recital.

"Come, my dear Miss Millbanks—or may I call you Serena?" Lady Hart continued, without waiting for her husband to answer. "We shall have a lovely coze during the drive to Winsor. You *are* driving with us, are you not?"

"Miss Millbanks is driving with me, Sophy," Hawk found himself cutting in firmly. He did not remember when the idea had occurred to him to take Miss Millbanks up in his curricle, which he had originally intended to share with Monroyal. But suddenly the notion of condemning her to being shut up in the Wolverton landau with the languid Mrs. Stella Waters and Lady Hart's inconsequential chatter seemed too cruel a fate. Besides, he though, watching her violet eyes turn dark with annoyance, he was already regretting having invited Stella at all and would not have done so had he known her loose screw of a brother would accompany her. Hawk had not missed the calculating glance George Waters had cast on both Lady Hart and Miss Millbanks, and felt an unexpected sense of responsibility for the naive chit from Yorkshire.

That same country chit now turned the full force of her guileless smile on Hawk, and he braced himself for the setdown he knew was coming. "Indeed?" she inquired with deceptive sweetness. "What a flattering invitation, sir. I must insist that you allow me to take the ribbons, however; otherwise, I would much prefer the company of Lady Hart."

"Touché, Hawk," Monroyal said lightly from beside him, and Hawk had the distinct impression that his friend was laughing at him. At that point, Stella's gay tinkling laughter drew all eyes to where she stood beside her brother and the other officer, who was gazing down at her possessively. "I must hand it to you, Hawk," Monroyal murmured laconically. "You do have a knack for collecting odd specimens. Gerald Lawson is hardly the kind of coxcomb I would want to invite to meet my family."

"Never met him," Hawk grimaced, thoroughly in accord with Monroyal's assessment of the tall, languid Bond Street Beau who was obviously one of Stella's latest admirers. "And Waters is hardly what I would call a gentleman either," he added under his breath. "Lord, I wish I had never let Aunt Bess embroil me in this fiasco!" he groaned.

Thus it was that before the cavalcade had gone more than two miles, Hawk's head began to ache. He wished he had thought to bring a flask of brandy with him. The outing, which had promised to be a welcome diversion from his perpetual round of drinking and gaming, had suddenly turned sour. And what the devil was he about letting a mere female and a plain one at that, drive his curricle? he thought disgustedly.

With a sinking sensation of déjà-vu, Hawk felt himself slipping inexorably into one of his black moods.

CHAPTER SEVEN

Lady on Horseback

Serena gave herself up entirely to the joy of driving the four superbly matched and gaited chestnuts hitched to the duke's racing curricle. Her small gloved hands, holding the ribbons with the light, firm touch she had learned so well from her father, soon established the fluid contact with each horse so that in a very short time Serena could tell, a second before he moved, what each horse would do next. Right from the moment Hawkhurst handed her the reins upon leaving Hyde Park Corner, Serena's attention was wholly taken up by the team, so much so that the presence of the man beside her receded into the background.

Once they had passed the turnpike and entered the Bath Road, Serena had imperceptibly allowed the horses to lengthen their stride until they were fairly flying along, the hedgerows a blur of autumn color beside her. It was not until they entered the village of Earling and she had to draw the team down to a walk to allow a heavy mail coach approaching from the direction of Bath to swing wide into the yard of the St. George's Arms that Serena realized that she had exchanged not a single word with her companion since leaving London.

She glanced at him now, startled by the black frown on his lean face. He regarded her with hooded eyes, gray as wet slate and equally hard. Serena had never seen Hawkhurst look so bleak, and wondered what she had done to anger him before she noticed that his eyes looked not at her but through her, as though she were invisible.

It also struck her that he appeared to be cold sober, and she wondered if this had anything to do with the haunted look she thought she detected in the turbulent depths of his eyes. This was not the laughing, drunken rogue who had kissed her that night at Lady Berkford's, the man whose hands had touched not just her body but some unsuspected core of her being that had threatened to undo her prized self control. Here was a man as far removed from the country girl she knew herself to be as it was possible to get and still inhabit the same world. Gone was the familiar teasing smile, the mocking glance, the easy repartee of Major Guy Hawkhurst, rake and libertine. In his place, Serena saw—perhaps for the first time—His Grace, the Duke of Wolverton.

Serena felt suddenly gauche and out of place. She pulled the team up by the side of the road and returned his stare calmly, although she was conscious of the pounding of her heart.

"What have I done to anger you, Your Grace?" she said huskily.

His eyes changed color and slowly focused on her face. Serena had the distinct impression that Hawkhurst had forcibly pulled himself back from a dark, desolate place in his mind where he had witnessed more pain than he could bear. Then he smiled, a fleeting grimace which, even as she watched, slowly turned to mockery. Serena felt her heart leap into her throat, suddenly aware that there was more to this man than she had imagined. She had written him off initially as a fashionable fribble, a Town Beau frittering away his life in the useless pursuit of pleasure. Now she wondered if perhaps behind the facade of profligate rakehell lurked a man she had yet to meet.

"Anger me?" he drawled in his lazy voice, his gaze raking her face. "Nothing you could do could anger me, my dear Serena. May I call you Serena? Such a relaxing name, although grossly inappropriate, of course, for a female whose left jab would put most men to shame."

Serena bristled instantly. "No, you may *not*," she snapped. "And that is the most outrageous whisker I have yet heard. I was named for my poor Aunt Serena," she rushed on, conscious of a flutter in her breast at his use of her name. "My father's sister. And Papa tells me that I am her exact image. She was a spinster," she added defiantly, raising her chin a notch.

"A spinster?" he repeated, his smile breaking into a grin. "And you plan to follow in her footsteps, I take it? Seems like a great waste to me." Again his eyes raked her face lazily. "But tell me, my dear, why is she *poor* Aunt Serena?"

"Well," Serena responded quickly, anxious to return their conversation to a more comfortable level, "for one thing, she has been dead for nearly ten years." She was rewarded by a rich chuckle from the duke. "But she was unfortunate enough to form an attachment for a French nobleman who was executed in the Terror. She was true to her first love until the day she died, my father told me."

"What a touching story," Hawkhurst remarked without his usual cynicism. "And what about you, sweet Serena? Are you wearing the willow for your first true love?"

Serena stared at him in surprise. "No, of course not," she replied unwarily. And to tell the truth, she had hardly spared a thought for Brian Westlock in weeks. "And I am not your sweet anything, sir," she added sharply.

"But you do have a true love, am I right?" For some odd reason he was no longer smiling, and Serena wondered why she felt no embarrassment talking about Brian to this man who was practically a stranger, yet no real stranger at all if one considered the intimacies they had shared.

"True love is perhaps not the correct term," she hedged, wondering how they had slipped into this highly personal subject. "And Brian never really noticed me, of course, being rather partial to simpering females with golden curls and pansy-blue eyes." She paused, her attention arrested by the troubling thought that she could no longer remember the color of Brian's eyes. She smiled to herself at this startling discovery, and then turned to her companion. "I should not keep the cattle standing around like this. Shall we continue?"

Hawkhurst only laughed at this abrupt change of topic and the rest of the journey was accomplished in comfortable silence. They arrived at Sutton House well in advance of the more cumbersome landau, and as she tooled the curricle up the oak-lined driveway, Serena felt the first flutters of trepidation at the ordeal awaiting her. What would Papa say if he could see her now, tooling the bang-up team of a duke? Or if he knew that his unprepossessing daughter was the guest of an acknowledged leader of the *ton* like Lady Lexington? And would the duke's great-aunt be as stiff-rumped as other aristocratic matrons she had encountered during her short sojourn in London, so conscious of their own consequence that they had barely deigned to acknowledge the daughter of an obscure baronet with neither beauty nor fortune to recommend her?

Her first glimpse of Sutton House, a stately Elizabethan structure, exquisitely proportioned and weathered to a warm amber glow in the afternoon sunshine, did nothing to assuage Serena's apprehension. The house had a sense of elegant permanence about it which bespoke countless generations of loving husbandry, and the grounds lay about it in a carefully contrived naturalness which owed nothing at all to nature.

Lady Lexington fit into this setting as though it had been created expressly to set off her own aristocratic beauty, and Serena's first sight of her hostess caused her to stop abruptly in her tracks as though she had seen an apparition. The lady who rose and came forward to greet them as they entered the spacious drawing room was nothing like the staid dowager Serena had anticipated. Lady Lexington was tall and slender, her eyes clear and intelligent, and her aristocratic nose softened by the generous mouth now curved in a welcoming smile. But it was her complexion that made Serena blink. Could this exquisitely beautiful woman, whose skin seemed—at this distance at least—to be as smooth and untainted as a young girl's, be the great-aunt the duke had spoken of?

She heard Hawkhurst chuckle deep in his throat as he nudged her forward with a hand lightly under her elbow.

"I know exactly how you must feel, my dear," he murmured, without any attempt at dissimulation. "My Aunt Elizabeth is a Diamond of the first water." He grinned affectionately at Lady Lexington and bent to salute her on the cheek. "Aunt Bess, allow me to present our intrepid horsewoman to you." He glanced down at Serena as she made her curtsy to the countess and then added *sotto voce*, "Now you can see for yourself where I get my good looks, Miss Millbanks. It runs in the family."

Serena threw him a startled glance. "Nonsense!" she exclaimed without thinking. "I see nothing of the sort. You overrate yourself, sir. What I do see is that you pale into insignificance beside her ladyship." She stopped abruptly and glanced guiltily at her hostess, conscious of the astonished expression on the countess's exquisite face. "Oh! I do beg your pardon, my lady, I did not mean—"

"Never tell me you did not *mean* it, my dear Miss Millbanks," the countess interrupted, her gray eyes—so like the duke's—twinkling with amusement. "It is not often I receive such a delightful compliment, and it is always a pleasure to see my nephew so neatly set down." She linked a slender arm through Serena's and drew her toward a gilt-legged settee. "Now come and tell me all about your father, my dear, before the rest of the party arrives. I knew him when he was a young hellion, you know. Is he still horse-mad?"

"I fear he is, my lady," Serena replied with a rueful smile.

"But since my mother died, Papa's luck has never been the same."

"Well, if he taught you all he knew in his salad days, I shall look forward to winning my wager with Guy, my dear."

Serena glanced up at Hawkhurst, who stood regarding her quizzically. "Oh, you may count on it, my lady," she replied gaily, suddenly glad that she had come. "You may indeed count upon it."

By the time the Wolverton landau arrived with the accompanying cavalcade of horsemen, Guy Hawkhurst heartily regretted his impulse to include Lady Hart and Mrs. Waters in the party. His aunt would have been adequate protection for Miss Millbanks's good name, he realized belatedly, and it was only Sir David's exaggerated punctiliousness in such matters which had compelled him to question Hawk's arrangements. And if the ubiquitous Stella were not present, he would not now be faced with the unpleasant task of keeping Serena safe from the unmistakable interest he had glimpsed in Captain Waters's languid glance.

Luckily his aunt had—in her intuitive fashion—taken stock of the situation and made it a point to keep the chit at her side. In this she was aided by Lord Monroyal, whom Hawk knew to be a special favorite of hers, and who seemed to have established an oddly protective attitude toward Miss Millbanks. Guy was not entirely sure he trusted the marquess's intentions, since in all the years he had known him, Robert had never expressed anything but contempt for single young ladies.

Even as he watched the practiced ease with which Monroyal kept Lady Lexington and Miss Millbanks entertained with his teasing banter, Hawk felt a light touch on his arm.

"Who is Monroyal's new flirt?" Mrs. Waters purred in her distinctively husky voice. "I cannot recall ever seeing his lordship so taken with a chit before. Not at all his usual style, I would say." Hawk saw her slanted eyes cast a disparaging glance in Miss Millbanks's direction. "Is our dear marquess so bored with what London has to offer that he must resort to seducing country dowds?"

Hawk glanced down at the petulant Beauty and reflected—not for the first time—the pleasure that Stella had afforded him in several occasions in the past was more than offset by the unpleasant nature of her company outside the bedroom.

Inviting La Waters had been a worse mistake than he had first imagined.

"I doubt Monroyal has any such intention," he said shortly.

Stella laughed her throaty, seductive chuckle, which had once held the power to stir his blood. In his present sober state, Hawk thought disgustedly, it sounded merely vulgar. "Ah!" she teased, a malicious inflection to her low voice, "don't tell me that you are also caught up in the chit's toils, my dear Hawk? How positively gauche of you. The girl is not even an innocent, unless I am very much mistaken," she added dismissively. "What do you think, Gerald?" she added, turning to the lieutenant, who had sauntered over to join them.

"About what, my sweet?" Lawson drawled, but Hawk deliberately turned aside in answer to a laughing query from Lady Hart, so he escaped having to listen to what he imagined would be the dandified officer's crude remarks. Had he been so foxed when he devised this outing that he had thought nothing of exposing Serena to the stares of rakes and the vicious tongue of a woman like Stella? And of course, he had insulted his Aunt Bess into the bargain, he told himself wryly, catching that lady's expressive glance across the room.

His awareness of these malicious undercurrents regarding Miss Millbanks did not improve Hawk's temper, for they reminded him too acutely of the rumors that had circulated among his fellow officers when Derek had arrived unexpectedly to join the campaign in Spain. His automatic response was to reach—as he had done ever since his return to England when these memories plagued him—for the brandy decanter. During the elaborate nuncheon Lady Lexington had ordered for her guests, Hawk was conscious of Monroyal's sardonic gaze upon him as he allowed the footman to refill his glass for the fourth time. He smiled thinly in response, and the marquess shrugged his elegant shoulders and turned his attention back to Lord Hart, who was expounding on the merits of a new hunter he had recently acquired at Tattersall's.

By the time the party removed to the stables to select mounts for the ladies, Hawk was feeling pleasantly abstracted from the unpleasantness he had overheard in the drawing room. The black humor that had plagued him earlier had dissipated, leaving in its stead a reckless nonchalance which he recognized all too well.

"Take it easy, old man," a voice said at his elbow as he was preparing to mount his gelding. Hawk turned and grinned

widely at Sir David Laughton, as the baronet regarded him
steadily, a silent question in his brown eyes.

"Do not fret, David," Hawk tossed off carelessly as he tightened the girth on his saddle. "I ain't bosky yet by a long shot."
He led his horse over to where Lady Lexington sat on her
long-legged bay Thoroughbred.

"I owe you an apology, Aunt," he confessed, fully aware
that Lady Lexington would stand for no roundaboutation.

His aunt did not pretend to misunderstand him. "It seems to
me that you own Serena an apology, Guy," she replied with
unusual sharpness. "She should not be obliged to consort with
females like Mrs. Waters, as you would have seen had you
given the matter any thought. And do not tell me that the creature is a baron's daughter," she continued acidly. "Lord Gower
was the world's worst libertine, and from what I hear, his
daughter is in a fair way to challenging that reputation." Lady
Lexington regarded him steadily, her wide gray eyes troubled.
"I am disappointed that you have seen fit to include her in the
ranks of your conquests, Guy," she remarked without embarrassment. "I would have thought you could do better for yourself than drink at a muddied fountain."

Accustomed as he was to his aunt's plain speaking, Hawk
was taken aback at this forthright condemnation. "I was
foxed," he mumbled, before giving any consideration to his
words.

"You are always foxed," Lady Lexington shot back force-
fully. "That is why I have asked Monroyal to keep a weather-
eye on Serena to see that she comes to no harm at Sutton
House."

Hawk felt himself bristle and his voice turned chilly. "I am
quite capable of taking care of Miss Millbanks without any
help from Monroyal," he said shortly. "And why Monroyal, if
I may ask, Aunt? A more confirmed care-for-nobody I have
yet to see." For some reason the thought of Serena in the marquess's care made Hawk's blood run cold.

"He is not foxed," Lady Lexington replied astringently.

"Neither am I, " Hawk growled, his black mood threatening
to overwhelm him again.

"You are in a fair way to becoming so," his aunt threw over
her shoulder, as she turned her horse and moved away.

The inside of Lady Lexington's well-appointed stables was
dim and warm, and Serena took a deep breath of the sweet hay

and leather as she followed the marquess down the long line of stalls, pausing to examine each animal that thrust a velvety nose out to greet her.

"Lady Lexington has a good eye for horses," she remarked after a particularly fine looking Arabian had nuzzled her hand playfully.

"It is her only real passion," Monroyal replied. "Always has been, or so I hear. The story goes that her ladyship refused Lord Lexington's suit for over a year until he agreed to allow her free rein in the stables and a curricle-and-four of her own."

Serena laughed. "I can understand that perfectly," she said with such feeling that the marquess glanced at her quizzically. "Her ladyship was lucky indeed to find a considerate husband," she explained. "Horses are better company than boorish gentlemen, I can tell you that, my lord."

Monroyal smiled one of his rare genuine smiles. "Horses have been known to be vicious and unmanageable, my dear Miss Millbanks."

"Ah, but there you have the real advantage of a horse over a husband, my lord," Serena replied gaily. "If a horse becomes vicious and intractable, one can always have the animal put down. Whereas if a female is saddled with a vicious husband, much as she might wish to do so, she could hardly have him put down, now could she?"

"Very true, my dear," the marquess said softly. "And is that the reason you have decided to eschew the married state?"

"I do not want a husband who arouses murderous instincts in me, that I *do* know," she replied spiritedly. "And I am afraid—judging from my brief sojourn in the Metropolis—that there are not many gentlemen like Lord Lexington to be found here." She smiled ruefully at the handsome marquess, wondering again what drove such men as Lord Monroyal and the Duke of Wolverton—men with wealth, position, and good looks—to fritter away their lives in pointless rounds of gambling, drinking, and wenching. She wished she had the courage to ask what demons drove them to destroy themselves, and in particular why Hawkhurst had seen fit to slip a flask of brandy into the pocket of his riding jacket after indulging liberally during Lady Lexington's luncheon.

"You are probably right, Miss Millbanks," the marquess said after a considerable pause. "But then again, I have it on impeccable authority that Lord Lexington was a very dull dog."

Serena was about to retort that she, for one, preferred dull dogs to drunk rakes when they were interrupted by Hawkhurst striding toward them in the penumbra of the stable. "Why are you not yet mounted, Serena?" he demanded. "Is Monroyal here trying to persuade you to select a less mettlesome nag and lose my wager for me?"

"You are too quick to malign your friends, sir," Serena responded calmly. "And I have yet to see this horse with the improbable name of Satan." Barely had the words left her lips than they all heard a commotion from one of the further stalls, accompanied by some choice curses from a groom.

"Barker!" the duke called imperiously, "is that you? Bring the beast out here, will you? The lady is ready to ride." He glanced down at Serena, who noted that his gray eyes were full of amusement again.

"Righto, Your Grace," came an exasperated voice from within the stall, and almost instantly the door was flung open and Barker himself appeared, holding tightly to the halter of the tallest horse Serena had ever seen. The animal snorted at the sight of the cluster of strangers and reared up, trying to dislodge the groom's hold.

Barker was stronger than he looked, however, and he coaxed the horse toward them, talking to him in muttered threats which seemed to calm the animal. "Are ye sure the lady would not prefer to take out Blueball instead, milord?" he inquired, eyeing Serena with a jaundiced expression. "I am afraid 'is nibs 'ere is a mite fidgety today on account of missing 'is exercise yesterday, milord. Now Blueball is a proper lady's mount. A real treat to ride, if I may say so, milady." This last was directed to Serena, who deduced from the disapproving tone of the groom's voice that he had a very low opinion of the ability of females to handle anything but the veriest slugs.

She gave the groom a dazzling smile. "I am sure the poor animal merely wants to stretch his legs, Barker. I am quite looking forward to a good gallop myself."

"The devil take it, Hawk," she heard the marquess mutter under his breath. "You cannot put a female up on a brute like that."

The duke appeared not to have heard his friend's remark. "Put one of her ladyship's saddles on him, Barker," he ordered. "And look sharp about it, or we shall be left behind."

"I doubt that, Your Grace," came the sour reply, but the

groom led the horse out and in no time at all—or so it seemed to Serena—Hawk had tossed her up into the saddle and adjusted the stirrups.

"Are you sure you want to do this, Miss Millbanks?" inquired Monroyal, who had drawn his own horse up beside her.

"Of course she does, Robert," Hawkhurst brushed the query aside impatiently. "And I shall be only too happy to pick up the pieces if Satan should prove too much for the lady to handle," he added with a smugness that caused Serena's hackles to rise.

"I see you wish to amuse yourself at my expense," she remarked dryly. "Well, we shall have to disappoint you, will we not, Satan?" She lowered her hands and the restless horse needed no further encouragement but broke instantly into a canter which soon lengthened into a gallop. In a very short time, Serena had caught up with the main party of riders, but her enjoyment of her spirited mount was vastly diminished when she found herself the object of Captain Waters's fulsome compliments.

"A very fine seat you have, Miss Millbanks," Waters said unctuously, pulling his horse so close to Satan that his knee brushed hers. "Very fine indeed," he repeated, his eyes sliding over her form with an undisguised leer. "I find there is nothing more intoxicating to a gentleman's senses than to see a spirited lady on a mettlesome steed. If you only knew how ravishing you look, my dear . . ." He allowed the sentence to taper off suggestively.

Serena looked at him coldly. "You are being quite absurd, sir," she said flatly and urged her horse into a canter. She was not to escape that easily, she soon discovered. Captain Waters caught up with her and continued as though she had not indicated any displeasure at his attentions. Serena glanced back, only to find that the party had split up into groups of twos and threes, and that the duke was apparently captivated by the lively banter of Mrs. Waters. Lord Monroyal rode with the Harts and Lady Lexington far behind the others. Colonel Laughton was nowhere in sight.

George Waters laughed unpleasantly. "I would not set your sights on Wolverton, my dear. Dukes do not wed impoverished baronet's daughters, you know. And if he is anything like that brother of his—a namby-pamby sort of fellow if ever I saw one—he will not be good for much else either." He paused to see if the significance of this oblique comment had struck home, then let out a crack of ribald laughter. "I never could understand what my sister sees in him. Now I am no slow-top with the ladies, my dear, and if it is a cozy niche you are looking for, you could do a lot worse than—"

"Thank you for your kind offer," Serena interrupted icily, "but I have not yet sunk *that* low." She shot the offensive captain a glance of pure disdain and then, without waiting for a response, urged Satan into a thunderous gallop which soon left the party far behind.

Over an hour later, having enjoyed the ride and exhausted herself and the horse by racing randomly over Lady Lexington's extensive estate, Serena found her way back to the stable yard, where an anxious Barker immediately came out to help her dismount. He looked faintly surprised to see her still on Satan's back.

"Right worrit about ye, we was, miss, and no mistake," the groom said with a glimmer of new respect, as Serena walked beside him into the stable and watched him put Satan into his stall and call a stable lad to wipe down the big horse's glistening hide. "But I see that old Satan 'ere 'as met 'is match." He patted the horse's rump affectionately.

"Where is everybody, Barker?" Serena demanded, noticing that most of the stalls were still empty.

"The ladies are up at the house, miss. But some of the gentlemen went out again when they 'eard ye were not back yet."

Serena wished she dared ask the surly groom which gentlemen had shown such concern for her safety, but instead she thanked him and turned away to find her way out of the sprawling building. The sound of a horse's arrival in the cobble-stoned yard made her quicken her step, but her hopes of encountering Hawkhurst were dashed when the figure who entered the dimly lit stable was much shorter than the duke.

"Well met, my lovely," the captain drawled, handing the reins to a stable lad and blocking Serena's way when she tried to slip past him. "Oh, no you don't, sweetheart," he murmured softly. Taking a firm grasp on Serena's arm, he half pushed, half pulled her into the nearest empty stall. "You and me have to finish that little talk we were enjoying, remember?"

"I do not recall enjoying any talk with *you,* sir," Serena replied coldly, although her heart was pounding with apprehension. "Quite the opposite is true, if you must know." She tried to pull free of his bruising grip, but the captain only laughed.

"I like my females with lots of spirit, sweetheart." He grinned down at her in the dim stall and—from the hungry look in his hooded eyes—Serena knew instinctively what was coming.

When he pulled her roughly against him and bent to kiss her, she was ready. The kiss never happened. Instead, Serena balled her fist and brought it up low and fast, catching the captain quite by surprise as it connected with his nose on its downward trajectory. The result was painful for Serena, whose knuckles jarred on impact, but infinitely more so for the captain, whose nose cracked ominously as he was sent reeling back against the wall.

"Let that be a lesson to you, Waters," an amused voice drawled from the open doorway. "Now get back on your horse and take your filthy hide out of here before I kill you."

The captain pushed himself upright and glared at the duke, one hand cradling his bleeding nose tenderly. With a snarl of pure fury, he launched himself at Hawkhurst. Serena held her breath as the duke moved unsteadily sideways to avoid the savage blow aimed at his head. Then he stumbled on the uneven floor, and Serena had a flash of intuition that made her freeze. His Grace was absolutely and utterly castaway. *Again,* she thought bitterly. A premonition of disaster flashed through her mind moments before the duke swung a powerful punch which went wide of the mark and caused him to stagger toward his opponent. The captain took full advantage of this opening to plant a crunching hook on the duke's nose, sending him crashing back onto the wooden floor of the stall.

A cynical laugh broke the momentary silence.

"Keep the bloody wench," the captain sneered. "And if you have any notion of making things difficult for me, *Your Grace,*" he added with a sinister emphasis on the form of address, "remember that I can tell the *ton* some very entertaining rumors about your actions at Vittoria, Wolverton."

He laughed again—the pure venom of it sending a shiver down Serena's spine—then turned to stride out of the stall.

Hawk struggled to rise, as if he had every intention of continuing the brawl, but Serena grasped him unceremoniously by his sleeve and tumbled him back into the hay.

"Do not be a complete lackwit," she snapped, her patience sorely tried by this show of masculine obtuseness. She knelt beside him, firmly keeping him in place with one hand on his chest and her full weight behind it, while she fumbled in his pocket for a handkerchief to stanch the bleeding.

"Let me up, you silly chit," the duke muttered stubbornly, struggling to raise himself on his elbows.

"Ahem!" A discreet cough came from the open doorway. "Forgive me for interrupting such a tender scene, my dear, but may I point out to you, Miss Millbanks, that the gentleman appears to be somewhat unwilling."

Serena swung around and stared up wrathfully into the sardonic gray eyes of the marquess, who lounged with deliberate nonchalance against the door frame.

"I trust you are not about to play the fool, too, my lord," she retorted scathingly. "One fool is all I can handle at a time, let me tell you. Now get in here and help me wipe all this blood off Hawk's face."

The marquess seemed rather taken aback by this abrupt address, but he did step into the stall and bend down beside the duke.

"Devil a bit!" he exclaimed under his breath. "Is his nose broken, do you suppose?"

"I certainly *hope* so," Serena replied with suppressed savagery. "We must get him into the house without making a fuss. Help me get him on his feet, if you please."

The marquess complied, but he could not repress his curiosity. "Did *you* draw his cork for him, Miss Millbanks?" he asked in astonishment.

"No," she replied succinctly. "Not this time."

"Then who—"

"That is a long story, and it will have to wait, my lord," she replied calmly. "Now hold still," she snapped at the duke, who was showing signs of resisting her ministrations. "We can hardly take you into the house with blood all over you. And over me," she added, glancing ruefully at her stained habit. "And I have a few things to say to you as soon as we get you patched up, which you will not like at all."

The duke groaned most piteously, but Serena refused to be moved. "Going to shoot the cat," he muttered inelegantly, his face a pallid mask in the dim stall.

"Serves you right," Serena remarked with considerable relish. "Luckily, there are no chrysanthemums here," she added, glancing up at the marquess's startled expression.

"Yellow chrysanthemums," she added sardonically, as though that explained everything.

CHAPTER EIGHT

Change of Fortune

Much later that night, after the duke's party had returned to London in varying stages of bewilderment at Hawkhurst's sudden indisposition that required the presence of Lady Lexington's personal physician, Serena sat in the dim sickroom listening to Hawk's heavy breathing. It was the first time she had enjoyed a few moments of quiet and privacy since she and Lord Monroyal had smuggled the duke up to a guest room hastily prepared by Lady Lexington's housekeeper, Mrs. Lovell.

With the unprotesting assistance of Lord Monroyal, Serena had thrown back the covers of the bed and proceeded to strip the duke of his cravat and ease him out of his elegant coat without wasting a moment's thought on the propriety of her presence in a gentleman's bedchamber. After one of her ladyship's footmen had been commissioned to remove the duke's boots, a wide-eyed maid instructed to find a suitable nightshirt for His Grace, and the phlegmatic housekeeper sent down to appraise her mistress of her great-nephew's plight, Serena found herself unbuttoning the duke's fine cambric shirt. The unprecedented vision of a gentleman's bare chest finally brought her to her senses, and Serena abruptly withdrew her hands as though she had been scorched. Her eyes flicked uncertainly at the marquess, and she blushed at the mockery she saw in his gray eyes.

"I wondered when the impropriety of your actions would impress itself upon you, Miss Millbanks," he drawled in his supercilious manner.

Serena's gaze dropped again to the supine form on the bed. Hawk's face was pale and tinged with a greenish cast, his hair was in complete disarray, the dark strands falling across his brow giving him a touchingly vulnerable demeanor. His eyes were closed, and as Serena watched, Hawkhurst shuddered violently and struggled to rise, his face screwed up in distress.

Instinctively, Serena reached for a blue Staffordshire bowl and held it under his chin, her right hand cradling his head. When the paroxysm spent itself, Serena calmly handed the bowl to the marquess and gently wiped the duke's face with a lemon-scented cloth. Hawkhurst groaned and sank back against the pillows.

Serena glanced at the marquess, her former embarrassment overshadowed by concern. "I think we should remove the rest of his clothes and get him under the covers," she remarked prosaically, wringing out the cloth in the lemon water provided by the housekeeper.

"I suggest you let me attend to that, my dear," Lord Monroyal remarked, relinquishing the bowl to Mrs. Lovell with a moue of distaste. "I hardly think Lady Lexington would approve of your doing so," he added with a touch of sarcasm.

"What would I not approve of Serena doing?" Lady Lexington demanded, sweeping regally into the room, a worried frown on her perfect features. She took one look at the man on the bed and her lips thinned noticeably. "Foxed again, nephew?" she said, the words more condemning than questioning. "Mrs. Lovell," she continued with hardly a pause, "get Holmes up here at once with one of the footmen. And tell cook to prepare some of that tisane she makes for my migraines. And you, my girl," she turned her speculative eyes on Serena's bedraggled appearance, "come with me. We will have to find a change of clothes for you."

Serena had protested, but Lady Lexington prevailed. She soon found herself installed in a luxurious guest room, where an efficient maid had prepared a warm bath and assisted her into an elegant emerald wool gown evidently belonging to her ladyship. By the time she returned to the sick room, the doctor had come and gone, pronouncing the duke's nose bruised but not broken, and prescribing complete rest for his noble patient.

Lady Lexington was no less adamant in her insistence that Miss Millbanks remain at Sutton House until her nephew was recovered enough to escort her home to Lady Thornton. She had detained her in the hall to inform her that the other members of the party had already departed.

"Monroyal has told me the whole, my dear," she remarked calmly when Serena protested that she could not impose upon her hostess any longer. "I could hardly send you back to London in a party including that jackanapes Waters, who has caused you so much grief," she explained in tones that brooked no argument. "And besides, Guy insisted that you re-main to tend his nose." Lady Lexington paused and raised a quizzical brow. "His very words, my dear," she said with an amused twinkle. "He refused to elaborate, so I cannot begin to understand his meaning, but he is most anxious to see you. I hope you will dine with me, my dear," she added as Serena turned to enter the sickroom. "I look forward to hearing the story from your own lips." She gave Serena a calculating glance. "Green suits you, my dear. You should wear it more often," she added unexpectedly before disappearing down the hall.

Serena thought Hawkhurst was asleep when she stepped quietly up to his bedside, and however much she might tell herself that the wretch deserved every discomfort he suffered, she could not help but feel a tug of pity for the lines of pain around his mouth. A damp cloth lay across his swollen nose and above it his eyes suddenly opened to regard her with un-comfortable directness.

"Did that scoundrel kiss you?" he demanded in a muffled voice.

Serena raised an eyebrow. "Which scoundrel are you refer-ring to, sir?" she inquired with a touch of sarcasm. "I seem to be surrounded by them."

She saw a flash of impatience cross his face. "Waters," he growled. "If that jackstraw harmed you in any way, I shall make him wish he had stayed in Spain."

"From the efficient way the captain dispatched you this af-ternoon, I fancy that is an empty threat," she pointed out with a certain amount of unholy relish.

"Well, did he?" the duke snapped, struggling to rise.

Serena firmly pushed him back, and the warmth of his chest under her fingers was an uncomfortable reminder of the dark curling hairs she had caught a glimpse of earlier. "There is no point in flying into the boughs over such a trifle," she said, pulling her mind away from these unsettling thoughts and meeting his gaze with aplomb. "It is hardly your concern, in any case, so pray do not tease yourself."

A gleam of annoyance flashed briefly in the dark gray depths of his eyes. "It most certainly is my concern if—through any fault of mine—your chances of snaring a suitable husband this Season are impaired."

Serena's mouth dropped open, and it was several moments before she recovered enough to take umbrage at this impertinence. Then the absurdity of Hawkhurst's words stuck her, and she burst out laughing.

"Chances?" she choked at last. "That's rich, indeed. To begin with, I never deceived myself into believing that I had any chances at all," she explained in answer to Hawkhurst's frown. "Secondly, wherever did you get the idea that I am on the catch for a husband? And thirdly, I must confess that I have yet to encounter any gentleman in London who would tempt me to consider giving up my freedom." She gave another chuckle. "Besides which," she continued mockingly, "I take exception to your use of the word *snare,* which—to my mind at least—implies deception and trickery, tactics I deplore in any form."

Hawkhurst regarded her with hooded eyes. Then a mocking smile twisted his lips. "Very commendable sentiments, my dear, I'm sure. But I have it upon excellent authority that your father is deeply under the hatches and expects you to make a credible match to pull him out of the hole."

Serena felt herself bristle. "That is a complete Banbury tale," she said stoutly. "I don't know where you got your information, sir, but there is no truth to it." She managed a slight smile. "I fully intend to return to Yorkshire in my single state to take up where I left off. And if my Papa had wished to snare—as you so rudely put it—a wealthy son-in-law, he would have entrusted such a mission to my sister Cecily. *She* is the beauty in the family. He was a fool to expect *me* to make a splash in London," she added, half to herself. "I simply could not do so, even had I the wish for it, which I assure you, I do not."

The duke looked at her oddly. "Have you received no offers at all?" he inquired bluntly.

Serena stiffened. "I hardly think that is any—"

"Yes or no?" he interrupted.

"No, of course not," she snapped back, angered at this high-handed interference in her affairs. "Leastwise, none that were at all to my liking."

Hawkhurst tried to push himself up on his elbows again and failed. "Who was he?" he said harshly.

"Lord Grifford, if you must know," she replied ungraciously.

Hawkhurst stared at her in astonishment, then let out a crack of laughter. "Grifford?" he repeated. "That old codger must be sixty if he's a day. Surely you are roasting me, my dear."

"Not at all," Serena said stiffly. "He was kind enough to tell me I reminded him of his first wife."

"And you declined the honor, I suppose?"

"Of course. Lord Grifford reminded *me* of my grandfather, who was a bad-tempered old tyrant."

"Ah, but Grifford is full of juice, my dear. Or didn't you know?" Hawkhurst drawled with veiled sarcasm. "Your father might have approved the match on that account."

Serena stared at him in amazement. "He most certainly would *not*," she declared. "At no time has my father pressured me to marry anyone." This was not quite true, of course, she thought ruefully. Her dear Papa had seemed unusually anxious for her to come to London, and had talked about getting her riveted—his very words—to a suitable gentleman. But at no time had he mentioned the need for a wealthy son-in-law. Could it be that her Papa had expected his daughter to understand what he had in mind without having to come right out and say it? He often did so, Serena remembered with a pang of nostalgia, especially if his intentions concerned something unpleasant. Could it be that the duke was right? she wondered, a prickle of fear knotting her stomach. It was certainly true, she suddenly remembered, that in each of his weekly letters, her father had inquired most particularly about her success on the Marriage Mart. Serena had taken this as her father's way of teasing her, but now she began to suspect that there may have been more urgency in his insistence on her London beaux—as he called them—than she had realized.

"Are you quite sure of that, my dear?" Hawkhurst's voice was no longer cynical but held a note of what sounded like real concern.

Serena was touched, and for the first time since arriving in Town, she felt that in this unlikely man—a dissolute, brandy-soaked, hardened libertine—she might have found a friend. She certainly needed one, if it was true that her father was ruined. Unexpectedly, she felt her eyes blur with tears.

"No, I'm not sure," she whispered after a moment in a subdued voice. "But it cannot be . . . Papa never said . . ." Her voice trailed off into uncomfortable silence.

"I'm afraid it is, my dear," Hawkhurst said gently. "I thought you knew how things stood. From what I hear, your father is in dire need of twenty thousand pounds if he is to avoid debtors' prison."

"Twenty thou— No!" Serena felt as though her world had

suddenly tilted beneath her. "Not Papa! He would never . . ." She struggled to overcome her sudden panic. "How do you know so much about my father's affairs?" she demanded abruptly, as the incongruity of the situation struck home.

Hawkhurst laughed ruefully. "My mother has me surrounded by officious busybodies who try to steer me away from fortune hunters. And by all accounts *you* are one of them, my dear."

Serena could not believe her ears. "Me?" she said in a strangled voice. "A fortune hunter?" She took a threatening step toward the bed and glared down at the duke, wondering how she could possibly have imagined that this obnoxious oaf was her friend. "You have maggots in your head, sir. Either that or the vast quantities of brandy you consume have addled your brains." Her voice shook with outrage at his unfair accusation, and she felt both the urge to slap him for his impertinence and an odd sense of disappointment at his lack of trust.

"Just look at you," she said, with a disdainful gesture in the direction of the bed. "You are quite the most disgusting man I know. Not only did you ruin my riding habit with blood stains, but you seem to become odiously unwell every time we meet."

"I shall buy you another habit, my dear—"

"You will do nothing of the sort," she stormed, incensed at this typical masculine nonchalance. After a moment, she turned resolutely toward the door.

"Where are you going?" he demanded sharply.

Serena glanced over her shoulder. Hawkhurst had pushed himself up onto his elbow, and the damp cloth fell away from his nose, revealing an ugly red swelling. His gray eyes held a silent appeal at variance with the autocratic tone of his voice. Serena relented and returned to rinse out and replace the cloth.

"Lie down," she said peremptorily. When he obeyed, she placed the cool cloth gently over his nose and smoothed it down against his cheeks. "I am going to make arrangements to return to Mount Street immediately," she informed him. "If what you say about my father's finances is correct, I shall have to make a push to snare a rich husband after all." She smiled with more confidence than she felt. "Perhaps Lord Grifford might be persuaded to renew his offer." She paused and regarded the man in the bed quizzically. "Are you acquainted with his lordship, by any chance? Perhaps you might see your way to dropping him a hint—"

"Do not even think of it," came the flat response.

"Why not? He did offer once, you know."

Hawkhurst ignored this comment. "You cannot return to London by yourself at this late hour. My aunt will never allow it. I shall drive you myself tomorrow morning, and we shall see what can be done about mending your father's fortunes."

Serena stared at him for a moment, conscious of an overwhelming desire to transfer her cares to this man's broad shoulders. Then she shook her head. "The doctor prescribed a full day's rest for you, sir," she pointed out as she twitched the covers into place. "And besides, my misfortunes are none of your concern."

"I have just made them my concern," Hawkhurst drawled in his familiar cynical voice, quite devoid—Serena noted with regret—of any hint of genuine warmth. "I shall find the role of White Knight vastly amusing, my dear. Humor me, I beg of you."

Overcome by a flood of mixed emotions, Serena did not trust herself to point out to the Duke of Wolverton that his proposal was both highly irregular and improper. Besides, there was a gleam of devilry in his eyes that she mistrusted. It hinted at intimacies between them she had tried to forget.

"I do not think your mother would approve of such nonsensical behavior," Serena said, steeling her heart against the slow, seductive smile that curled the corners of his mouth. She gave the quilted eiderdown one last, lingering pat and turned to leave. Hawkhurst and his managing ways would have to wait till morning.

By the time they were halfway back to London, Hawk's nose throbbed painfully, but he was mercifully free of the black mood that had plagued him the previous afternoon and every other sober moment since returning from the Peninsula. As he had predicted, Lady Lexington adamantly refused to allow Serena to leave Sutton House alone or to provide a suitable abigail to accompany her back to Mount Street. His great-aunt had even protested vigorously at Hawk's plans for an early departure for the Metropolis, insisting that she was desirous of enjoying another day of Miss Millbanks's company.

"Thanks to that unspeakable fellow, Waters, we have not had time or opportunity for a comfortable coze, my dear," her ladyship pointed out with evident displeasure. "And if my pesky nephew insists upon dragging you away so arbitrarily, I demand that he bring you to Sutton House again before you return to Yorkshire. I would like your opinion on a young bay colt I am tempted to purchase from one of my neighbors," she added, casting a warm smile at her guest.

"You are very kind, my lady," Serena replied politely. "But I fear there are urgent family matters I must attend to in London."

With that his aunt had to be content, although Hawk was amused to see that Lady Lexington insisted on wrapping Miss Millbanks in a warm fur robe and ordering hot bricks to be placed at her feet.

"Aunt Bess seems to have taken a shine to you, my dear," Hawk remarked as he tooled the curricle past the twin stone pillars of Sutton House. "She always wished for a daughter of her own, you know, but that never happened, so she has to make do with me."

"A sorry exchange indeed," Serena remarked, rather acidly Hawk thought. He glanced down at her enigmatic profile and wondered—not for the first time—what sort of female lay behind the placid exterior Miss Millbanks chose to parade before the world. Was she really as indifferent to the *beau monde* as she professed to be? And what had so set her against marriage? True, she was no beauty, he had to admit, his eyes flicking over her quiet profile, but she possessed a calm and restful presence that Hawk found extraordinarily appealing. She had none of the nervous fluttering of hands and lashes that drove him to distraction in so many young chits on the town every Season. It was as if they believed in perpetual motion as the most effective way of attracting attention to themselves. Whereas Serena—he always thought of her by that soothing name—could sit for lengthy periods in complete silence, making no demands, expecting no adulation, withdrawn yet always composed, complete and self-contained in her own private world.

Hawk envied her this ability to withdraw into an inner space, away from the ugliness of a world which he himself could only escape through drink. He often wondered what kind of peace she found there, evidently so different from the temporary relief he found in his drunken excesses. He shot another quick glance at the girl beside him. Perhaps her private world was not so very different from his after all, he thought, noting the slight droop of those delicate lips, whose texture of warm silk he suddenly recalled in all their sensuous softness against his own. Now if all his memories could be so pleasant, he mused, entranced by the sudden quiver that shook Serena's lower lip. Merely the sight of her made his own ugly memories fade into the background of his mind, he realized with a start. And he was stone sober, too. So unlike that delicious interlude on Lady Berkford's terrace when he had held her, and kissed her, and forgotten everything but the imprint of her body against his, and her lips . . . And all in a drunken haze that defied him to separate reality from illusion. Had the sharp-tongued Miss Millbanks actually felt that good, he wondered, or had it been a figment of his liquor-soaked brain?

Well, he thought cynically, his eyes drawn once again to his passenger's full lips. He was sober now—a rare enough feat for him this late in the morning. And there was only one way to find out if Serena was the sensuous witch he had imagined, or the managing virago who had called him disgusting to his face. He would have to kiss her again. Now. While he was still sober. He grinned down at her in anticipation.

Abruptly, he found himself gazing into a pair of violet eyes, wide with alarm, and felt a small hand grasping his arm.

"My lord!" Serena cried out, shaking him out of his pleasant fantasy. "Watch what you are about, sir. You will have us both in the ditch."

Shocked by the urgency in her voice, Hawk glanced at his team and saw that they were bearing down—with no evidence of slackening their headlong pace—on a rickety gig full of squealing children, driven by an old groom who evidently hadn't the sense to pull aside to allow the approaching curricle to pass.

Averting disaster by a hairsbreadth, Hawk guided his team into a rutted farm road, where he pulled them to a standstill. He turned to look down at Miss Millbanks, whose extraordinary violet eyes now held a gleam of indignation. Sensing that he was in for another tongue-lashing—well deserved this time—Hawk slipped off his driving glove, and when Serena's lips parted to speak, he placed a finger firmly across them.

"Before you inform me that I am a clumsy oaf, my sweet, allow me to apologize for giving you such a scare. It was unforgiveable of me. I am not usually so distracted."

"You were wool-gathering on the King's highway?" she demanded in appalled tones, brushing his hand aside. "Like some mere whipster fresh down from Oxford? You might have killed us both."

Her obvious distress made Hawk incautious. Without thinking, he laid a hand on her muff and smiled down at her. "Actually, I was thinking of you, Miss Virago," he said softly, watching her eyes change color as the implications of his words sank in.

"You are off the mark if you think to turn me up sweet with Spanish coin," she warned him, her voice unsteady.

"More specifically, I was thinking of this," he whispered gruffly, cupping her chin in his hand and brushing her lips with his. Her mouth parted in surprise, and the temptation was too much for Hawk to bear. With a muffled groan, he put his free arm about her and pulled her close, his mouth savoring the warmth of her. Warm silk. He had not dreamed it after all, he thought irrationally before losing himself in the pliant softness of the embrace. Her apparent compliance incited him to probe the sweetness of her mouth with his tongue, but this invasion caused her to stiffen, and Hawk reluctantly raised his head.

Apart from that sudden stiffness, Serena rested passively against his chest, and as Hawk gazed intently into her eyes, he thought he detected a flicker of apprehension before she dropped her lashes. Long, silky lashes, Hawk thought idly, unwilling to break the precious moment of peace and well-being this woman had given him. Why hadn't he noticed them before? What else had he failed to notice about this strange creature who had challenged him as no other woman ever had? Serena often made him feel like a naughty schoolboy with her sharp tongue; she had told him to his face what a rotten excuse for a man he was; she had refused to toady to his rank and fortune, or to throw out lures and flirt with him as every other woman he knew did automatically. And when provoked, she had landed him a facer to put him in his place. The memory of that encounter still made him chuckle. Was she contemplating another such punishment? he wondered, searching her pale face for signs of incipient violence.

Hawk relaxed his grip on her shoulders. "Please do not hit me, my sweet," he murmured, mock remorse in his voice. "As you see, my nose is already mashed."

She looked up at him then, reluctant amusement in her eyes. "It was my understanding that you only forced yourself upon defenseless females when foxed, sirrah," she said accusingly. "I wonder if Lady Lexington was aware that she entrusted me to the company of a depraved rogue who thinks nothing of embracing females in broad daylight on the King's highway."

Hawk withdrew his arm from around her and grinned. "Please accept my humble apologies, Serena," he said penitently. "And you are right; I do not make a practice of abusing young ladies when I am sober." His gaze drifted to her lips again, which immediately thinned in disapproval. He felt a definite urge to repeat this particular abuse on this particular young lady, but her voice cut sharply across these pleasant thoughts.

"I suggest that you steer your mind away from such reprehensible pursuits and apply yourself to getting us out of this muddy lane," Serena said acidly. "We have already attracted too much undesirable attention from the locals."

It was then that Hawk noticed that they were indeed being subjected to the amused scrutiny of several pairs of curious eyes belonging to a group of small children hanging over the dry wall on one side of the narrow lane. He winked broadly in their direction, causing a gale of nervous laughter among the rag-tag urchins, as he carefully turned his horses back the way they had come.

The rest of the journey was accomplished without mishap, but upon entering Mount Street from Berkeley Square shortly before noon, Hawk's attention was caught by the bustle of activity occurring outside Lady Thornton's residence.

"Whatever can have happened?" Serena murmured anxiously as Hawk drew up his curricle behind a cumbersome, old-fashioned coach standing before the front door. "That is my aunt's traveling carriage. But we had not planned to return home before the end of next week."

It was obvious to the duke that the vehicle was being readied for an imminent journey, for there were various trunks, valises, and sundry other pieces of luggage already strapped to the roof. As they mounted the shallow steps, the front door was thrown open and a harried looking Simmons ushered out two footmen struggling with yet another trunk.

"What is going on, Simmons?" Miss Millbanks demanded, following the butler back into the front hall, where a confusion of bandboxes, valises, and heaps of traveling rugs were strewn about. Before the butler could reply, an agitated voice floated down to them from the first landing.

"Oh, Serena, my love!" Lady Thornton cried out in a voice fraught with hysteria as she tottered down the stairs. "How relieved I am that you have returned. The most terrible thing . . ." She suddenly caught sight of the duke, and even her obvious distress did not prevent her from executing a wobbly curtsy. "Oh, Your Grace," she babbled nervously. "Such an honor to welcome you to this poor house again. I trust you found Lady Lexington in spirits? Simmons," she added, turning distractedly to gaze about the wreckage in the hall. "Simmons? Oh, there you are. Have some refreshments sent up to the Yellow Saloon for His Grace—"

"I assure you that is not necessary, Lady Thornton," Hawk hastened to interject. He had no desire to add to the burdens already inflicted on the aggrieved-looking butler, but he had every intention of finding out what had upset Serena's aunt. "I merely wished to deliver Miss Millbanks safely to you, ma'am, and to convey Lady Lexington's most sincere appreciation of your kindness in allowing your niece to visit Sutton House."

Lady Thornton was momentarily diverted. "So very gracious of her ladyship to invite Serena, Your Grace," she simpered, casting her eyes upward in mock ecstasy. "Simmons," she exclaimed suddenly, as the butler came down the stairs carrying a lady's fur cloak and muff, "is Miss Melissa returned yet? Send her to me at once, if you please. She will not wish to miss the pleasure of renewing her acquaintance with His Grace."

"But what is happening here, Aunt?" Serena interrupted, gesturing at the cluttered hall. "Surely you do not intend to set out for Yorkshire so soon? I understood you to say you wished to attend Lady Berkford's—"

"Oh, my dear child!" Lady Thornton exclaimed, apparently recalling her niece's presence. "Such terrible news, my love. Such terrible, terrible news. I do not quite know how to tell you." As if to emphasize the impossibility of this task, Lady Thornton abruptly dissolved into tears and threw herself into her astonished niece's arms.

For a brief moment, Hawk met Serena's alarmed gaze over Lady Thornton's heaving shoulders and read in it a silent plea for help.

"Come, Lady Thornton," he said bracingly, stepping forward to take the weeping woman by the elbow. "Let me assist you into the library." Without waiting for a reply, Hawkhurst steered Lady Thornton down the hall and installed her gently in a yellow brocade settee before a fire which had been allowed to burn itself out.

"There," he said, as soon as the door was closed behind them. "Tell us what has happened to distress you so."

Lady Thornton pulled a damp kerchief from her pocket and dabbed delicately at her eyes. "I am completely overset, Your Grace," she murmured. "Completely overset. I received a disastrous message from Reverend Wells, Serena," she added, glancing nervously up at her niece.

Hawk noted that Miss Millbanks stiffened perceptibly. "And what did the vicar have to say, Aunt?" she asked calmly. "Is anything wrong at Millbanks Hall?"

Lady Thornton immediately burst into fresh tears. Serena sat down beside her and took her aunt's limp hand in hers. "Tell me, Aunt, is it Cecily?"

"Cecily?" her ladyship repeated as though she had never heard of her second niece before. "No, no. Cecily is well, as far as I know."

"What is it, then?" Hawk demanded bluntly, tired of this display of overwrought sensibilities.

"It is your father, Serena. Your poor father." Having said this much, Lady Thornton buried her face in her wet handkerchief and sobbed uncontrollably.

Hawk glanced at Serena and saw that she had gone very pale. "What has happened to Papa?" she whispered through bloodless lips. "Tell me at once, Aunt," she continued, shaking Lady Thornton by the arm.

Hawk strode over to the sideboard and poured a shot of brandy, which he carried back to Serena. "Here, drink this," he said gruffly, holding the glass to her lips. She gulped once and then turned back to her aunt.

"Is that why we are leaving Town?" she demanded. "Papa has been taken ill, is that what it is?"

There was a long pause, punctuated by Lady Thornton's hiccups. Then she raised her tear-stained face resolutely and caught Serena's hands in a desperate grasp.

"No," she muttered incoherently. "Henry is not ill, my dear." She dabbed ineffectually at her red eyes. "He is dead."

CHAPTER NINE

End of Innocence

Serena opened her eyes to find herself reclining on the cracked leather sofa in her aunt's library. She blinked up at the gentleman leaning over her, a glass of brandy in one hand, and assayed a wobbly smile.

"Never say that I swooned like some silly schoolroom chit," she murmured, mortified at the thought of such unprecedented missishness. "I *never* do so, you know."

"I know," Hawkhurst said gently, his frown dissolving into a fleeting smile. "And I swear I shall not tell a soul. Now drink up, lass." He pressed the rim of the glass against her lips. "Your sensibilities sustained a severe shock, I am afraid."

Something in his voice jogged her memory, and Serena struggled unsuccessfully to sit up. "My father? It is true then?" She searched the gray eyes, willing Hawkhurst to deny the appalling news, but his gaze did not waver, and after a moment Serena sagged against the leather bolster, her eyes fluttering shut. If her dear Papa were really gone, she mused—not wanting to accept it but impelled by the look of pity she had seen in Hawk's eyes—she could not afford to lie about like some spineless creature. There would be scores of tasks to take care of, the most pressing perhaps being her immediate return to Yorkshire.

Her mind balked at the finality of this thought. How pleasant it would be if she were indeed such a pathetic, spineless creature, she mused; one who dissolved into tears at the least sign of adversity. Exactly as her poor Aunt Hester was doing now. How comforting to allow someone else to shoulder all the responsibilities she would soon be saddled with. Someone with broader shoulders than hers, who would stand by her in the trying times ahead and look at her with the gentleness she had seen in Hawkhurst's eyes.

Resolutely, Serena dragged herself back from this maudlin quagmire and opened her eyes. No, she thought; she was not the spineless, clinging sort of female who aroused protective instincts in gentlemen. If truth be told, she would not wish to be one. She would have the greatest difficulty curbing her runaway tongue, for one thing. And Hawkhurst was merely being kind, Serena told herself firmly. By tonight he would probably be thoroughly foxed again and, if rumors were any indication of his debauchery, in the company of some Cyprian with more beauty than morals.

No, Miss Serena Millbanks would have to stand on her own two feet, she thought wryly. She sat up abruptly, her equanimity restored.

"I must see to the rest of the packing," she said prosaically, glancing at Lady Thornton, who still sniveled disconsolately into her damp handkerchief. "You have been most kind, sir," she murmured as Hawkhurst assisted her to her feet and stood, one hand on her elbow, much too close for comfort.

"The deuce take it, Serena," he said with a wry grin, "you will not fob me off with that farradiddle, let me tell you. Besides, everything has been taken care of, so sit down and drink this like a good girl."

"I do not need strong spirits to sustain me, sir," Serena replied sternly. Or a gentleman either, she added silently, although the warm pressure of his hand felt oddly comforting. "And you know very little about traveling with females if you imagine that anything can be accomplished without considerable planning."

"Well, you are right on that head," he admitted, "but do not tease yourself over it, my dear. Steele knows all about such things, and he is taking care of everything."

Serena stared at him in amazement. "You confuse me, sir. I know of no Steele, and he certainly does not have my permission to—"

"John is my secretary," the duke interrupted smoothly. "An excellent fellow. You may trust him to make all the arrangements."

"I do not need anyone to make my arrangements for me," Serena protested hotly. She had the distinct impression that if she did not assert herself immediately, this overbearing man would order her life to suit himself.

Hawkhurst greeted this remark with a derisive laugh. "I suppose you intended to set forth in that old tub of a coach standing at the front door?" he said sarcastically. "And arrive in Yorkshire about four days hence?" When Serena could find no argument to deny this accurate assessment of her intentions, the duke continued in a gentler tone. "You will travel in my chaise, my dear. It will get you home in two days at most. Steele will arrange all the details, and I shall accompany you."

Serena gaped at him. This was beyond anything she had ever experienced. She knew that men of wealth and rank often rode roughshod over the wishes of others, but the impertinence of Hawkhurst's assumption that she would meekly bow to his commands set her back up.

"Most obliging of you, I am sure," she said icily, "but I prefer to make my own arrangements." She glanced pointedly at the clock on the mantel, but the odious man did not take the hint that he had outstayed his welcome.

"Lady Thornton has already accepted my assistance, love," he said mildly. "She seemed to be quite overwhelmed by my generosity and thoughtfulness."

Serena could quite see why. The temptation to leave everything in his capable hands was so strong that she actually contemplated giving in to it. But only for a moment.

"Lady Thornton is in no condition to make such a decision," she said firmly, removing her elbow from his grasp. "Furthermore, there is absolutely no need for you to inconvenience yourself in this matter, sir. I am sure you have a dozen engagements that require your presence, so I will not keep you any longer."

She turned away dismissively, but the sound of his chuckle told her more plainly than words that he was not to be dissuaded so easily.

"If it is a test of wills you are looking for, my dear," he drawled in an amused voice, "you have picked the wrong man. So do not pull caps with me. It is all settled."

Serena whirled to face him, her temper simmering, but her response to this piece of high-handedness was cut short by a flurry of pink that hurtled into the room.

"Mama!" the new arrival shrieked hysterically. "What is this that Simmons tells me? Surely you cannot mean to leave London *now*? Just when I am beginning to *take*? How can you be so *cruel*?" Her voice rose querulously at the end of each question.

There was a moment of horrified silence, during which even Lady Thornton forgot her tears. Then Melissa became aware that her mother was not alone, and she blushed charmingly.

"Oh, dear!" she exclaimed in agitated tones. "I do beg your

pardon, Your Grace." She sketched a shy curtsy. "I had no idea—"

"It is your cousin's pardon you should be seeking, Miss Thornton," Hawkhurst said curtly. Serena felt his hand on her elbow again and heard him mutter an unflattering remark about unmannerly chits under his breath.

"Melissa!" Lady Thornton exclaimed in a distraught voice. "Did Simmons not inform you that your Uncle Henry—"

"Of course, he did, Mama," Melissa interrupted quickly, her lovely mouth drooping into an appropriate expression of sorrow. "And I am quite devastated, of course. I was rather fond of Uncle Henry, you know. But it was too bad of him to choose the middle of my first Season to . . . t-to . . ." She paused, suddenly becoming aware of the presence of her thoughtless uncle's grieving daughter, Serena reflected uncharitably.

There was another uncomfortable pause, while Miss Thornton appeared to be assessing her next move. Serena could almost hear her cousin's mind weighing the possibilities, and was not the least surprised when Melissa suddenly burst into tears and threw herself into Serena's arms.

Serena met Hawkhurst's eyes over her cousin's fair curls and was oddly comforted by the exasperation she saw there.

It was well past two o'clock by the time the Duke of Wolverton's well-sprung traveling chaise pulled away from Number Seven Mount Street.

The timely appearance of his secretary and battle-scarred batman with a hastily packed portmanteau had diverted Hawkhurst from his sudden impulse to throttle the spoiled chit, whose outburst of tears had not fooled him for a moment. Nor did it escape his notice that Miss Thornton's selfish remarks had caused her cousin more pain than Serena had acknowledged. Hawk had seen the shock in her expressive violet eyes, and the unfamiliar urge to protect her that welled up in him had taken him by surprise.

This odd reaction also caused him to reassess his initial impulse to accompany Lady Thornton's party up to Yorkshire. Hawk knew himself to be reckless, accustomed to indulge even the most outrageous of his inclinations at a moment's notice, with nary a thought for the consequences. How else could he go on living at all after he had lost Derek? Insensibility had seemed the logical answer at the time. So he had sought it in the mindless pursuits of his class, losing himself in French brandy, wild and reckless wagers, and in the arms of a string of willing females whose faces blurred together in his mind before fading into oblivion.

And now he was off to Yorkshire with Miss Serena Mill-banks.

On the surface this appeared to be yet another of his freak-ish starts, undertaken without a thought for anything but a con-venient escape from the demons that had pursued him since that day in 1813 when Wellington had taken Ciudad Vittoria at the cost of his brother's life. But Hawk could not deceive him-self. There was something else involved here. Call it pity, compassion, even a sense of gratitude for the brief respite from those demons that Serena had brought into his feverish exis-tence with her honesty and lack of guile. Hawk could not say for certain. All he knew was that—contrary to her heated protestations—the self-sufficient Miss Millbanks needed his assistance.

He could barely recall the last time he had felt a sense of purpose in his life. The war on the Continent had given him that feeling, but Derek's death had deprived him of that, too. As sole survivor of a long line of Hawkhursts, he had been barred from the battlefields. Nobody—least of all his family—seemed to understand that he needed to expiate his guilt in the only way a soldier knew, by fighting. Debauchery was a poor substitute, but he had thrown himself into it with a vengeance.

Until Miss Millbanks had come along and landed him a facer. Hawk grinned to himself at the recollection. How could he leave such a female in the lurch? he wondered.

From a disjointed account extracted from Lady Thornton after Serena had gone upstairs with the tearful Miss Thorn-ton—who had attempted several times unsuccessfully to claim his attention—Hawk had learned that the intrepid Serena faced anything but a blissful future in Yorkshire. Sir Henry's heir was—if her aunt could be believed—a thoroughly nasty piece of work, but his mother, the widow of Sir Henry's younger brother, was a great deal worse.

"Never did take to Serena, Your Grace," Lady Thornton ex-plained with unusual frankness. "Too hoydenish by half, Gladys always called her. Lacking in all those ladylike airs and graces she sets such store by. And much as I love my niece, I cannot say Serena is your usual mild-mannered, obedi-ent young lady." The lady shook her head dolefully, whether at her niece's lack of social graces or her uncertain future at Millbanks Hall, Hawk could not decide, although he certainly agreed with the former.

"Not that Gladys Millbanks is what you might call a lady herself, Your Grace," Lady Thornton added with a sniff of disapproval. "Married above her station, she did, when she caught Henry's brother George. Never had an ounce of sense, did old George. Always a roving eye, he had, if you will forgive me for saying so, Your Grace, but no discrimination at all," she continued, warming to her subject. "His odious son takes after him, I hear. And when Gladys would not be bought off, George up and married her. Against his brother's advice, I might say." She paused to sigh gustily. "It was a sad day in more ways than one when Henry left his daughters at the mercy of that old harridan."

"But at least your nieces will have a home, will they not?" Hawk demanded, unwilling to think beyond that elementary point.

"Oh, that is true enough," Lady Thornton agreed. "Poor things," she added with another sigh. "Gladys will doubtless enjoy having two unpaid servants about the house."

"Could you not offer them a home with you, my lady?" the duke suggested gently.

Lady Thornton blew her nose noisily. "Oh, indeed, I intend to, Your Grace, but Serena will not agree to it, you may be sure. She is all too conscious of how pinched my purse is. And after all," she added, casting a calculating glance at the duke, "it is not as though she will have to support herself at some genteel occupation, which no Millbanks has ever had to do, I can assure you, Your Grace."

Hawk rather thought that Miss Millbanks would be doing precisely that as her aunt's unpaid servant, but he said nothing. The notion of Serena's being reduced to supporting herself at all did not sit well with him, and Hawk vowed that he would do something—what that might be he did not at the moment perceive—to prevent that fate from overtaking the only female in England who had made his nose bleed.

He would give his undivided attention to the matter, Hawk thought as he climbed into his saddle a scant two hours later. Between London and Yorkshire he would have more than enough time to find a suitable solution to a rather prickly situation.

*   *   *

Serena remembered little of the journey except her aunt's sly hints—repeated with annoying regularity as the duke's luxurious traveling chaise bore them swiftly northward—that if she played her cards right, she might well find herself settled for life, and very comfortably indeed. After the third such remark, delivered in a complaisant tone, the gist of her aunt's meaning dawned upon her, and Serena cast a curious glance at the tall figure riding beside the carriage. Aunt Hester was off the mark, of course, she thought wryly. Of all the possible reasons for Hawkhurst's perverse insistence upon accompanying them, any interest in either Melissa—who was still sulking at the abrupt interruption of her London Season—or herself was too ridiculous to be considered. Regretfully, Serena dismissed it from her mind.

True to his word, Hawkhurst had indeed taken care of all the tedious details entailed in traveling on the King's highways. As a result, Serena had far too much idle time to dwell on the future. The picture was anything but bright. She was too realistic to imagine that her Aunt Gladys would welcome her with open arms. Ever conscious of her lack of breeding, Mrs. Millbanks had made up for it by aggressively aping the manners and foibles of the world to which her marriage had given her entrée. Serena shuddered at the thought of how impossible her aunt would be now that she was mistress of Millbanks Hall.

Serena soon discovered that her worst fears came nowhere near the state of affairs she encountered when the fashionable chaise drew up before the doors of her old home—as she had begun to think of Millbanks Hall—on the evening of the second day. Much to the consternation of Lady Thornton—who had relished the prospect of flaunting her connection with a real live duke of the realm in Gladys Millbanks's face—Hawkhurst had insisted upon eschewing the use of his title, and it was as plain Major Hawkhurst that Serena presented him to her sister, who was the first to greet them.

"Oh, Serena," Cecily wailed, throwing her arms around her sister's neck and bursting into tears. "I am so glad you have come. That dragon is too horrible to bear. She has moved into Mama's room and rearranged all the furniture and ordered Mrs. Porter to cook the most ghastly food imaginable and . . . oh, Serena, she has dismissed Higgy without a reference. Please tell her she cannot do so—"

"Hush, darling," Serena murmured, interrupting the tearful

rush of words. "Aunt Gladys is mistress here now, Cecily, and there is nothing I can do to stop her making all the changes she wishes." She stroked her sister's soft rumpled curls gently, her own eyes misting over in spite of her brave words. "We must learn to accept it, dear." Her gaze encountered Hawk's over her sister's bowed head, and she drew strength from the steady gray stare.

"Come, Cecy," she continued, brushing a wayward strand of pale flaxen hair from her sister's cheek, "where are your manners, dear? Here is Aunt Hester come all the way from London to sustain us in this sad time. And Cousin Melissa. And this is Major Hawkhurst, whose kindness has been beyond anything wonderful."

She threw a grateful look at the major and was surprised at the odd expression that greeted this remark. However, she had little time to ponder the matter, for at that moment Aunt Gladys's falsetto took over, banishing all else from Serena's mind.

The sight of her Aunt Gladys standing in the open doorway of Millbanks Hall brought home to Serena as nothing else had the realization that her life could never be the same again. As she listened to Mrs. Millbanks greeting Lady Thornton and Melissa with that false civility tinged—as it always was with Aunt Gladys—with a hint of condescension that grated on Serena's nerves, she found herself wondering how she would endure her aunt's petty, overbearing, bullying ways for the rest of her life. It would not be easy, she thought, and far from pleasant, but for Cecily's sake she must learn to be submissive, docile, and impervious to the open attacks on her pride that were sure to come.

Serena gritted her teeth, fixed a vacuous smile on her face, and turned to introduce her aunt to Hawkhurst. She winced at Mrs. Millbanks's covetous glances at the major's glossy equipage, at his horse, at the neat uniforms of the two grooms and driver, and finally at the gentleman himself. Hawkhurst was dressed in a sober brown coat and buff breeches, but the gloss on his tall black boots and his curly-brimmed beaver labeled him a gentleman of means. This fact was not lost upon Aunt Gladys, whose voice became a shade more fawning as she welcomed the stranger to her modest home.

"My dear Hester," she cooed, offering a roughed cheek to Lady Thornton, "surely this is not your carriage, my dear. I seem to recall a rather ancient landau—"

"The chaise belongs to the . . . t-to Major Hawkhurst," Lady Thornton replied, stumbling slightly over the name, "who was kind enough to offer his escort when he heard of our sad loss."

"Indeed," Aunt Gladys murmured, and Serena could almost hear the wheels of her aunt's avaricious mind churning furiously. "In that case, I must insist that you rack up with us, my dear sir." Her gimlet gaze skipped from Hawkhurst to Lady Thornton, resting briefly on Serena before pausing on the enchanting face of her niece Melissa. She smiled, and Serena guessed her aunt had drawn the wrong conclusions regarding Hawk's presence in Yorkshire.

The notion was oddly disconcerting, for Serena herself was not at all sure of the major's motives. She suspected he had acted on the spur of the moment, perhaps out of boredom, and was even now regretting this ill-advised entanglement with the family of an obscure baronet in rural Yorkshire. Well, she thought wryly, it served him right for disregarding her wishes. Had she not told him unequivocally that she preferred to manage on her own? Did it really matter that, in this case, she had told a small fib?

As she followed the party into the house, Serena heard Aunt Gladys quizzing Hawkhurst about his connection with the Millbankses. She listened with a slight smile as the major confessed to a long-standing acquaintance with her father. His entanglement with her had led him into a masquerade that was getting more complicated by the minute, she thought, knowing that Aunt Gladys would not rest until she had extracted the last, most insignificant detail from the hapless Hawk. Serena doubted that the major would have the patience required to maintain such a deception for any length of time. Particularly if he got himself foxed after dinner. She must convince him that his presence was no longer required at Millbanks Hall, and that the sooner he shook the dust of Yorkshire from his expensive boots the better it would be for him.

If not for her, she added with crushing honesty.

This resolution was more difficult to carry out than Serena had supposed. Having established in her own mind that Major Hawkhurst belonged to the cream of the *ton,* Mrs. Millbanks stuck to him like a leach. And when his mother was distracted from her quarry for even a moment, Serena's cousin, the newly elevated Sir William, made it his business to monopolize Hawkhurst's attention. He mortified her with his impertinent questions on the cost and quality of the major's clothes, the precise manner in which he tied his cravat, and the name of the polish his valet used to bring his Hessians to their high gloss. It amused Serena to note that Hawk answered none of these questions, choosing instead, in a drawling, supercilious tone that Sir William attempted unsuccessfully to imitate, to deride country life and extol the various pleasures offered by the Metropolis.

It was not until early the following morning, when Serena had escaped from the house with an ecstatic Jollyboy frisking at her heels, and walked briskly across the small park and up the hill to her favorite spot beneath the old oak tree, that she had a chance to be private with him. She had not planned it that way, but she had not been there more than ten minutes before she heard footsteps in the grass behind her. Fearing it was her Cousin William, she jumped to her feet and prepared to return to the house.

"Oh, it is you," she said when she saw the major, and smiled fleetingly. "I thought it was William."

"Has that bandy-legged jackstraw been bothering you?" Hawkhurst demanded, taking one of her gloved hands in both of his. "Would you like me to cut him into small pieces and feed him to the dogs?" he added, his eyes searching her face keenly.

"Oh, no, at least not enough to signify," she responded briefly. "William has always fancied himself a lady's man, although no female I know of would be taken in by his odious starts. And as for your kind offer, sir, I rather imagine no self-respecting dog would touch him."

Her smile deepened as she withdrew her hand and adjusted the old bonnet she had thrown on haphazardly when she left the house. "I am glad you are up early," she said quietly. "I needed to talk to you last night, but my aunt seemed to be deliberately keeping you to herself."

"That was none of my doing, let me assure you—"

"Oh, I know that," Serena interrupted quickly. "You should have seen the expression on your face." Quite unexpectedly she giggled, and just as quickly caught her breath on a sob.

Immediately his arms came around her, and Serena felt herself crushed against Hawk's chest. Without conscious thought, she snuggled her face into his coat, careless of her bonnet that fell off into the grass, and closed her eyes. How could she bear to send him away when she needed him so much? she won-

dered. The urge to cry rose up in her so strongly that Serena
had to swallow several times before she overcame it.

"I did not mean to be such a silly goose," she whispered in a
choked voice, "but I have had no time to cry for my father."

His arms tightened around her and she felt his lips on her
hair. "Why not cry now, love?" he said softly. "Believe me,
you will feel better if you do. The hurt will always be there; it
always is when you lose someone you love, Serena. But crying
will ease your heart."

Hawk spoke with such unfamiliar emotion that Serena
raised her face and gazed up at him. His expression was
painful to watch, and his eyes stared blindly as though he saw
a ghost out there on the desolate moors that stretched away behind them to the skyline.

Serena's heart went out to him. She knew instinctively that
Hawk had lost someone very dear to him, and that he had spoken to her from his own experience.

Finally he seemed to pull himself together and looked down
at her. The gray eyes were clouded and his mouth twisted into
a parody of a smile. Serena dropped her gaze and stepped
away from the comfort of his arms.

Hawkhurst picked up her bonnet and held it out to her, a
quizzical expression on his face. "What did you wish to say to
me, my dear?"

"You may well stare, sir," she said, taking the bonnet and
brushing off a piece of grass. "I image you rarely see bonnets
this old and ugly. But it brings back good memories, so it is
dear to me."

"And you wished to talk to me about your old bonnets, is
that it?" His smile became less strained as he talked, and Serena was able to relax.

"No, of course not," she chided. "What an absurd notion. I
merely wished to thank you before you leave Yorkshire for
your assistance. I shall never forget your kindness, sir. It
means everything to me."

"You are giving me my congé, I take it?"

Her eyes flew open in surprise. "Of course not. But you cannot wish to stay long after the funeral this morning. As a long-
standing acquaintance of my father's," she said with a touch of
irony, "you will wish to attend that, of course. But I cannot expect you to tolerate another day of my aunt's pretentious prattle."

He gazed at her for a long moment, and Serena hoped he

would not pretend a concern for her welfare he could not possibly feel.

"You wish me to leave?"

"You have done far too much for us already, sir," she responded, avoiding the question. "I can never repay you."

"As far as I recall, I did not ask to be repaid, Serena," he murmured. "And I am not yet convinced that you and your sister should remain here with that abominable female. I know she is your aunt, Serena, but a worse termagant I have yet to see. What kind of a life will you have here? Can you honestly say you will be happy?"

What did happiness have to do with anything? Serena asked herself cynically. At least she and Cecily would have a roof over their heads, and with a little patience and restraint she might even learn to deal peaceably with Aunt Gladys. What more could two destitute females of good birth and no fortune hope for? But she could not say so to this man who had never lacked for anything in his life, she thought.

"We shall manage very well," she said briskly, surprised that she could still muster a smile.

Hawkhurst stared at her skeptically, and Serena knew he would not be fobbed off so easily.

"I would prefer to see you in Norfolk with Lady Thornton. She is of the same mind, I take it."

"My Aunt Hester has indeed offered us a home with her, but that is impossible. My uncle left her in straightened circumstances, and I will not add such a burden to her meager resources."

"You choose to stay here as an unpaid servant?" he asked with such bluntness that Serena flinched. "Until your father's debts are paid off, there will be little enough for you here."

"I would be in much the same position in Norfolk, sir," she retorted crossly. "Aunt Hester is a tyrant in her own way, you see. And I must consider Cecily's future. In two more years she will be seventeen and with her looks is sure to find a suitable husband."

"If your precious cousin does not get her first," Hawkhurst said with brutal frankness.

Serena felt the blood recede from her cheeks as the significance of the duke's warning sank in. She had not considered, fool that she was, that Cecily's pale beauty would attract the unsavory attentions of their cousin. But only last night she had caught William in the upstairs hall with his arm around a frightened maid. What was to stop him from extending his lecherous marauding to her innocent sister?

"You cannot really believe that William would . . ." She hesitated, unwilling to put the horrible thought into words.

Hawkhurst's grin was savage. "You are such an innocent, my dear Serena. Have you not yet learned that there is no limit to the depravity of men?"

CHAPTER TEN

Clifftop Manor

By ten o'clock, a cold drizzle began to fall, and as the funeral procession edged its ponderous way through the fresh mud, Hawk cursed himself for refusing Lady Thornton's offer to join her and the three young ladies in his own chaise. He had chosen, against all common sense, to ride Hercules instead, just as he had three years ago at the last funeral he had attended.

Mrs. Millbanks and her son rode behind them in Sir Henry's coach, while the Millbanks staff—such of them as had been given grudging permission to accompany their old master to his grave—brought up the rear in Lady Thornton's ancient landau, graciously offered for the occasion. The entire proceedings were indescribably depressing, Hawk thought, wiping a drop of water off his nose as he stood by the open grave. It reminded him too vividly of that other funeral. His brother Derek's. It had rained then, too, and Hawk still remembered the cold wind that had whipped the vicar's surplice around his thin legs, and the cold water that had dripped down on the coffin containing what remained of his beloved twin.

Yet none of that had come close to the coldness in his heart, he recalled. And to the emptiness that he had carried about with him ever since he had been forced to accept that Derek was gone forever. Hawk could guess at the pain and loneliness Serena must be feeling as she stood beside Lady Thornton, one arm about the sobbing Cecily, and a look of desolation in her violet eyes.

As far as Hawk knew, she had not yet cried for her lost father. From the tense expression on her face, Hawk guessed that Miss Millbanks had been too busy comforting her sister to take a moment for that private grieving. Hawk knew all about grieving. He had cried himself dry over Derek, but none of it had erased that dreadful memory of his twin's body on the battlefield at Vittoria, caught up in the inescapable throes of death. A death that should have been his, he recalled grimly.

With a conscious effort, Hawk jerked his thoughts back to the present. Death had come and gone again, this time leaving two young girls to face an uncertain future alone. He had been ravaged by death himself, and had found a convenient escape in recklessness, but he knew that Serena had no such escape open to her. She needed protection from the world, but did she not deserve better than to spend her days as a drudge in a household that had once been her own?

A novel idea took root and grew in his mind, and by the time the family had returned to Millbanks Hall and partaken of a cold collation in the bleak formal dining room, Hawk had devised an idea which he hastened to lay before Lady Thornton when he caught her alone in a rare private moment that afternoon.

That lady's first reaction was to stare at him as though he had grown two heads.

"Your Grace cannot have considered the possible ramifications of such a scheme," she said with unwonted severity. "And I will countenance nothing that will bring disgrace or even the suggestion of impropriety down on my nieces' heads."

"You are to be commended for your noble sentiments, my lady," Hawk said soothingly. "But surely you agree with me that something must be done to remove Miss Millbanks and her sister from this house. I do not scruple to tell you that Sir William is not to be trusted to behave appropriately."

It appeared that Lady Thornton had harbored similar reservations about the new baronet, but Hawk had to exert his considerable charm to persuade her to fall in with his hastily devised scheme.

"And exactly where in Norfolk is this minor estate of yours, Your Grace?" she demanded cautiously.

"I cannot tell you exactly, my lady, because I have never visited the place. But I believe it is just outside the village of Weybourne. I understand the house stands on the cliffs above Sheringham and has been empty—except for the caretaker and his wife—ever since my Great-Aunt Amelia Hawkhurst died there in 1807." Clifftop Manor was also reputed to be haunted, but Hawk thought better of confiding this piece of local gossip—which he set no store by—to a fainthearted, elderly lady like Serena's Aunt Hester.

When Lady Thornton appeared to hesitate, Hawk threw in his last ace. "Of course, I will personally escort you to Clifftop Manor, my lady, and see you comfortably installed there before returning to London."

"You do not intend to stay there, I take it, Your Grace?" The question surprised him, and Hawk thought he detected a hint of censure in the lady's voice.

"Only until you and the young ladies feel you can dispense with my presence," he answered ambiguously.

"Hmm," the lady demurred, regarding the major with a calculating stare. "I cannot find anything improper in such an arrangement—provided that Serena agrees to it, of course."

Hawk relaxed and gave Lady Thornton one of his rakish smiles. "I depend entirely on your powers of persuasion, my dear lady," he murmured, "to convince Miss Millbanks that you have her best interests at heart."

And with that, the battle should be more than half won, Hawk thought complaisantly, strangely pleased with the success of his benevolent impulse.

"But Rufus is *mine*," Cecily exclaimed loudly as the ladies settled themselves in the drawing room that evening after dinner. "Papa gave him to me for my tenth birthday. What do you *mean*, I cannot take him with me?"

"Do not shout, my dear Cecily," Aunt Gladys said in her sweetly cloying voice that Serena knew to be as false as the smile on her aunt's plump face. "Young ladies should be demure and modest and speak only when spoken to. They do not make demands, child, particularly not in *this* house," she added with unmistakable emphasis.

There was a distinctly hostile pause, during which Serena prayed that her sister would exercise some restraint. The atmosphere at the dinner table had become uncomfortably tense after Lady Thornton had announced her intention of departing the Hall on the following morning, taking her two nieces with her.

"I can see no reason whatsoever for the girls to leave Millbanks Hall," Aunt Gladys had expostulated, the harshness of her voice betraying her annoyance. "This is their home, Hester. You cannot wish to deprive them of their rightful place. In fact, I expressly oppose it."

Rightful place, indeed, Serena thought cynically. In the short space of time she had been back, her aunt had made no bones about establishing the places she and Cecy might expect to occupy at Millbanks Hall. Serena had been told that, since she had done so for years anyway, she might oversee the running of the house, subject naturally to her aunt's instructions. Poor Cecy was to become, in everything but name, their aunt's personal slave, destined to be at her beck and call for any task that the mistress of the house considered beneath her. Serena could well understand her avaricious aunt's reluctance to lose them.

Lady Thornton was not to be deterred by her sister-in-law's rudeness, however. "We shall try it for a few months, Gladys," she replied calmly. "If the girls become homesick, I shall of course send them back to you."

"I do not like it above half," Aunt Gladys snapped back, her veneer of civility slipping noticeably. "And if you think you can take either Rufus or that chestnut gelding with you, Serena, you are sadly mistaken, my girl. All livestock is considered part of the estate and the horses are mine, although that little roan is too small to be of much good to anyone. I shall probably have to sell him off," she added waspishly.

Listening to this spiteful remark caused Serena's temper to rise. Before considering the consequences, she turned to her aunt. "If you plan to sell Rufus, Aunt," she said, attempting to keep her voice pleasant, "what price would you take for him? Perhaps I can see my way to purchasing him."

"Oh, Serena!" Cecily gasped, clapping her hands to her cheeks. "Would you do so? How splendid of you."

Mrs. Millbanks stared intently at her eldest niece. "How did you come by that much money, miss?" she demanded sharply. "I assume your father gave it to you as pin money. As such it belongs to the estate, of course, and since you will no longer be needing it, I insist that you return it immediately."

Serena flinched at the pure venom of her aunt's tone, and shook her head. "What little Papa gave me is long spent, Aunt," she lied. "I had hoped to borrow enough from Aunt Hester to purchase Rufus." She knew better than to confess that she had wagered and won over a thousand pounds from one of London's most notorious rakes.

"Borrow from Hester?" Mrs. Millbanks repeated scornfully. "You are being absurd, Serena. Your aunt lives in genteel poverty as it is, and how she intends to fit the four of you in that poky little house of hers in Attleborough is beyond me." She paused and her face took on a crafty expression. "Now if you decide to make your home here with us, my dear," she said, her voice softening considerably, "I am sure that my dear William will not object to Cecily's riding Rufus occasionally. If she is a good girl, naturally. As for the gelding, I suppose that could be arranged, although William has taken rather a fancy to the horse himself."

The thought of her cow-handed cousin riding her beloved Jason made Serena shudder, but before she could utter the unwise response that trembled on her lips, the drawing room door opened and her cousin entered, accompanied by Hawkhurst and the Reverend John Wells, who had been invited to dinner.

Sir William came in rubbing his long, bony hands together, evidently much pleased with himself. "Talking about me again, are you, Mama?" he smirked. "And which horse have I taken such a fancy to?"

"I was just telling your cousins that Rufus and that bay gelding you like so much belong to us now, dear. Poor Cecily was under the impression that she could take Rufus with her. Can you imagine such innocence? And as for the gelding—"

"Belong to *me,* I imagine you meant to say, Mama dear," Sir William corrected her rather pointedly. "And as for that gelding, I have just sold him to Major Hawkhurst here. Took quite a fancy to him when we were down in the stables this afternoon. Paid every penny I asked, too," he added, patting his coat pocket significantly. "Perhaps I should have asked more." He winked broadly at Hawkhurst and accompanied his witticism with a raucous laugh.

Serena hardly heard it; she was staring at Hawkhurst, whose gray eyes were fixed on her enigmatically. As she watched, the major raised one eyebrow and smiled his lazy smile. Serena's heart did an odd flip in her breast and she lowered her gaze, wondering if Hawkhurst might not be foxed again. Disguised or not, she thought irrelevantly, the rogue had a devastating smile, one that she suspected had beguiled more than his fair share of female hearts. An exclamation from her sister brought her back from this dangerous line of thought.

"Oh, Major Hawkhurst!" Cecily cried with what Aunt Gladys would undoubtedly have called unladylike exuberance. "How perfectly splendid of you to purchase Jason." She threw a saucy glance at Serena, who had little warning of what was to come. "Now if only you could see your way to purchasing Rufus as well," Cecily added, dancing across the room to lay her hand coaxingly on the major's sleeve. "Oh, do say you will, sir."

Serena struggled to find her voice. She could well imagine the melting look her shameless sister was at this very instant directing at the bemused gentleman.

"Cecily!" she exclaimed sharply. "What an outrageous thing to say. I tremble to think what Mama would say if she were here to listen to you. I insist that you apologize to Major Hawkhurst this instant."

Hawk raised his eyes from her sister's face and gazed at her with evident amusement. "I imagine I would cut a very odd figure indeed riding about the countryside on Rufus, my dear. My feet would undoubtedly drag on the ground and ruin my boots in no time at all." He grinned down at Cecily, who still clung to his arm. "Besides," Hawkhurst added, "I suspect Sir William would not part with that pony at any price."

"No, he would certainly not," Mrs. Millbanks cut in sharply. "I have a fancy to keep Rufus for myself."

Sir William gaped at his mother, his slack mouth falling open to reveal two chipped teeth. Serena held her breath. Could there be a rational explanation for the major's odd behavior? she wondered.

"Are you feeling quite the thing, Mama?" the lanky baronet demanded none too politely. "You appear to have taken leave of your senses, Madam. You would look mighty peculiar riding the pony yourself, if I may say so. Unless you wish to make us the laughingstock of the neighborhood," he added with a cynical curl to his lip. "Which I can assure you, I will not tolerate. If Major Hawkhurst wishes to put down his blunt for the brute, let him do so, I say." He turned to his guest with a crafty smile. "The animal is yours for a mere fifty pounds, sir."

"F-fifty pounds?" Serena gasped. "Rufus is not worth half that price, William. Do you wish Major Hawkhurst to think you are trying to gull him?"

Sir William looked disconcerted at Serena's blunt accusation. "I will take forty, then," he blustered. "But only as a favor to you, sir. The horse is sound enough, I can guarantee it."

Serena rose to her feet and moved to stand beside her sister. "There is absolutely no need for you to do this, sir," she said repressively. "And please forgive my sister's lack of manners. She does know better, I assure you."

Hawkhurst grinned down at her, a circumstance Serena did her best to ignore. "I have always wanted to have a pony of my very own," he remarked in a perfectly serious voice. "I never did as a child, you know. Forty it is, Millbanks, if you throw in Jollyboy," he added, addressing the baronet, although his gray eyes had a definitely teasing gleam in them, Serena noted.

"You will not get away with this, you know," she muttered under her breath, while Cecily gave a shriek of delight and thanked the major very prettily.

She would repay every penny, Serena told herself silently as she turned away to help her aunt with the tea-tray.

"I warned you when we set out from London that traveling with a bevy of females and a retinue of servants was no easy undertaking, Major," Miss Millbanks reminded him as they rode down the drive of Millbanks Hall together the following morning.

Hawkhurst glanced at his companion and grinned. Serena was still pale, he noted, and her dark riding habit and black beaver made her appear remote and unapproachable. He envied her the calm detachment she had displayed at leaving behind not only her home, but everything else that had defined her small world and given her stability and happiness. Hawk had seen her going from room to room—when she imagined no one was looking—running her fingers over the old furniture, gently tracing the shape of a figurine or vase, touching the keys of her mother's pianoforte, plumping a cushion here, twitching a curtain there. All with a loving tenderness that had touched a chord within him he had thought stilled forever.

She had been happy growing up here, Hawk realized, and leaving it, perhaps forever, must be a wrenching experience. But Miss Millbanks had uttered not a single word of complaint. Unlike her younger sister, who had cried copiously as their trunks were loaded onto the chaise, and her cousin, who had never ceased lamenting her lost London Season, Serena had busied herself with directing the operation with a military precision that rivaled the stalwart Sergeant Slowe's. Hawk's admiration for her had tripled.

"You were a tower of strength in my hour of need, Miss Millbanks," he remarked lightly. "As I remember quite distinctly you have been on several other occasions." He was gratified to see the faint blush rise to her cheeks and knew she was thinking of the interlude they had shared on Lady Berkford's terrace. As he was himself, Hawk thought wryly, remembering the silken feel of her lips under his.

"You exaggerate, sir," she murmured. She leaned forward to pat the gelding's sleek neck with her gloved hand. "And your gratitude should go to Sergeant Slowe, not to me. I do not consider the small service I was able to extend to you while you were . . ." She hesitated, and glanced at him, her violet eyes glinting with amusement.

"While I was disgustingly disguised?" he suggested, inexplicably warmed by her ability to laugh at him.

"Yes," she agreed at once. "Odiously foxed. I do not consider such service of any significance. Anyone might have done the same."

He grinned at her until she blushed and turned away. "I fear I must disagree with you, my dear. I seem to recall an exceedingly painful attack on my nose, which no other female I know would have dared to deliver."

"You deserved it, sir," she retorted spiritedly, her color still high. "And I do not wish to be reminded of it, if you please. More to the point," she continued, abruptly changing the subject, "I must insist that you allow me to repay the price you paid for Jason and Rufus. Unless, of course," and here the irrepressible laughter twinkled in her eyes again, "you really wish to fulfill that childhood dream of owning a pony of your own."

"Oh, no." He chuckled. "We had innumerable ponies at Wolverton Abbey, Derek and I. I can still remember the time . . ." He stopped abruptly.

Hawk could not remember the last time he had spoken to anyone of his childhood with Derek. Even his mother had learned over the past three years to let those memories lie undisturbed. Only Lady Lexington had the temerity to bring up his brother's name. His great-aunt had loved them both as her own sons, Hawk knew, so he had tolerated the intrusion into his private sorrow. Now here he was confiding his memories to a stranger.

Hawk turned to meet Serena's gaze, ready to cut short any impertinent question she might venture to utter with a sharp set-down. But he could detect no vulgar curiosity in those violet depths, and instinctively he knew that she would ask nothing. He relaxed.

It dawned on him quite abruptly that Miss Serena Millbanks was no longer a stranger to him. In the past few days, he had learned more about this female, he realized with a start, than he knew of his own sisters. Hawk had never really paid much heed to them as a youngster; it had always been himself and Derek. Then they had gone away to school. He and Derek. And then it had been the Army. After their father's death, he recalled, Derek had been caught up in the business of being a duke. Hawk had felt lonely for the first time in his life. Lonely and left out. So he had struck out on his own. Derek had begged him not to, Hawk recalled with a flash of the old bitterness. Fool that he was, he had imagined the title as a wedge driven between them. There had been no wedge, of course, and in trying to make him see this, Derek had joined him in Spain.

And lost his life in the attempt.

"My brother," he heard himself say in a tight voice.

Still she said nothing, merely looking at him with those huge violet eyes he wished he could drown himself in.

"My twin brother. He died at Vittoria."

She did not even mouth the conventional words of sorrow, Hawk noted with a sense of relief. He had had to endure so many meaningless phrases of condolence after he returned from the Peninsula that he had wanted to scream. The pain he had suffered was beyond sorrow, but nobody seemed to understand.

Except perhaps Miss Millbanks, who said nothing at all.

By midafternoon of the second day, Serena caught the first salty tang of the sea. She pulled her heavy cloak closer about her shoulders to keep out the damp breeze that had been blowing inland since they had stopped for refreshments at an ancient inn outside Fakenham.

"You should be riding in the carriage, Serena," the major said, pulling his own horse to a stop and frowning at her. "As your Aunt Gladys would say, it is not seemly for a gently bred female to ride around the countryside in this weather."

"Fiddlesticks!" Serena exclaimed, drawing Jason to a halt and glancing over her shoulder at the cavalcade that trailed half a mile in their wake. She dared not confess that she would much rather be out here riding with him—however chill the wind—than squashed into the comfortable chaise listening to Miss Higgenbotham lecture on the migratory habits of seabirds native to this region of England.

"It was kind of you to allow poor Miss Higgenbotham to accompany us, sir," she said softly, her attention still focused on the two carriages toiling up the incline toward the cliff from which they would catch their first glimpse of the sea. "She is such a dear, although I know you must find her a dreadful bore, always prosing on about the classics and that summer she spent as a girl touring the Greek islands with her father."

When he did not answer, Serena glanced at Hawkhurst and found his gray eyes fixed upon her. She smiled. "Higgy was my governess, too, you know. She taught me to appreciate the classics and gave me a love of all things Greek that I treasure to this day. I had this ridiculous dream when I was sixteen of sailing the Aegean Sea in a ship similar to those that carried the Argonauts all the way to Colchis and back." She omitted adding that the captain of that ship in that long-forgotten dream had been the blond, godlike Brian Westlock.

"I see now how Jason got his name," the major remarked, his eyes laughing at her. "And dreams are rarely ridiculous, my dear. One should pursue them vigorously."

"That is all very well for you to say," Serena retorted, turning Jason's head toward the cliff again. "Gentlemen are allowed to go where they please, but females are expected to stay at home and amuse themselves with dull occupations like embroidery and watercolors." Besides which, she reminded herself without rancor, Brian had had eyes only for the beautiful—and wealthy—Priscilla Winston.

He laughed at that, and Serena rejoiced at the sound. Hawk had been unusually withdrawn since yesterday morning, when he had talked so briefly and painfully of his twin brother. Serena suspected that he had not intended to mention anything so personal, and from his subsequent silence, she sensed that the subject was not one he would broach again.

"You are off the mark, my dear, if you think I can do as I wish," he said after a pause. "I wanted most urgently to join Wellington's army in Brussels when a decisive encounter with Napoleon was inevitable. But my family joined ranks against me, and I was forced to follow the action in the newspapers. A poor substitute for the battlefield, let me tell you."

"From what I know about Waterloo, I wonder that anyone would willingly have been a party to that slaughter. It sounds perilously like a death wish to me, sir."

"It was," Hawkhurst replied shortly. "One that unfortunately was not fulfilled."

Touched by the despair in his voice, Serena turned to observe the duke's grim profile. "I am thankful indeed that it was not, sir," she said with feeling.

"And why is that?" He looked at her directly as he spoke, and Serena shuddered at the emptiness in his eyes.

"I have no wish to think of you as dead, that is why," she responded calmly, wondering what demons this man carried in his heart that compelled him to such somber thoughts.

"And yet quite recently—if I remember rightly—you expressed an unholy desire to dance on my grave, did you not, Serena?"

Her eyes opened wide as she recalled the scene he spoke of, and she blushed. "That was very rude of me," she murmured. "And naturally I did not mean a word of it. I am always tempted to be rude to gentlemen who drink themselves into a stupor, sir."

"Touché, my dear." He smiled then, but Serena thought she had rarely seen a sadder smile on any man. She felt tempted to reach out and touch him, but he urged his big chestnut into a canter as they neared the top of the cliff, and the moment was lost.

The sight of the sea took Serena's breath away.

"I know exactly how you feel," Hawkhurst said after they had sat in silence for an interminable moment. "The sea always makes me feel so small and insignificant. A very sobering thought, actually."

"Salutary, too," Serena could not resist adding. "One's troubles also fade into insignificance. I confess that mine have done so already." She met his gaze and smiled encouragingly. "The sea air does not reduce one's appetite, however, and I for one am quite famished. Where is this house of yours, my lord? I declare it must be nearly teatime."

CHAPTER ELEVEN

The Portrait

Norfolk, Winter–Spring, 1816–1817

The first week at Clifftop Manor was so filled with the impressive task of making the house habitable after what appeared to be years of neglect that Serena hardly noted its passing. Her Aunt Hester had taken one look at the faded carpets, the cobwebs in the corners of the drawing room, and the mildew growing rampant on the damp ceiling of the library and thrown up her hands in despair.

"My dear Serena," she moaned, pulling the Holland covers off an elegant but shabby settee and allowing her considerable bulk to sink into the faded cushions, "the duke must be all about in the head if he expects me to spend a single night in this dreadful place. I wager the beds have not been aired in months, and we shall all catch our death of cold. I shall insist upon putting up at that inn we saw in the village earlier today, although I rather suspect the sheets will be damp there, too."

"Oh, Mama, is that not a spider I see there?" Serena turned from uncovering a beautiful escritoire in the corner to find her fastidious cousin pointing a trembling finger at the ceiling, an expression of pure horror on her pretty face.

Lady Thornton clapped a hand to her mouth to stifle a squeal. "Do not go near the horrid creature, dearest," she warned in a shaky voice, as if there was any real possibility of her timid daughter's doing anything so audacious.

After that inauspicious beginning, things got progressively worse, as Serena discovered that the elderly housekeeper had taken to her bed upon being informed that not only her ducal master but also a party of five other guests would expect to sit down to dinner that evening. Her equally ancient husband, who had served Hawkhurst's great-aunt until her death nearly ten years ago, threw up his hands and declared that cooking for a houseful of guests was not a responsibility he was willing or able to undertake.

Serena cast him a look of disgust and marched down to the kitchen to assess the situation. What she found there convinced her that if anything were to be done, she would have to do it herself. So she donned an apron, requested both Cecily and Higgy to join her, and set about making an inventory of the pantry. Hawkhurst found her there an hour later.

"What the devil are you doing here?"

At the sound of that familiar voice, Serena turned from the long trestle table, where she was chopping carrots into neat cubes, and smiled at the man standing in the doorway.

"Your language, sir, is offensive to our tender ears," she retorted, reveling in the amusement that flashed briefly in Hawk's gray eyes. Behind her at the sink, Cecily giggled, and Miss Higgenbotham tittered nervously.

"I thought I was addressing Cook," the duke drawled, dwarfing the large kitchen with his presence. This brought another chuckle from Cecily, who had developed—much to Serena's dismay—an uninhibited hero worship for the man who had restored Rufus to her.

"My sister is an excellent cook," Cecily announced between giggles, "but I fear she is rather squeamish about wringing necks."

"Wringing necks?" the duke repeated, perplexed. "I am happy to hear that your sister has enough delicacy to stop short of wringing *my* neck."

"Chickens' necks, silly," Cecily corrected him.

"And I gather that you have no such scruples, brat?"

"Of course not," Cecily replied scornfully. "I have wrung hundreds of necks. And I am not a brat."

"A blood-thirsty brat, at that," he murmured, coming to stand beside Serena. "Where are all the servants, my dear? I do not like to see you toiling away on my behalf."

"Do not deceive yourself, sir," Serena retorted, all too conscious of Miss Higgenbotham's interested presence behind her. "We are not toiling on your behalf but rather on our own. If we do not cook, we do not eat tonight. And as for the servants, there are none, except for those we brought with us. I do not count that useless Billings and his poor-spirited wife. She took one look at us and retired to her bed with a megrim."

"At least let me help you peel the potatoes," the duke said, surprising Serena so much that she paused to stare at him. "I *can* peel potatoes, you know, love," he murmured, the glint of amusement she loved to see clearly visible in his eyes. "I have done a stint in the Army, you know."

"But not peeling potatoes, I would be willing to wager, sir," she shot back with a smile. "If you are serious about helping, you might revue the troops upstairs. I set your driver and grooms to bringing wood inside and lighting fires in all the rooms. They were not too pleased to be doubling as footmen, let me tell you."

"They shall double as whatever you say, my dear," came the warm response. "Leave them to me."

So, with the assistance of Sergeant Slowe, who was not above acting as butler, the party sat down to a hot meal that first evening, and—thanks to the efforts of Miss Higgen-botham and Serena's abigail—they slept in beds that were not as damp as Lady Thornton had feared.

Serena herself carried a warming pan up to the duke's bed-room later that evening, after Robin Slowe had stoked the fire burning brightly in his master's marble hearth.

She derived an inexplicable satisfaction from performing these mundane tasks for the gentleman who had brought about such a drastic change in her life. From a rather inauspicious encounter on Lady Berkford's dimly lit terrace, their relation-ship had slipped into an unusual sort of friendship that Serena had come to treasure more than she cared to admit. His pres-ence always managed to comfort her, and the sound of his voice buoyed her spirits and made her heart sing more than it had ever done for the elusive Brian Westlock.

That childhood dream was well and truly lost to her, Serena thought, astonished that the loss of her first love did not elicit even a tremor of anguish in her heart. She had dreaded facing Brian at the funeral—which he was bound to attend with his father, their closest neighbor—but when he had approached her with his condolences after the service, his marvelous blond hair misty with the light rain and his manner as charming as ever, Serena had been strangely unaffected.

It was as though her friendship with Guy Hawkhurst had filled a void in her heart that Brian had never been able to touch. Except in her dreams, of course, Serena mused, drawing back the heavy curtains from the duke's bed and thrusting the warming pan beneath the covers. And dreams were all very well for schoolroom chits, but at her advanced age, Serena had learned to mistrust them.

So caught up in her task was she, that Serena did not notice Hawkhurst's presence until he spoke.

"Toiling again on my behalf, I see." His voice came from the foot of the bed, and to Serena's heightened senses, he appeared very much as he had that first time she had seen him lounging in the doorway of Lady Berkford's ballroom. He had exchanged his black pantaloons for buckskin breeches, but they were equally efficient in defining his long, lean legs in their tall riding boots. His coat was a bottle-green corduroy, but the broad shoulders were equally impressive. And the lithe grace was the same Serena remembered so vividly from their first encounter. She was struck again by the impression of coiled power he exuded as he leaned casually against the bed-post.

He was smiling at her, and Serena took refuge in raillery. "You are full of delusions, Your Grace," she said gaily.

"Do not call me that, Serena," he surprised her by saying. "I never want to hear you call me that, my dear. My name is Guy, or Hawk if you wish. But none of this stiff title nonsense from you, I beg you."

Serena gazed at him a moment before responding with a smile, "If that is what you wish, sir."

"It is exactly what I wish, love. And surely I am not deluding myself in believing that, thanks to you, Serena, my bed will be a great deal warmer tonight."

Serena's heart leapt into her throat at the duke's suggestive words, and she was mortified at the vivid blush that invaded her cheeks. Had it not been for the deliberately provocative tone of his voice, which had dropped to a seductive murmur that could not be misinterpreted, Serena might have ignored the erotic overtones to a perfectly natural remark. As it was, her heightened color betrayed her, as she searched frantically for an innocuous response to Hawk's highly improper remark.

Nothing even vaguely appropriate came to mind, of course, and Serena was wondering how she might escape from the room without giving the impression of running for her life, when he stepped across the carpet and laid a restraining hand on hers. To her consternation, his other hand cupped her chin and raised her face.

Determined not to give way to strong hysterics, Serena lifted her eyes defiantly and met his gaze. Never in all her twenty-three years had she wished so fervently that she had been born beautiful, or that she had, at least, mastered the art of light flirtation that would have defused her present predicament into an exchange of friendly banter. Conscious that her best—perhaps her only acceptable—feature was the unusual color of her eyes, Serena allowed the duke to look his fill.

After an endless, paralyzing moment, she saw a slow, lazy smile curve the fullness of his mouth. "Forgive me, my sweet Serena," he murmured, so close that his breath moved a wayward curl that had escaped her chignon. "It was wicked of me to make you blush like that. But you are wicked, too, love, for thinking exactly what I intended you to think." His grin widened. "I love to see you blush." He lowered his head and deliberately brushed his lips across her mouth, pausing for the briefest moment, his lips resting lightly against hers.

Serena could have willingly stood there forever, offering up her lips to the intoxicating heat of his mouth, but all too soon, he turned away and sauntered over to the hearth. "I do not like to see you doing menial things for me, my dear," he remarked, quite as though they had been exchanging mere pleasantries instead of a shattering kiss that had left Serena trembling. "First thing in the morning, I shall send Robin down to Weybourne to hire more staff." The casual remark disconcerted Serena; it also made her angry, a circumstance that enabled her to regain her composure.

"Menial but necessary, sir," she answered dryly. "That is, if you do not wish to catch an inflammation of the lungs from the damp sheets." She withdrew the warming pan with a flourish and pulled the covers back into place.

"No chance of that happening with you to take care of me, love," he murmured nonchalantly. "Of my health, I mean," he added quickly when Serena whirled on him, the copper bed warmer clutched menacingly in both hands.

Hawkhurst's teasing grin did not fool her for a moment. Could it be that the odious man was feeling the absence of his London Cyprians? she wondered. But if he thought to indulge his perfidious appetites in dalliance with her, he was all about in the head.

Clutching at this thought as though it were the proverbial straw in the maelstrom of her emotions, Serena marched out of the room and shut the door firmly behind her.

As the days slipped by, Hawk's admiration for Miss Millbanks increased considerably. Not only did she adamantly refuse his offer to remove to the comfort of the Green Stag Inn in the bustling town of Sheringham when it became apparent that Clifftop Manor was in a serious state of disrepair, but she quickly mustered what servants they had brought with them to set the house to rights. An impossible task, Lady Thornton had declared in piercing tones no sooner had she crossed the threshold, but one that Serena had taken on without a qualm.

"We could 'ave used the likes of that lass in Portugal, Major," Robin commented one morning in his forthright manner as he helped his master into his coat and smoothed it across Hawk's broad shoulders. "Nothing mealy-mouthed about Miss Serena, let me tell you."

Hawk glanced at his hulking batman skeptically. Robin was not given to idle praise, particularly concerning females, whom he tended to mistrust on principle.

"I fear that Miss Millbanks has been saddled with more responsibility than I like," the major said after a pause. "She and her sister appear to be running the household without any assistance from her aunt. I want you to relieve her of as much as you can, Robin."

The sergeant let out a crack of laughter, his brown eyes twinkling with amusement. "Aye, Major, and that I 'ave tried to do, and got me 'ead bitten off fer me pains. But ye be right about the old gel and that brazen daughter of 'ers. Not overly fond of gettin' their pretty 'ands dirty, if ye were to ask me, sir."

Hawk could not agree more. He had himself expressed his displeasure at the menial tasks she did for him, but Serena had always brushed him off with a practical answer. He had caught her in the kitchen slicing carrots, in the garden digging turnips, and up on a stepladder dusting the chandeliers in the dining room. And in his bedchamber warming his bed, Hawk recalled, smiling to himself at the memory of the sweet kiss he had given her upon that occasion. Her lips had been as soft and warm as he remembered them, but his own reaction had surprised him. He had experienced none of the licentious impulses he was accustomed to under similar circumstances. Instead of tumbling her onto the bed, he had found himself begging her forgiveness for causing her to blush.

And then he had kissed her. But not as he had planned, and certainly a far cry from that heated embrace they had shared on Lady Berkford's terrace. Serena had looked up at him with such an expression of trust in those amazing violet eyes of hers that Hawk had been overcome by an odd sense of reverence he had never experienced with any of the females of his acquaintance.

It had been a sobering experience, actually, Hawk thought as he made his way down to the breakfast room at the back of the house. And strangely frightening, too, he admitted reluctantly. Not much in this world frightened him, but that defenseless look in Serena's eyes had shaken him down to the pit of his stomach. Hawk was not at all sure he liked it. But he was even less sure what to do about it.

On one hand, he found life in rural Norfolk a pleasant change from the drunken debauchery of London. He certainly enjoyed the crisp sea air and invigorating tramps along the cliff with the Millbanks sisters and their indefatigable dog. On the other hand, he knew that he should leave; that the growing affection he felt for Serena might not be as innocent as he imagined; that sooner or later he would be tempted to kiss her again, and then, if he were not careful, he might do something they would both regret.

The fear of bringing unhappiness to the one female he had set out to rescue from a life of humiliation and genteel poverty gave Hawk the impetus he needed to make up his mind. He would leave at the first opportunity, he decided. Not today, of course, for he had promised the ladies a trip into Sheringham to do some shopping. And perhaps not tomorrow either, since they were promised to dine with old Viscount Babbington and his lady on the other side of Weybourne. But quite possibly the day after, if the weather held fair.

It was not as if he lacked an excuse, Hawk told himself as he set off for a brisk walk down to the beach with Jollyboy romping wildly at his heels. Only yesterday his secretary had written to remind him that his mother was counting on his presence in Hampshire for the Christmas holidays. Wolverton Abbey seemed miles away—both geographically and emotionally—from Clifftop Manor, Hawk realized with an unpleasant start. The ducal seat was a world apart, a world he had until now associated with Derek and shunned—as he had shunned the title—because of the painful memories it represented.

A world in which Serena Millbanks had no place at all.

The thought took Hawk by surprise. His mind recoiled from it instinctively, for he knew what it implied to be impossible. His mother would have a monstrous attack of the vapors if she so much as suspected that he had entertained the notion of such a mésalliance. But he had not really considered it at all, had he? he argued.

For the first time, Hawk allowed himself to examine his feelings for Miss Millbanks. They were, to say the least, hopelessly muddled, and his unsuccessful attempts to untangle them as he trudged along the windy cliff only strengthened his resolve to return to London. He would tell her so this evening, Hawk thought, and once that was settled, perhaps this nagging uneasiness would leave him.

But it was not until late afternoon three days later that Hawk forced himself to seek out Miss Millbanks. Clifftop Manor was fully staffed by now, so the major no longer expected to find her either chopping vegetables or dusting chandeliers. He came upon her unannounced in the formal drawing room in the east wing, directing two of the new footmen in the removal of a large picture from its prominent place above the fireplace.

She started when he strode in and glanced apprehensively at the linen-draped picture leaning against the damask settee. She did not appear any too pleased to see him, he thought fleetingly.

"What scheme are you up to now, my dear?" Hawk drawled, stopping to gaze at one of the footmen poised precariously on a ladder in the act of removing a rather hideous painting of a herd of cows drinking from a village pond at twilight.

"It was meant to be a surprise, sir," Serena responded. "I was cleaning out the attic yesterday and came across this wonderful portrait. I did not recognize the painter, but Billings assures me he is a local artist who has since set up in London. I did not think you would miss the cows," she added, the gleam of amusement he loved to watch returning to her eyes.

"You are absolutely on the mark there," Hawk remarked. "But tell me, Serena, whose is this wonderful portrait you discovered in the attic?"

"I told you, sir, it is a surprise. So do go away and let us put it up. And no peeking, please."

To humor her, and because the notion of allowing Miss Millbanks to order him around in his own house was an oddly intimate experience he found enjoyable, Hawk removed himself to the hall outside.

She did not keep him waiting long. First the footmen came out bearing away the offensive pastoral scene; then Serena

herself appeared in the doorway, her face glowing with anticipation.

"You may come in now, sir."

Hawk was amused. One of the things he particularly liked
about Serena was the ease with which she brought a smile to
his lips, and a lift to his too often heavy heart. He followed her
into the drawing room now quite prepared to tease her, to
compliment her, to praise her taste in portraits, even to kiss her
if the opportunity arose.

What he saw drove all these fanciful thoughts from his
head.

The dead face of his brother stared down upon him from
above the mantel.

Hawk felt as though the breath had been driven violently
from his lungs. The unknown artist had captured Derek's likeness so accurately that, for a fleeting moment, Hawk imagined
himself face-to-face with his twin. The haunting sadness of the
smile tore at his heart and transported him back to that last
time he had seen his brother alive. The screams of dying
horses, the groans of wounded men, the acrid smell of cannon
smoke, the noise and stench of battle hung about him as he
knelt in the bloody dust, his twin's twisted body cradled in his
arms.

"What a goddamned, bloody awful, stupid thing to do,"
Hawk had yelled at Derek above the bedlam that raged around
them. He had felt an enormous wave of fury welling up inside
him at what his brother had done. But he should not have been
surprised. He would have done the same himself had their
roles been reversed. That was what being a twin was all about,
he thought bitterly.

And then he had noticed the dark stain of blood on Derek's
red uniform. But no, he remembered, the uniform of a major
of the 18th Hussars that his twin was wearing that day at Vittoria was not Derek's at all. The bloody uniform had been
Hawk's. The uniform he should have been wearing. The uniform Derek had obviously put on in his stead, and which was
even now soaking up his twin's life blood.

It was at that moment that Hawk had sensed that his brother
was dying. "Why in bloody hell did you *do* it?" he had yelled,
terrified by the still paleness of Derek's face.

And his beloved brother had smiled, the same sweet, sad
smile of the portrait. Then he had sighed and closed his eyes.
Hawk had heard himself begging over and over for his

brother's forgiveness, his voice hoarse with emotion and fear, and that implacable loneliness that had begun that day at Vittoria and taken up permanent residence in his heart.

He would never know if Derek had heard him.

"You do not like it?" he heard a voice inquire tentatively from what seemed like miles away. "I thought it was such an excellent likeness of you, sir. I could not bear to leave it hidden away in the attic."

Hawk stared at her for several moments before what she had said stirred his befuddled brain. He let out a crack of bitter laughter.

"That is not my likeness," he said heavily, turning away and making straight for the sideboard where the liquor decanters were lined up invitingly.

"That is my brother, Derek." He unstoppered a decanter and sloshed a generous measure into a glass. "My dead twin brother, remember?" he added with quite unnecessary cynicism, he realized after it was said. "The brother who died at Vittoria," he continued mercilessly. "And I do not want his portrait hanging on my wall. Do I make myself clear?"

When Serena made no reply, Hawk raised his glass in a mock salute and downed the contents in one long, desperate gulp.

Serena did not wait to see the duke pour himself a second glass of brandy. She was quite sure that he would do so, but had no desire to see the man she cared for more than she wished to admit drink himself into a stupor. She went in search of Sergeant Slowe.

"Like as not the major will not listen to me, lass," the brawny batman said wryly when Serena had laid the whole before him. "Hawk has never forgiven 'imself for 'is brother's death, ye see. And when 'e gets into these black moods, 'tis best to leave things be. Gets downright vicious, 'e does, lass."

Serena clasped her hands tightly to keep from trembling. "But you will at least try, will you not?" she pleaded. "I should have realized that the portrait could not have been Hawk's. He told us that he had never visited Clifftop Manor. It is all my stupid fault."

When the duke did not put in an appearance at the dinner table, Serena sought out Robin again.

"Yes, lass, I talked to the major, just as ye asked me to," the batman replied to her inquiry. "But all I got fer me pains was a string of oaths the likes of which I dinna think ye want to 'ear."

"Then I shall talk to him myself," Serena declared, her own temper beginning to simmer. "This behavior is nothing but a childish tantrum, and so I shall tell him. Where is the major, anyway?"

"Where ye left 'im, lass. Sittin' there gazin' at 'is brother as though 'e could bring the poor lad back from the dead. I would not go near 'im, lass, if I was you."

In the end, Serena reluctantly followed the sergeant's advice and retired early to her room, pleading an incipient headache. But she could not sleep. She had not really expected to, for her thoughts were with the man downstairs who had been reminded, because of her own stupidity, of the most shattering event in his life. Serena wished fervently that she had never decided to venture into the attic, never discovered the portrait among several others under the linen cloth, never had the temerity to imagine she could hang it on the duke's wall quite as if she were the real mistress of his house.

The notion of being mistress of one of Hawkhurst's establishments had wormed its insidious way into her thoughts only recently, but once there, Serena had been quite unable—or perhaps unwilling—to dislodge it. It was, after all, a harmless fantasy, she told herself. There was no earthly way such a wild daydream might come true. Was she not eminently unsuitable for such a splendid position? she reminded herself. As a duke, Hawk would be expected to choose . . . But Serena did not want to think about what Hawk was expected to do; that was beyond her control. She much preferred to dream about what he *might* do if given the opportunity and a little encouragement.

At this point, her dreams would come to an abrupt halt. Such sinful thoughts—for what else could her secret wantonness be called?—could only lead to shame and disgrace. Was she prepared to throw her good name, her spotless reputation, her precious innocence away for a fleeting glimpse of desire in a pair of gray eyes?

Serena liked to tell herself that, as a practical female, she would not stoop to ruin for any gentleman, however bewitching his eyes might be. But her heart was not so easily convinced. It was lucky for her, she thought wryly, glancing at the clock on the mantel as she heard it strike midnight, that her heart was generally ruled by her common sense.

The pressing issue at present, of course, was not her virtue or the fear of losing it, but the need to apologize to Hawk for her terrible blunder and obtain his forgiveness. Serena did not think she could ever be comfortable again if he refused to speak to her, doubtless blaming her for the renewed pain and desolation he must be feeling at this very moment. If he had not already drunk himself into a stupor, she thought ruefully.

The notion of her dear Hawk once again besotted with drink and quite possibly feeling very ill indeed caused Serena to climb out of bed and slip into her warm dressing gown. Nervously, she paced to and fro in front of the fire.

What could she do? she wondered. It would be unseemly for her to go downstairs, as she wished very much to do, to determine the exact state of her host's inebriation.

Serena was torn between throwing discretion to the winds and going downstairs anyway, and getting back into bed on the off chance she could persuade herself that Hawk's troubles were none of her concern, when she heard a muffled curse from the landing.

Without stopping to consider the consequences, Serena rushed to the door and flung it open.

The duke was standing at the head of the stair. He appeared to be sober, but Serena mistrusted the rakish glint in his eyes. He clasped a half-empty decanter in one hand, a glass of brandy in the other. As she watched, he took a careful step toward her, and Serena did not hesitate. With an exclamation of impatience, she tried to remove the glass—which he was waving at her, slopping the contents on the carpet—from his fingers. He resisted, and Serena found herself tugging at it angrily.

"Let go this instant," she hissed under her breath. "Are you trying to kill yourself?"

"Yes, love," he drawled nonchalantly. He would not release the glass, and Serena found that her tugging had backed them both into her room. "Unless of course, my dear," he added with a rakish grin, "you can think of any good reason why I should want to go on living?"

Serena could think of a dozen reasons to keep Hawk alive, but none of them seemed quite appropriate at the moment.

His grin became a grimace. "You see, love, not even my sweet Serena can persuade me that there is any sense to life after what happened at Vittoria." He turned abruptly toward the door, spilling more brandy on the floor.

Before Serena could stop herself, she had caught him by the sleeve. "You are going to end up in Bedlam unless you learn to live with your brother's loss," she said bluntly. "You cannot go on blaming yourself for his death," she rushed on, ignoring the coldness that abruptly banished the humor in his eyes.

He glared at her for what seemed like an eternity. When he spoke, his voice cut through her like shards of ice. "Yes I can, indeed," he growled, his lips taut in an ugly grimace. "Because I *am* to blame. If I had been there when I should have been, none of this would have happened. Derek was not a soldier, you see. He died for me."

Serena could think of nothing to counteract the starkness of this confession. She took the glass out of his unresisting fingers and placed it on the dresser. "I refuse to believe that your brother would wish you to drink yourself into an early grave on his account," she murmured, prying the decanter away and leading him to the settee by the fire.

"Tell me about it," she suggested gently, after Hawk had sat gazing into the flames for ten minutes.

Serena had not expected him to confide this deepest of his secret sorrows to her, but finally he did, speaking in a low, hoarse voice she had to strain to hear.

He talked steadily for more than an hour, and when he stopped, as abruptly as he had begun, Serena knew the answers to all the questions she had so often wondered about.

CHAPTER TWELVE

The Seduction

A half-consumed log shifting among the embers of the fire roused Serena from the spell Hawkhurst's voice had woven around her in the dim room. His account of his brother's death and the circumstances leading up to it had moved her beyond tears. Her gaze drifted from the flickering flames in the grate to the man sitting silently on the settee beside her. His head was buried in his hands, and his shoulders stooped forward in an attitude of such profound dejection that Serena had to resist the urge to reach out and comfort him.

At least she now knew the reason for that dejection, and perhaps understood a little of the compulsive guilt that drove the duke to embrace the reckless, dissipated life he had displayed to her in London. Here in Norfolk he had been almost a different man, she realized, and she had not seen him foxed since that memorable visit to Lady Lexington in Windsor, over a month ago.

Except for today, she thought. Today he had begun to drink again. All because of her own stupidity. She had reminded him, by bringing Derek's portrait down from the attic, of his brother's ultimate sacrifice. And of his own guilt—or what Hawk seemed to imagine was his guilt—in bringing about his twin's death.

Serena had learned something about guilt that afternoon. Hawkhurst's drawn face and bitter laughter had branded it on her soul as they stood together before Derek's portrait. Together, but never more far apart, Serena sensed with sudden insight. The enormity of her error, her incredibly hurtful blunder, had come crashing down on her when Hawk had picked up the decanter and poured his first glass of brandy. How many more he had consumed that evening, Serena did not want to speculate, but the number must have been considerable. And with every glass, her guilt had grown, until she felt the impossible weight of it compressing her heart, strangling her mind, choking her emotions. Yes, she thought ruefully, she knew something of what Hawk was suffering.

Except for the occasional falling ember, the room was silent until the clock in the hall below struck two.

Two o'clock! With a start, Serena realized she had been shut in her bedchamber alone with a gentleman for two hours. The impropriety of this circumstance caused Serena to fidget nervously. She must be utterly mad, she thought, lost to all sense of propriety.

These proper thoughts flew her mind when Hawk suddenly raised his head, and Serena saw that his cheeks were wet. His glance flickered over her and settled on the brandy decanter. He rose abruptly and walked to the dresser, but before he had reached for the half-empty glass, Serena was beside him, her hands clasping his arm. She gazed up into his gray eyes, her own misty with unshed tears.

"*Please* do not do this, Hawk," she pleaded, her voice breaking with emotion. The visible evidence of his grief had unsettled her badly. She was not accustomed to seeing gentlemen express their pain so tangibly. Yet, after the first shock of seeing his tears, Serena felt a surge of joy that he had trusted her enough to share this intimate moment with her.

"Are you referring perchance to my unmanly behavior?" he quipped with a self-deprecating smile.

Serena shook her head and swallowed. "No, of course not," she whispered, her voice catching in her throat. "I meant the drinking, Hawk. I do not believe Derek would have wished to see his sacrifice come to naught, do you?" Her own daring amazed her, and she was not surprised to see the gray eyes turn cool.

"You know nothing at all about what Derek would wish." There was no mistaking the dismissive tone of his voice, but Serena was past caring.

"Oh, but I do," she insisted. "Your brother loved you above life itself. He faced almost certain death to save your honor. How can you believe . . . ?"

"Honor?" Hawk spat the word out as though it tasted foul on his tongue. "I have no honor, Serena. Did you not hear what I was doing while my brother was dying for me on the battlefield?"

"Oh, yes, indeed," Serena retorted sharply. "You were drinking and wenching with some anonymous Spanish señorita."

"Two, actually," he observed cynically, his eyes fixed on her face. "Señoritas, that is," he added, when Serena looked perplexed.

She blushed instantly as the picture of Hawk rolling around on a rumpled bed with two unclothed Spanish beauties rose to mind. Or perhaps it had been in some stable or behind a hedge or . . . Serena soon ran out of places where such carnal encounters might occur, her experience being deplorably limited. And why two of them? she wondered, the possibility of such depravity never having occurred to her before. Her blush deepened as her fertile imagination ran wild.

A flicker of amusement in Hawk's eyes warned her that he had guessed her wayward thoughts. Serena dropped her eyes and snatched her hands away from his arm as though she had been burned.

"I have to agree with you, sir," she said stiffly. "You lack even the minimal vestiges of honor." She turned away, quite unable to look at him without that distressingly erotic vision dancing before her eyes. "To say nothing of decency," she threw over her shoulder. Serena walked to the door and jerked it open. "I must ask you to leave at once." She gestured toward the hall.

Setting the glass back on the dresser, Hawk walked deliberately over to the door, took her limp fingers from the knob, and closed it firmly. Serena gasped as he leaned back against the door and brought her fingers up to his lips. There was something about the sad smile he gave her that reminded Serena of the portrait downstairs in the drawing room. It was indubitably Derek's smile, and it brought a lump to her throat.

"Do not wash your hands of me, Serena," he said in a tired voice. "I suspect you really do understand about Derek. Perhaps better than I do myself." Gently, he drew her against him until her resistance evaporated, and Serena let herself go limp against his chest, her nose buried in his cravat.

"Talk to me about your impressions of my brother," he murmured after a short pause, during which Serena felt his arms go around her.

She sighed. "I think he must have been very different from you," she began. "You looked identical, of course, hence my mistake about the portrait, but inside he must have been more serious and responsible, less the rakehell you obviously were."

She heard him grunt in acknowledgment, his hands caressing her back. "What else?" he murmured against her hair.

"The obligations of his rank must have weighed upon him more than he liked, I imagine," she said thoughtfully. "Perhaps he envied you your freedom, Hawk. But I see him as a man of principle and tradition; his life had been determined for him from birth, and he would have carried the title proudly. He had all the right qualities for it, I would say."

"Unlike me," Hawk whispered, his warm breath teasing her cheek, "who have none of them. Is that what you are implying, you saucy minx?"

"We are not talking about you, sir," she retorted. "But I do know that, had your fortunes been reversed, Derek would not have crippled himself with self-pity to the point of ignoring his duty to his line."

Serena felt Hawk go rigid and wished that she had moderated her words. She raised her head and saw that his eyes were clouded with pain rather than anger.

"Is that what you really think of me, Serena?"

"Yes," she said gently. "Is it not true that you leave the running of your estates to stewards?" she continued, knowing that her honesty was painful to him. "How often do you visit your principal seat, sir? Once a year for a week at Christmastime, or so rumor has it. And have you not heard what the gossips say about you in Town?" she went on implacably, ignoring the wry, twisted smile he was having difficulty maintaining as he stared down at her. "None of this is what Derek would have wished for you, Hawk. And I can assure you that this is not the Guy Hawkhurst he died for."

Appalled at her temerity, Serena closed her eyes and waited for the duke's wrath to fall upon her head.

For a paralyzing moment that stretched out interminably, Hawk stood stock still listening to Serena's damning questions echo in the silent room. Her accusations echoed in his head, too, and he had the uncomfortable premonition that they would stay with him for a long time to come. By rights he should be angry, he thought, but the only anger he could summon up was at himself. For what Miss Millbanks had said was true. He would be a fool, and dishonest to boot, to deny any of it.

Hawk allowed his gaze to rove over the face of the woman in his arms. Serena rested against him with the touching trust of a woman who knows she will not be harmed. The notion brought a lump to his throat. Trust had never entered into his relationships with females before, and he found it immensely reassuring to know that this one had found something worthwhile in him despite the glaring faults she had enumerated.

Her eyes were closed, and Hawk suspected that were she to open them, their violet depths would be filled with apprehension. Serena would expect him to be angered by her plain speaking. But in truth she had humbled him. In her forthright way, Serena had put her finger on the crux of what ailed him. He was not the man his brother had died for. By indulging himself in his grief to the exclusion of all else, Hawk had betrayed Derek's trust. He had become a disappointment to his brother, to his family, and to himself.

He had even disappointed Miss Millbanks.

Abruptly, Hawk realized that she had opened her eyes and he saw that he had been right. There was apprehension in them, but there was also strength, and trust, and something infinitely sweet that flickered briefly and disappeared before he could identify it.

"Do you think I could become that man again, love?" he murmured almost inaudibly, and was filled with delight at the smile that leapt into her eyes.

"I do not doubt it for a moment," she responded with a confidence that touched him deeply. "If you really wish to, naturally. It will depend on you, Hawk, but I know you can do it."

And there was the rub, he mused, watching the certainty in her eyes and wishing he possessed one half of it. Did he have the determination and dedication that his twin had expected of him? Hawk wondered. Could he, in short, step into his brother's shoes in the fullest meaning of the word? With a start, he recognized that he had always doubted his ability to—what had the perceptive Miss Millbanks called it?—carry the title proudly. Could it not have been this fear of his own inadequacy as much as his feelings of guilt that had prevented him from becoming the man Derek had died for?

Serena was still smiling up at him, and Hawk was beset by the odd fancy that life would be far less threatening—and yes, he admitted reluctantly, less frightening, too—if Serena was always there to smile at him just so. Better yet, she always seemed to know right from wrong, and did not scruple to say so. Robin had been right about Miss Millbanks, Hawk reflected; there was nothing mealy-mouthed about her. Quite unexpectedly, he was overcome with the desire to share this woman's strength, to capture her smile in his heart, to take away with him some of her confidence and trust.

The silence of the room was broken by the clock downstairs striking the half hour.

Serena moved in his arms, and Hawk felt her slim body tremble against him. Without conscious thought, he tightened his arms about her until he could feel every sweet curve of her pressed into him. As he watched, her eyes changed color, darkening with emotion, and the world outside that room where the two of them stood together as one vanished, until all he could see or feel or touch was there in her amethyst gaze.

With no thought for the consequences, Hawk lowered his mouth over hers and gave himself up to the silken softness of her lips.

Much as he might have wished to do so, Hawk could not afterward lay the blame for his actions that night on the brandy. For one thing, he had not imbibed with his usual heedless abandon. Halfway through the first glass, he had made the astounding discovery that mindless swilling of strong spirits no longer held the attraction it once had. Since his departure from the Metropolis, Hawk seemed to have lost the knack of drinking himself into a stupor. Since his intention—upon coming face-to-face with the haunting smile of his dead twin in the portrait—had been to immerse himself, as quickly as possible, in that blissfully immune state, Hawk was dismayed to find that he no longer had the stomach for it.

That first glass, knocked off in one gulp before Serena's reproachful gaze, had fallen on his stomach like a ton of bricks. He had forced himself to pour the second glass, but the thought of actually drinking it had made him shudder with distaste. In the end, Hawk had nursed it through the rest of the afternoon, and it was not until after he heard the dinner gong that he had poured the third. At midnight he was only halfway through his fourth, a record of moderation he reflected morosely, since he could still propel himself unaided up the staircase, and the decanter was only half empty.

And then a door on the landing had flown open and Serena had stood there, her hair an auburn cloud around her shoulders, her violet eyes wide with concern.

Concern for him, Hawk remembered thinking at the time, his heart warming at the miracle of it.

They had tussled over the glass, he recalled, and some of the brandy had sloshed down his coat and onto the carpet. And then he was sitting before a blazing fire in his shirtsleeves—he had no recollection of divesting himself of his damp coat—and suddenly he had begun talking about Derek.

Hawk had never opened his heart so completely to a female before, but abruptly the need to confide in Miss Millbanks had overcome his natural reticence, and he had shared his intimate memories of Derek with her. Not only his twin's tragic final moments, but from the very beginning, when they were boys together at Wolverton Abbey. He told her about their dogs, and their ponies, and the rabbits they had kept one summer in the old chicken house behind the barn. About their infrequent squabbles, and their frequent infatuations—at fifteen they had fallen in love with the same woman, the tapster's daughter at the Stone and Arch inn. About their stint at Eton, and their wild summers riding the farthest reaches of their father's estates. And the more sobering experience of Oxford—sobering because Derek had insisted upon taking their quest for knowledge seriously. Hawk had gone along with his twin, although he had also managed to indulge in the kind of outrageous wagers that were later to color his reputation in London.

He talked about their father's death, and his brother's sudden accession to the title. Somehow, Hawk had not been prepared for that breach in their friendship. Derek had fervently denied any such breach, but Hawk had felt—or imagined he felt—the shadow of that august title wedging itself between them. He talked about the Army, where he had sought to assuage the pain of losing touch with his twin. Ironically, of course, it had been in the Army that Hawk had lost his brother irrevocably and forever.

And finally Hawk spoke of Derek's death, and the humiliating part he had played in it. He had never revealed this secret to anyone before, and he did not spare himself. Aside from Robin Slowe, and possibly Colonel Sir David Laughton, his commanding officer, who may have guessed the truth, Serena was the only person who knew the dishonor and guilt that had hung over his head since that day at Vittoria.

And now she was in his arms, and he was kissing her. Again.

Oddly enough, Hawk had not considered the possibility of her resisting him, and she did not. After the initial moment of shock, Hawk felt her body relax into his embrace, and he ran his hands slowly, caressingly over her pliant form, molding her into his own hardness as though he would make them one.

Her lips parted under his, and with a groan of desire, Hawk slipped into her, tasting her, exploring her, moving over her, against her, and inside her quite as though he had never kissed a woman before.

And perhaps he never had, he reflected, dazed by the strength of his reaction. At least no woman quite like this one. Serena opened beneath his tender assault as if she had been waiting all her life for this moment. Had he not been waiting for this same moment himself? he wondered, thrilling at the sense of completeness she brought to him. His hand slipped inside her dressing gown and touched the swell of her breast beneath the silk of her night rail. He felt her tremble as he gently explored its contours, his thumb teasing the nipple until she sighed against his mouth and pressed herself into his hand.

The world seemed to explode around him, and before he knew what he was about, Hawk had slipped the dressing gown from her shoulders and pressed his heated face into the sweet curve of her neck. When he felt her hands slide up his arms and around his neck, he claimed her lips again, seeking in the sweetness of her mouth the answer to his loneliness, the culmination of his desire.

His reason blurred by passion, Hawk swept Serena up in his arms and carried her to the bed, setting her down gently among the rumpled sheets. As he lowered himself beside her, he marveled at the surrender he saw in her eyes. She was his, he thought, so dazzled by his good fortune that he refused to dwell on anything but the warmth of her skin under his kiss, the curve of her hip under the slow caress of his hand, and the deep violet of her magnificent eyes that seemed to promise everything that he needed to be whole again.

Gently, Hawk untied the ribbons at her throat, pulled open her night rail, and buried his face in the warm valley of her breasts. He could hear her heart distinctly, fluttering wildly against his cheek in a rhythm that matched his own. He trailed his mouth up to the hollow of her throat, where he felt her pulse beating against his lips. He found her utterly enchanting and wished that this precious moment of their coming together would last a lifetime.

Something about this fantasy disturbed him, but Hawk dismissed it.

He raised himself on one elbow to observe her reaction to the leisurely path his fingers were tracing from her lips, down her lovely throat, across her breast, cradling her hip and descending with a lingering, sensual touch to her left knee. Her eyes were luminous in the candlelight, Hawk noticed, and held within their violet depths the salvation he sought.

Slowly, so as not to alarm her, Hawk slid his hand to the inside of her knee and began the tantalizing exploration of her inner thigh. Her skin was petal-soft, and as his fingers inched upward, Hawk's imagination leaped ahead to the heady delights that awaited him. His breathing became shallow, and as he gazed down at the woman beneath him, he saw the awakening of passion in her eyes.

Then, without warning, Serena reached up to him, pulling him down for her kiss. "Oh, Guy," she murmured against his mouth, her voice ragged with passion. "Oh, Guy, I do love you so."

A chill hand seemed to grip Hawk's heart as he listened to this artless confession, and all desire fled, leaving him cold sober. Abruptly, he disentangled himself from Serena's arms and sat up, swinging his legs over the edge of the bed.

With superhuman effort, Hawk fought his surging emotions until he felt his fevered pulse gradually slow to a heavy pounding in his head. A cold sweat broke out on his brow as he realized just how close he had come to committing the irrevocable act of seducing the very female he valued above all others. No matter that she had been willing, even eager for his caresses, he told himself bluntly. Serena was an innocent, and it was his responsibility to keep her out of harm's way. And that included himself.

And he had almost failed her.

Not trusting himself to speak, Hawk stood up, picked up his coat from the chair by the fire, and strode out of the room.

The sound of the chamber door closing behind the duke echoed like a shot through Serena's head, a shot that seemed to go on forever, piercing her heart and shattering all her dreams. She lay perfectly still, rigid with anguish, and mortification, and an immense sorrow that washed over her trembling body in icy waves.

What a weak, romantic fool she had been to imagine that plain Miss Serena Millbanks could attract a man like the Duke of Wolverton, even for a brief, illicit encounter such as the aborted one she had just experienced, Serena reflected somberly, listening absently to the clock downstairs tolling the hour.

Three o'clock. Serena shuddered with a chill that had nothing to do with the cooling of her fevered skin. The past half hour had witnessed her greatest joy and her most intense grief. Hawk had kissed her again, and she had allowed it; nay, she had reveled in it. Lost in the miraculous ecstasy of his touch, she had allowed herself to forget who she was. Who he was. To forget the practical world beyond her chamber door where life was regulated according to strict social and economic rules, where fortune and rank determined relationships, where the yearnings of the heart were regarded as too common by half. An implacable world in which dukes put their obligations and duties above everything else. Even above love, Serena mused disconsolately. Especially above love.

Not that Hawk . . . No, she must not think of him with such intimacy if she were to get through the rest of her life. The Duke of Wolverton had never loved her, she reflected; that had been made perfectly clear to her tonight. He had pitied her, found amusement in her rustic innocence perhaps, and certainly he had been kind to her. In return she had listened to him pour out his guilt and despair. He had needed to share that terrible burden, Serena suddenly realized, and he had chosen her. Poor comfort that was, of course, when she had wanted to give him so much more. She would have done so, too, she mused. Her heart had been too full of love to deny him anything, and had he wished . . .

But all too clearly he had not wished to avail himself of what she so freely offered, Serena thought, her throat constricting with unshed tears. And perhaps, in the lonely years ahead, she might even grow to thank him for not dishonoring her. For there could have been no honorable outcome to the magical moment they had shared—but never consummated—together. There could be no offer of marriage from a duke for Miss Millbanks. And anything less—and Serena admitted in her heart of hearts that she had been prepared to accept less—would have branded her an outcast and destroyed her sister's chances of making a suitable match.

No, Serena forced herself to admit, any connection with Major Guy Hawkhurst, the Duke of Wolverton, had been unsuitable in every way, and if she were sensible, and practical, and reasonable, and in full possession of her wits, she would be grateful to the man for walking away when he did.

But of course she was none of these things, nor was she

suitably grateful for being saved from disgrace, and her heart bled silently as tears began to course down her pale cheeks.

Hawk had rejected her. That was the only truth that seemed to matter at the moment.

And the knowledge of it hurt most dreadfully.

CHAPTER THIRTEEN

The Separation

Hawk had not even attempted to sleep during what remained of the night.

When Robin came up at six o'clock, in answer to his master's summons, Hawk instructed him to start packing, for he intended to leave after breakfast.

The batman raised a shaggy eyebrow, but all he said was, "Shall ye be taking the chaise, sir?"

"No. I prefer to ride. Hercules is fresh, and we can make better time," Hawk replied curtly, omitting to add that he did not wish to leave Miss Millbanks without a carriage. "I wish to be in London by nightfall."

Robin raised his other eyebrow, but said nothing. He set out the major's clothes and departed in search of shaving water.

Hawk sat down at the elegant escritoire by the window and moved the candle to augment the thin winter daylight that was beginning to filter into the room. The pristine blankness of the paper daunted him. What could he possibly say to her that would erase the memory of his perfidy? he wondered. He shook his head, impatient at his own stupidity. What he wished to do was clearly impossible. Who better than Guy Hawkhurst to know that memories—good or bad—could not be erased? Nevertheless, he must at least make the effort to set the record straight.

As if the record of what had occurred between Miss Millbanks and the Duke of Wolverton could ever be set straight, he thought morosely. There was no way he could right the wrong he had done her—or *almost* done her. At least no way that was open to him, Hawk amended grimly.

Hawk took a firmer grip on the pen and scrawled, *My dearest Serena.* He stopped abruptly. How could he dare call her *his,* when she would never be anything but a stranger to him? Well, not exactly a stranger, he corrected himself with a cynical flash of humor. Never a stranger. In actuality, it was damned painful trying to remind himself that he would never see Miss Millbanks again. She would be here in Norfolk, and he would be . . .

He paused to stare out at the gray dawn, a wave of dark thoughts flooding his mind at the prospect of losing her bright presence. He would be in the Metropolis, briefly, but would stay clear of his usual vices, Hawk had vowed to himself during those cold morning hours after he had fled the warmth, and comfort, and passion of Serena's bed. It had taken every ounce of self-control he possessed, and a strength of will he had not known he had, to stay away from that bed. And from that violet-eyed woman, who seemed to offer the reprieve and redemption he had never expected to find after Vittoria.

Abruptly, Hawk crushed the paper in his fist and reached for another sheet. *Dearest Serena,* he began, but that did not seem appropriate either. Not that she was not very dear to him indeed. He could at least admit that to himself. But the endearment suggested intimacies between them that were best left undisturbed, unacknowledged, unremembered.

As if he could ever forget, Hawk thought grimly, crushing the second sheet and hurling it after the first onto the floor. The devil fly away with the whole world, he muttered viciously, staring at yet another blank page.

In the end he merely wrote, in his bold, slanting scrawl, the briefest essence of his message to Miss Millbanks.

Serena, forgive me.

He signed his name with a flourish and quickly folded the paper before his emotion betrayed him into maudlin sentimentality.

After a silent breakfast—for the ladies were still abed at that early hour—Hawk forced himself to mount the stairs to the formal drawing room where Derek's portrait still hung. He placed his note to Serena on the mantel beneath the picture and then looked up into his brother's gray eyes.

Had Serena been right about that, too? he wondered. Had Derek—expecting more from his twin than Hawk had been prepared to give—died in vain? A sobering thought, and one that would plague him for the remainder of his life. Unless Serena had also been right in her assessment of his power to change the course of that life. *I do not doubt it for a moment,* she had said. And when he was with her, he had not doubted it either.

Only time would tell, Hawk reflected, descending quickly to

the hall and allowing Billings to help him into his many-caped greatcoat.

It would all depend on him, she had told him in that clear, confident way she had of facing life's vicissitudes. But in that his dear Serena was mistaken, Hawk decided, striding out to the waiting horses. Taking his reins from Robin, he flung himself into the saddle and checked Hercules's nervous prancing. His success, if indeed he attained any success at all in overcoming the demons that had plagued him since Vittoria, would depend largely upon her. Had the outspoken Miss Millbanks not enumerated—in highly unflattering terms to be sure—the long list of his faults?

And after acknowledging every one of them, what kind of man would he be if he made no push to correct them?

Certainly not the man Miss Millbanks clearly expected him to be, he reflected wryly. Nor the man for whom his brother had died.

Hawkhurst turned his horse's head toward the gate. Without a backward glance, he urged Hercules into a canter.

Deep in his heart, he feared that if he looked back, he would not be able to leave at all.

And he must. Honor and duty and family obligation demanded it.

As did Miss Serena Millbanks.

"I cannot understand why His Grace left us in such a bang," Lady Thornton remarked at the breakfast table—as she had every morning for the past sennight since the duke's departure. "One might almost imagine that the bailiffs were after him." She sniffed audibly at the notion. "Why did he not let us know he had urgent business in Town, I wonder?"

"Quite possibly because it is none of our concern, Aunt," Serena replied patiently. She knew perfectly well why Hawk had disappeared from Clifftop Manor so suddenly, but of course she could not tell her aunt. It did not bear thinking on.

"I think it was very poor-spirited of him," Melissa interrupted with a delicate pout on her rosy lips. "I was quite counting on him to escort us to the New Year's Assembly in Sheringham, Mama. Sally Caldwell tells me it is all the crack. Everyone who is anybody attends. I do think he might have considered my feelings before he went haring off in the middle of the night." She sighed, then added ingenuously, "I did so wish to make an entrance on the arm of a real duke."

Serena gave her beautiful cousin a thoughtful look. If only Melissa would occasionally consider something other than her own appearance and convenience, she might conceivably achieve an eligible match in the near future. Indeed, even without two thoughts in her head to rub together, her cousin might well dazzle a gentleman of rank and fortune—like Sir John Walker—enough to bring him up to scratch. Not that there were many eligible *partis* in this region as far as she knew. Not now that Hawk had shaken the dust of Norfolk from the heels of his elegant boots.

Resolutely, Serena dragged her mind back to the breakfast table.

"I fail to see how that would signify, dearest," Lady Thornton was saying mellifluously. "Even if Wolverton so far forgot himself as to offer you his arm instead of me, as protocol dictates, how is the world to know one is dancing with a duke if the rogue insists upon going about as a mere major?"

"Oh, they all know who he is, Mama," Melissa remarked, with a coy little laugh. "He is so like his brother, you see. Everyone saw it immediately but dared not say so for fear of setting his back up. I think it silly of him not to use his title, especially such a grand one."

"Well, it is a moot point, anyway," Lady Thornton remarked, motioning the footman to serve her a second helping of kippers. "By the New Year you and I shall be home in Attleborough, love, so you should concern yourself with plans to attend the Assembly there instead. No doubt there will be swains aplenty languishing for your return, dear, even if Sir John Walker does not keep his promise to visit us." She turned to her eldest niece, who had set down her empty cup and risen from the table. "I do wish you would reconsider and accompany us, Serena, my dear," she added. "I do not like to think of you and Cecily staying here on your own."

"We shall not be alone, Aunt," Serena pointed out. "Miss Higgenbotham has agreed to stay on as long as we need her." She threw her old governess a quick smile and escaped from the room.

Christmas came and went without a word from Hawk. Not that she had expected any, Serena kept telling herself when her spirits flagged. After Aunt Hester and her daughter had made their departure in the antiquated landau, amidst the usual commotion and false starts, and with Lady Thornton's last-minute recommendations to her nieces still ringing in her ears, Serena felt that a particularly harrowing chapter of her life had come to a conclusion. The next chapter would be focused upon her sister Cecily and the task of establishing her creditably.

Ruthlessly, Serena put all thoughts of the duke out of her head. And if this was not entirely successful, at least she made a valiant effort to forget the emotionally shattering encounter they had shared in her bedchamber the evening before his precipitous departure from Clifftop Manor. With fierce determination to heal her battered heart, still cringing from the unpalatable conclusion that Hawk had actually run away rather than allow himself to be compromised by the unsuitable Miss Millbanks, Serena threw herself into the role of chatelaine with single-minded intensity.

Was it not the best—and certainly the most honorable—course he might have taken? she repeated to herself when the memory of Hawk's caresses intruded—as they frequently did—upon her consciousness. Then why did she feel—whenever she allowed herself the luxury of reliving those precious moments with him—so unutterably miserable?

By the end of January, Serena had learned to think about the duke without being quite overcome with the desire to weep. She forced herself to focus on his kindness and generosity.

In this she received the unexpected assistance of John Steele, who wrote soon after the New Year—on direct instructions from His Grace, the duke's secretary informed her—to thank her for accepting the task of making Clifftop Manor habitable again. His Grace was deeply in her debt, Mr. Steele claimed in his elegant copperplate, and begged Miss Millbanks to oblige him further by considering the manor her home for as long as she remained in Norfolk. As an afterthought, or so it seemed to Serena, the secretary mentioned that a draft had been remitted to a branch of the Bank of England in Sheringham which she was specifically requested to draw upon to cover household expenses and all charges arising from her stewardship of the duke's property.

Flabbergasted at the discovery that she had, without so much as a by-your-leave, become the official stewardess of Hawk's estate, and more than a little miffed at the prospect of finding herself joining the ranks of his pensioners, Serena had applied to Miss Higgenbotham for solace and advice. Her old governess had surprised her, however.

"You are being uncommonly missish about this arrangement, my dear Serena," she remarked immediately.

"You do not think it improper for the duke to send us money, Higgy?"

Miss Higgenbotham shook her head emphatically, sending her tight brown curls into a frenzy of motion. "Oh, no, my love. It is entirely proper for His Grace to defray the normal costs of maintaining all his establishments. Only think, Serena, his estate must have been doing so for years. Ever since his great-aunt died, I would wager. Perhaps even longer if the old lady had no income of her own."

"By rights I should be paying rent for the place," Serena pointed out stubbornly. "And it is not as though we are quite penniless. I still have most of the money I won from the Marquess of Monroyal, you know. That should last us for several years, I hope."

"Now that is positively absurd, love. Can you honestly say that you would have rented the manor in the deplorable condition it was when we arrived here? I must confess I was skeptical myself about ever getting the place put to rights, Serena. It is pure folly to imagine paying for the privilege of living in a damp, dilapidated, drafty barn. Why, the chairs and settees were literally rotting on their frames, dear. I can well understand that the duke feels he is in your debt."

"There is still much to be done to restore it to its original charm," Serena admitted, glancing up at a large damp spot on the ceiling of the morning room where they sat enjoying a cup of tea. "For one thing, the house needs a new roof if it is to last through the spring rains."

"That is exactly my point," Miss Higgenbotham cut in. "And surely you do not intend to pay for that yourself, dear."

Serena could not argue with that, and let the matter drop. On their next trip into Sheringham, however, she was curious enough to visit the bank—ostensibly to withdraw a small sum from her own account—and discovered from the manager that the estate had received the sum of one thousand pounds, which the Duke of Wolverton had placed at her discretion.

"One thousand pounds!" she exclaimed to Miss Higgenbotham the moment they climbed back into the carriage. "Does he imagine he is housing a regiment at Clifftop Manor?"

"The duke is doubtless accustomed to providing far greater sums for the upkeep of his principal estate, dear. Besides, he is rumored to have very deep pockets. No doubt this is but a paltry sum to him."

Paltry or not, Serena was determined to keep a strict accounting of every penny she expended on the duke's account, and as a result spent many an afternoon sitting behind the huge walnut desk in the library, tallying the columns of figures in the ledgers she had purchased for that purpose. It pleased her to imagine the self-imposed task as a tenuous link with Hawk.

It was here that Cecily found her one particularly chilly afternoon in mid-March.

"Oh, Serena!" her sister exclaimed, bursting into the room with her usual exuberance. "You will never guess who is sitting downstairs, as large as life, drinking tea with Higgy."

Serena's heart leapt wildly, and she felt herself grow pale. "Do try to act like a lady, Cecily," she said instinctively, shying away from the name that jumped immediately to mind.

"Pooh! I can be ladylike when I want to, Serena. You know that. And this afternoon I shall give you a special demonstration of my airs and graces. There are *three* gentlemen downstairs," she confided in thrilling tones, "And Higgy sent me to fetch you down immediately."

"Three gentlemen?" Serena's heart gave another lurch.

"Yes. Of course, one of them is Lady Babbington's pimply grandson, Nevil, but the other two are neighbors of the Babbingtons—Sir James Lockhart and his nephew Christopher. Sir James is rather old, of course, but Christopher is . . . is so . . ." She seemed to be at a loss for words, and Serena laughed.

"I see your heart has been enthralled again, Cecy," she chided. "You really must learn to be less transparent, dear. Gentlemen feel threatened by the merest hint of pursuit, you know."

"Is that why Hawk ran away to London? Because Melissa made sheep's eyes at him all the time, and threw out the most disgusting lures?"

Serena's amusement faded. "The duke did not *run away,* dear. And I fancy he was more than a match for our totty-headed cousin. He merely had business that required his presence in Town." Surprised at her growing ability to prevaricate, Serena wished that this innocuous explanation were closer to the truth.

Her sister regarded Serena with a look far too knowledge-able for her years.

Not wishing to hear another of Cecily's disturbingly percep-tive remarks about the duke, Serena rose from behind the desk and took her sister's arm. "I presume that Lady Babbington is also present, dear?" she inquired. "What a happy coincidence. I have found that recipe for Mama's rosemary salve her lady-ship wished to try for her stiff joints."

Cecily's lovely face took on a mulish aspect. "I trust you do not intend to sit there all afternoon talking about smelly salves and stiff joints with Lady Babbington while three perfectly eli-gible gentlemen sit around eating all Cook's damson tarts."

"I am sure that other inconsequential topics will occur to me, dear," she answered blandly.

Moments later, Serena found herself encompassed in Lady Babbington's motherly embrace and enduring the nervous salutation of her grandson, Nevil, who was clearly besotted with Cecily but so tongue-tied at the sight of her that he could do little but stammer responses to Serena's greeting. Cecily had been correct in her estimation of Christopher Lockhart, Serena had to admit, watching the excessively handsome young gentleman exert himself in a truly polished bow for her benefit. His blond perfection and languid blue eyes, no less than his excessively modish attire, must surely bewitch all but the most exacting of females.

Serena found him oppressively foppish. Her own taste ran to gray eyes and lean features. Unconsciously comparing the young man's willowy, tightly encased figure in pale blue su-perfine, brilliantly white pantaloons, and tasseled Hessians with the casual elegance of the well-muscled man who haunted her dreams, Serena wrote the younger man off as in-consequential.

She smiled politely at young Lockhart's flowery, insincere compliments, and raised her eyes to examine the third gentle-man, standing quietly before the fire.

She found herself the object of an amused gray stare. Cecily had been mistaken in her description of Sir James Lockhart, but Serena could see why. The baronet—at thirty-five or -six, she guessed—must seem a veritable ancient to a fifteen-year-old. His brown hunting jacket was well-worn but unobtru-sively well cut and hung comfortably on his wide shoulders. He was not as tall as Hawk, and unlike his flashy nephew, his buckskin breeches showed no sign of padding.

As he stepped forward to acknowledge Lady Babbington's

gushing introduction, Serena realized with a start that Sir James had read her evaluation of his nephew in her eyes. Thank goodness it had amused him, she thought, conscious of a faint blush rising to her cheeks.

"I am happy to make your acquaintance, Miss Millbanks," he said soberly. "Lady Babbington has no doubt told you that I am a close neighbor of hers and have been in Scotland for several months attending my brother's sickbed. Happily, he is now recovered, and I can return home, bringing my eldest nephew with me. Christopher has a mind to spend a Season in the Metropolis."

During the conversation that accompanied the passing of teacups and plates of sandwiches, Serena learned that Sir James was not of a mind to accompany his nephew.

"I have no liking for the frivolity that pervades the Metropolis," he confided with a slow smile.

Serena felt a glow of sympathy for this plain-spoken man. "I must agree with you, Sir James, that if one is not drawn to the gambling, the drinking, the gossip, or . . ." She paused, briefly before adding, "or other forms of vice, one is sadly out of place in London."

His gray eyes did not glitter with amusement at her near *faux pas* as Hawk's would have done, but then—she reminded herself regretfully—Sir James was not Hawk.

"You have been to Town, I assume, Miss Millbanks?"

"Briefly during the Little Season, with my aunt, Lady Thornton. But my father was taken from us in November, so we cut short our stay." Serena marveled that her brief but eventful experience of London's pleasures and perils might be rendered in such a bland description. Had it not been for one very disguised duke on a dark terrace, she thought wryly, her taste of London might had been quite as dull as she made it sound.

"I am told that Wolverton was here, too. I am sorry to have missed him."

Something in the baronet's tone when he made this casual remark set off warning bells in Serena's head. Could it be that Lockhart had heard gossip in the village regarding the duke's sojourn at Clifftop Manor? Surely the presence of her Aunt Hester and Miss Higgenbotham, to say nothing of a houseful of servants, had precluded the kind of rumors that might reflect adversely on her reputation? Or perhaps they had underestimated the prudery of rural Norfolk?

Serena felt her temper stir. She would not sit tamely by and endure sly innuendoes from this backwater baronet, would she?

"His Grace left months ago," she said, meeting Sir James's gaze coolly. "Before Christmas actually. My cousin was most put out." She permitted herself a faint smile. "Melissa had the cockeyed notion of parading Hawkhurst about at the New Year's Assembly."

His eyes still did not register amusement. "Ah, that is understandable. It must be no small triumph for a female to parade a duke around by the nose."

Serena stared at him and then burst out laughing. "It seems you know nothing at all about this particular duke, sir," she explained. "Hawkhurst is not the kind of man to be led around by the nose. By anybody," she added emphatically.

Sir James seemed to find nothing amusing in this response either, for his gray eyes remained serious and faintly quizzical. "I assume you must know Wolverton extraordinarily well, Miss Millbanks," he said in his carefully neutral voice.

Serena merely stared at him, biting her tongue to avoid throwing this impertinence back in his face.

After a long moment of enduring her cool stare, Sir James must have realized that he had committed an indiscretion. "I shall look forward to meeting the duke when next he comes into Norfolk," he added with a slight stammer, his color high under his tan.

"I would not count on it, sir," Serena remarked dryly. "As far as I know, His Grace has no intention of returning any time in the near future." Without waiting for his response, she rose and joined Lady Babbington on the settee.

How dared this country rudesby assume anything about her relationship with Hawk?

For the remainder of the visit, Serena carefully maintained her distance from the baronet. Luckily, Lady Babbington was only too happy to dissect her many ailments, and when she found herself discussing her mother's famous salve and her ladyship's stiff joints, Serena could not resist a glance at Cecily, who gave her an exasperated grin.

She was not to escape so easily, however. A week later, the three ladies arrived at the Babbingtons' to keep a dinner engagement only to find Sir James and his flamboyant nephew already installed in the drawing room.

Thanks no doubt to Lady Babbington—whom Serena suspected of wishing to try her hand at matchmaking—she found herself seated next to Sir James at the dinner table, with the unpalatable alternative of his nephew on her left. She noted with some amusement that the baronet made no mention whatsoever of Wolverton, but kept the conversation on neutral subjects, proving himself an able and interesting table companion. Still, Serena could not quite bring herself to forgive his unspoken insinuations about Hawk.

After joining the ladies in the drawing room, Sir James had immediately come across to where Serena was seated at the pianoforte.

"Lady Babbington tells me you are an excellent pianist, Miss Millbanks," he remarked.

"I do play a little," Serena responded with deliberate modesty. "Are you partial to music, Sir James?"

The baronet murmured his assent, but he seemed preoccupied. "I fear I have offended you, Miss Millbanks," he said at length, his deep voice serious. "And I do beg you will forgive me. It was never my intention to do so."

Serena could not doubt his sincerity, and she respected him for the direct way in which he broached the subject. But perversely, she succumbed to the urge to punish the baronet for daring to cast aspersions on Hawk's integrity. "Offended me?" she repeated in feigned astonishment. "Now what makes you imagine that, sir?"

He hesitated, but only for a moment. Then his eyes did light up with amusement, and Serena felt her heart turn over, for the baronet's eyes were as gray as Hawk's, and the twinkle she saw in them reminded her forcibly of the duke's.

But never the same, she mused, lowering her eyes to the keys to hide her thoughts. No man would ever be the same. No one could.

"I do believe Sir James has developed a *tendre* for you, Serena," Miss Higgenbotham remarked as they drove home in the duke's elegant carriage. "Lady Babbington tells me that he is well respected in the region. He has a tidy estate over beyond Weybourne, with over three thousand a year. Takes great pride in his house, they say."

"And why should I be interested in Sir James when I am perfectly comfortable where I am," Serena answered more sharply than the subject warranted.

Cecily glanced at her oddly. "Because you cannot *wish* to

become an ape-leader, Serena." Her sister's innate honesty was as irrefutable as her logic. "I most certainly do not intend to. It is rather a pity that Christopher Lockhart has no title, but I would certainly consider him seriously should he make me an offer."

Serena glared angrily at her little sister. "You are far too young to be thinking of marriage yet, Cecily, so I suggest you put that painted popinjay out of your head."

"Well, one of us must start to think of it," Cecily retorted. "We cannot live at Clifftop Manor forever. What if Hawk discovers he has an ancient relic in need of a roof over her head. Where do you suppose he would send her if not here, as far away as possible?"

Much as her heart rejected the notion of another man, Serena had to acknowledge the truth in her sister's words. She looked appealingly at their governess, but Miss Higgenbotham only shook her head.

"Cecily is quite right, my dear. There is no denying the precariousness of your position. And one should not look a gift horse in the mouth," she added ominously.

"Of course, Sir James cannot hold a candle to Hawk," Cecily added with scathing honesty. "But much as I adore Hawk, he is more like a brother than a prospective suitor. Would you not agree, Serena? Besides," she continued without waiting for a response, "he is quite above our touch. Now Sir James is much more your style, Serena. In fact, he quite reminds me of Papa."

Serena took these disconcerting remarks to bed with her that night, and as a result did not sleep a wink until the gray dawn poked its dim fingers through a crack in the curtains.

If she had needed a final, devastating blow to any fantasies she had harbored about the absent duke, Cecily's honesty had demolished them entirely.

CHAPTER FOURTEEN

The Cautious Suitor

By the middle of April, it was definitely established among the local gossips that the unassailable bachelor, Sir James Lockhart, was paying court to Miss Serena Millbanks. There was no doubt in anybody's mind, Miss Higgenbotham reported at the breakfast table one morning.

"But I have it upon the highest authority, love," the governess insisted in response to Serena's quizzical stare. "Only yesterday, Mrs. Crompton accosted me at the Sheringham Library to discover which day you had set aside for the nuptials."

"I trust you informed that old busybody that my mythical nuptials are none of her concern."

Miss Higgenbotham's plain face brightened perceptibly. "Mythical nuptials? Then you are decided to accept Sir James, love?"

Serena frowned. "I believe the issue of nuptials is premature, Higgy. Sir James has yet to show any signs of wishing to embark on the perilous seas of matrimony." She knew this to be patently untrue, but Serena felt an odd reluctance to allow herself to be carried along by the tide of public opinion.

"That is arrant nonsense, dear, and well you know it," the governess exclaimed in a rare show of annoyance. "The man is practically living in your pocket, as it is, Serena. What other reason would he have for haunting Clifftop Manor, can you tell me?"

"Perhaps he has become addicted to Cook's damson tarts," Serena offered facetiously.

This was not an argument she could expect to win, of course. Protest as she might, it was plain as a pikestaff that Sir James Lockhart had made her the object of his particular attentions. He had been exceptionally discreet about it, she had to admit, but there could be no denying the partiality he displayed for her company whenever they met. And meet they did, with alarming frequency. Serena could count on running into him at every musicale, card party, soirée, or dinner engagement she attended, and this in itself gave rise to considerable speculation, for Sir James had garnered, over the years, the reputation of a man not given to excessive sociability.

"Who is addicted to Cook's tarts?" Cecily wanted to know. She had that instant entered the breakfast room with her usual impetuosity, and now flung herself down in a chair in a hoydenish manner that caused Miss Higgenbotham to utter an exclamation of protest.

"Your sister was referring to Sir James, dear," the governess explained. "But let me remind you that—"

"Oh, Higgy, do not pinch at me so early in the morning. Especially when I have such important news to impart." Cecily glanced around the table to make sure she had everyone's attention.

"I have been perusing the *Morning Post,*" she announced in suppressed excitement, as she waved the newspaper at her sister, "and you will never guess what Hawk has been up to."

Serena's heart grew cold. She herself had occasionally scanned the social pages of the newspapers sent regularly by the thoughtful Mr. Steele, but as time passed with no word from Hawk—at least no direct word, for his secretary's missives arrived with predictable regularity—Serena had had to desist. The mere mention of the duke's name had caused her such agitation of the nerves that she resigned herself to getting the London news through Miss Higgenbotham, who read the *Post* zealously.

It now appeared that her little sister read it, too.

"Oh, do tell!" Miss Higgenbotham's curls bobbed excitedly. Serena gritted her teeth and waited for the ax to fall.

"It appears that any day now we shall have to wish him happy," Cecily announced gleefully. "The rogue is about to get himself leg-shackled to a Lady Maria Shelby, eldest daughter of the Earl and Countess of Westhaven," she read directly from the column.

Serena was glad she was sitting down. Her whole world appeared to tip crazily, and she felt decidedly unwell. If her companions did not change the subject instantly, she feared she would dissolve into tears.

"If you do not bring Sir James up to scratch very soon, Serena," her heartless sister continued with blithe disregard for Serena's distress, "Hawk will beat you to the altar."

This was more than Serena could endure. With a choked excuse, she rose precipitously and swept out of the room, her eyes filming with tears and her heart in tatters.

A turn about the rose garden helped to restore her equanimity, but Serena had little hope of regaining her usual poise. Only time would heal the rude buffeting her emotions had suffered at the news of Hawk's imminent betrothal. The discovery—from an exhaustive perusal of the *Morning Post,* which she had carried with her into the rose arbor—that he was not yet actually betrothed to Lady Maria had done little to assuage her distress. It would only be a matter of time, she concluded—judging from the glowing description of the duke's chosen lady—before the irrevocable announcement would appear in print. And then her foolish fantasies would be truly over.

But not her life. There was always Sir James, she reminded herself resolutely. But the sight of the baronet making his way across the terrace in her direction a short time later did little to restore her spirits.

She was able to dredge up only the vestige of a smile for him when he greeted her with his customary formality. His gray eyes regarded her with concern, and Serena saw them turn somber as he caught sight of the fateful newspaper lying abandoned on one of the stone benches.

"I see you have been catching up on the London news," he remarked in his neutral voice, when Serena could think of nothing to say. "Lady Babbington called my attention to the announcement of Wolverton's betrothal." He paused, but Serena seemed to have lost the use of her tongue.

"I expect you, too, have seen it, Miss Millbanks."

"Yes." Her voice was little more than a whisper.

Had he come to Clifftop Manor expressly to talk about Hawk's betrothal? she wondered. Sir James had not mentioned the duke since their first encounter, when Serena had snubbed him for his impertinence. Did he now intend to plague her with more questions regarding her association with Hawk? She fervently hoped not.

"I trust we can all wish the duke well in his choice of a bride," he said tentatively, his voice still neutral.

Serena could find nothing to say to this.

There was a considerable pause, during which Sir James cleared his throat several times. Abruptly it dawned on Serena that perhaps the baronet was finally preparing to make his formal declaration. The time could not be more inappropriate, she thought, wildly casting about in her mind for words to put him off. She was not ready for this. Her heart was not prepared to listen, much as she knew she eventually would, to words of love from any other man.

She glanced up at him. Her distress must have been evident, for all he said was, "Do *you* wish him well, Miss Millbanks?"

Relieved that a declaration had not been forthcoming, Serena answered without thinking. "I doubt that what I wish matters one way or the other, sir."

"It matters to me, Serena," Sir James said instantly, taking both her hands in his. "It matters very much indeed. But you must know that, my dear."

It might have been his use of her name, Serena thought afterward, or it may have been the endearment—an endearment she had heard so often from Hawk's lips—but whatever it was, it brought sudden dampness to her eyes. Before she could stop them, the tears were running freely down her cheeks, and Sir James was staring at her, a look of horror on his face.

"My dear Miss Millbanks," he murmured, retreating into the safety of formality, "I did not mean to discompose you." He glanced wildly about him. "Here," he snatched his handkerchief from his pocket and held it awkwardly out to her.

Had Sir James been the duke, her traitorous heart whispered, she would be in his embrace by now. Hawk's arms would be around her, her wet face buried in his snowy cravat, his hand gentling her with tender concern. His lips might even brush her hair, and his voice most certainly would have been telling her not to be a silly goose. And her tears would have turned to watery smiles under the warmth of his gray eyes.

But Sir James was not Hawk, her reason pointed out prosaically. So Serena took the baronet's proffered handkerchief and dried her own eyes, wondering if he had even the faintest inkling of the opportunity he had lost of taking what he apparently wished for.

Hawk would never have missed it.

"I beg you will forgive this unseemly outburst, Sir James," she stammered, handing back the damp kerchief. "I am not feeling quite the thing today."

And instead of the warm amusement she would have expected in Hawk's eyes, Serena saw only acute embarrassment in the baronet's as he made his excuses and strode back to the house.

Sir James took himself entirely too seriously, Serena mused as she took another turn round the rose arbor, which still showed more promise than actual blossoms this early in the season.

She would have to cultivate a seriousness of mind that was foreign to her if she meant to accept the baronet's offer.

Not *if*, she corrected herself. *When* she accepted his offer.

If indeed she did, her heart insisted perversely.

"Did I not know differently, my dear Serena," Lady Babbington remarked slyly two weeks later as the ladies sat drinking tea in the morning room of Clifftop Manor, "I would be led to believe that you had never attended a ball before." She shot an amused glance at her hostess and helped herself to yet another slice of seed cake.

"Pooh!" exclaimed Cecily. "My sister has attended hundreds of balls in London, my lady. Far grander than this one promises to be, too."

"That is a slight exaggeration, Cecy," Serena said mildly. "Aunt Hester escorted us to a few, of course, but we spent most of our time at more sedate gatherings, like musicales."

But even at sedate affairs she had not been safe from Hawk, she thought, remembering his unprecedented appearance, together with that rake Monroyal, at Mrs. Easton's musicale, where they had tricked her into that reckless wager. And then Hawk had taken her out to Winsor to meet his great-aunt, Lady Lexington, who had treated her quite as though she belonged to their exalted set. Which of course she did not, Serena reminded herself quickly. There was no place for Miss Millbanks, a plain and penniless baronet's daughter, among the wealthy, titled members of the *ton* who flocked around the Duke of Wolverton.

But when he was hurt, he had called for her. She smiled to herself at the memory of that odious Captain Waters and the look on his face when she had cracked his nose for him. And Hawk had started a mill with the captain, even if he had received a bloody nose for his pains. Because he had been foxed again. But he had sent for her. *Demanded* her attendance at his bedside to soothe his hurt.

None of his fine friends had been able to do that.

"You are wool-gathering again, Serena." Miss Higgenbotham's voice cut into these pleasant memories and jerked

Serena back to reality. "You were not listening to Lady Babbington's suggestion about your gown, dear."

"Oh, indeed, I was," Serena lied quickly, casting a smile at her rotund guest, whose plump fingers reached eagerly for another damson tart. "I agree wholeheartedly with her ladyship," she added rashly, hoping the viscountess had suggested something she would be expected to second.

"You *do?*" Cecily's astonishment told Serena that she may have committed an error.

"What do you think, Higgy?" she countered, turning to the elder lady for support.

Miss Higgenbotham smiled delightedly. "I am glad to see you are showing such good sense, dear. And I certainly agree with her ladyship that it is high time you put off your blacks, Serena. It is six months now since poor Sir Henry was stricken, and I see no harm at all in getting on with your life. A lilac or deep violet silk, trimmed discreetly with cream lace, would be just the thing, I believe. Do you not agree, my lady?"

Lilac silk? Serena shuddered at the thought. She had worn her new lilac silk gown that first time she had encountered Hawk at Lady Berkford's ball. Serena had known that the style was a little out of fashion, but she had not been prepared to discover that her country modiste had turned her out to look more like a dowd than a girl attending her first Season.

"Violet sounds nice," she said quickly. "And not silk, Higgy. I think something in satin would be more suitable, if we can find it here in Sheringham. Perhaps with a narrow skirt and a single flounce at the hem."

"And may I have a new pink muslin, Serena?" her sister begged, her blue eyes huge with longing. "Sally Caldwell is to have one made up especially for the ball. Do say I may . . ."

"In white, my dear," Lady Babbington interrupted with awful finality. "White is *de rigueur* for a young miss. But your sister should take particular care with her gown. Only think, my dear Serena. This is a heaven-sent opportunity to flush Sir James out into the open. The time for all his coyness is long past. You must dazzle him into making his declaration during the ball, dear."

"I must?"

Serena felt uncomfortable with the direction Lady Babbington's remarks had taken. Had it been a mistake to listen to the matchmaking viscountess's proposal for a small dinner party at Clifftop Manor? Or to allow her to lend her name and support to the event? That small dinner had since grown to include thirty guests, and dancing had been added as an enticement to the younger crowd. Now it appeared that the after-dinner dancing had become a ball to rival any London affair, and an orchestra had been engaged in Norwich—Serena had discovered quite by accident—to supplement the pianoforte and harp originally planned.

And now she was expected to rig herself out in all her finery to entrap poor Sir James. What had started out as a simple dinner party among friends was turning into a circus before her eyes, and Sir James was to be the performing bear, teased and tricked into taking a step for which he might not yet be entirely ready.

Serena experienced a flash of panic. Was she herself prepared for that irrevocable step? she wondered. Or would she prefer to spend her remaining years pining for a man she could not have, and who assuredly did not want her? Faced with that blunt alternative, Serena saw that Fate had left her little choice. What practical female—and Serena had always prided herself on her resourcefulness—would hesitate to accept a perfectly suitable match with a man of admirable qualities who appeared to hold her in high regard?

If Sir James was indeed poised—as everyone seemed to agree he was—on the brink of a declaration, merely awaiting, in his unhurried, cautious manner, for a clear sign that she welcomed his offer, then why was she dithering like a silly chit at the prospect of her first kiss? Serena knew well enough what it would take to push him over the brink. Little as she liked to flirt, she knew precisely the sign Sir James was waiting for.

All that stood between her and wedded bliss, Serena reasoned the evening of the momentous event, as she made her way downstairs with Miss Higgenbotham, was the determination to take that step. And tonight she would do so. There was no point in waiting any longer, as Cecily had pointed out with unthinking callousness only minutes before, when she had come to show off her new white muslin gown.

"And Hawk will want to know the wedding date, of course," she had announced out of the blue, sending Serena's heart on one of its jerky leaps into her throat.

Serena had gaped at her sister in disbelief. "I thought I told you not to pester the duke with your absurd starts, Cecily. And I forbid you to mention anything about Sir James to Hawk."

"I already have," her unrepentant sister had calmly informed her.

Serena took a deep breath. "What did you say?"

"That you are about to make a most suitable match with a rather stuffy baronet with a respectable income."

Well, her little sister had the right of it, Serena had to admit as she entered the drawing room with Miss Higgenbotham, who was attired in her new dove-gray silk, to await their dinner guests.

Lady Babbington and her grandson were already there, and Nevil caused Serena a pang of sympathy when he lapsed into stammering admiration at the sight of Cecily in her new finery.

Sir James did not stammer when he arrived minutes later with his peacock of a nephew in tow, but he wasted no time in coming across the room to take both Serena's hands in his and raise them to his lips for a warmer greeting than the formal salute he normally bestowed upon her.

"My dear Miss Millbanks," he murmured, his voice unusually husky, "you are in magnificent looks tonight. I am quite speechless with admiration."

Conscious that everyone's eyes were upon them, Serena found herself blushing. "You are a great tease, Sir James," she said lightly, smiling up into his eyes.

What she saw there made her start and quickly lower her lashes. The baronet was most assuredly primed to burn his bridges behind him tonight, and Serena suddenly knew that she would have no difficulty at all in bringing him up to scratch during the course of the evening. An innocent remark on the stifling heat of the ballroom, and surely he would take her out onto the terrace. And there he would kiss her. Serena hoped he would kiss her. She needed to be kissed by a man who loved her. A man who could make her forget those other kisses from a man who did not. The heated glance in Sir James's gray eyes had given her a jolt, conjuring up as it did even warmer glances in those other eyes she had vowed to put behind her.

After tonight she could put Hawk out of her mind for good. Sir James would doubtless take care of that. He might not invade her bedchamber at midnight and ravish her as Hawk had almost done, but tonight she had—for the first time—glimpsed passion in his eyes. After they were married—and suddenly Serena found herself reconciled to the notion of marriage to

Sir James—he would not leave her to languish alone in her cold bed.

With a flash of insight, Serena felt the future settle around her with a comforting certainty, stretching out into the years to come with familiar monotony. There would be no drastic ups and downs with Sir James, no drunken brawls, no reckless gambles, no kisses on the King's highway in plain view of every passerby. And no bloody noses to tend, she thought with a vague regret.

She would put all these wild things behind her tonight, she promised herself. When she gave Sir James the answer he wanted.

An answer she herself wanted, too, did she not?

"The devil fly away with the skitter-brained widgeon!"

Hawkhurst threw down the missive he had been reading, crossed and recrossed in a childish scrawl, and scowled at the only other occupant of the library, sprawled elegantly in a leather fauteuil.

"The Incomparable Maria run away with the groom, has she? Better now than after you are married at any rate, old man."

Hawk glared at his friend and waved dismissively. "I wish she would," he growled. "That chit is getting to be a downright nuisance. Last night at the Mansfields' she had the temerity to confide that her dearest wish is to have a June wedding. And I am not even close to thinking of weddings myself." He paused, then added in a harsh undertone, "At least not to Lady Maria Shelby."

The Marquess of Monroyal laughed. "Then may I suggest that you desist from sitting in her pocket, Hawk. You provide fodder for the tattleboxes and are in grave danger of finding yourself riveted to the silly chit."

"If you were any kind of a friend, Robert, you would throw yourself into the breach. Dazzle the lady with a light flirtation—"

"Nothing would induce me to take such a rash step," the marquess interrupted instantly. "Even for you, old man. Besides, it would look mighty odd if I started dangling after the Shelby chit. Everyone knows I cannot abide virgins. Not enough return for the effort, I always say."

Hawk paused at Monroyal's careless words, his mind slipping back to his last encounter with a virgin. There had been no effort at all on his part, he remembered with a pang of regret. And the returns had promised to be beyond anything he had ever experienced with a woman. Her violet eyes had promised passion enough for any man's dreams, and she had also offered comfort, and safety, and an understanding rare in a woman.

And she had spoken of love.

Aside from the glib protestations of that tarnished emotion from his numerous paramours, which he discounted as lip service to the rites of Eros, Hawk had little experience with the tenderer side of his nature. The intense rush of emotion that overrode any thought of lust at the sight of Serena's tears had come as a surprise to him. He refused to put a name to it, choosing to see it as gentlemanly deference to her obvious innocence. But the memory of it had followed him in his headlong escape from Norfolk, stayed with him during his months at Wolverton Abbey, and after a mere week back in Town, had turned him into a near recluse.

He picked up Cecily's almost illegible letter and poured over it again. Her garbled description of an aging baronet, a courtship that had set the countryside on its ears, an impending offer of marriage, and an upcoming ball at which the happy event would be announced and celebrated had jolted Hawk out of his lethargy.

The chit's congratulations on his own forthcoming marriage had also stunned him. He had no intention of offering for Lady Maria Shelby. That had become abundantly clear to him two days into the lady's extended visit to Wolverton Abbey during the Christmas season with her parents. He had no fault to find with either her looks or pedigree. Lady Maria was startlingly beautiful, and he had been momentarily blinded by the glitter of it. However, aside from a distressing inability to hang two words together without tittering, and an annoying habit of continually fluttering her long lashes at him, Lady Maria never looked at him directly.

She was—as the duchess pointed out to him whenever she could catch him alone—docile, obedient, impeccably well-bred, and beautiful. What more could a man of rank and fortune wish for in a wife? Hawk might have told his mother that he wanted warmth and passion in *his* wife. He wanted a lively female who would not hesitate to stand up to him if she thought he was wrong. A female who could talk to him intelligently without flaunting her wiles. A female who would look at him with violet eyes he could drown in.

In short, a female his mother would never countenance.

As this state of affairs became increasingly apparent to him, Hawk found himself on the horns of dilemma. His mother's choice of bride was unacceptable to him; the woman he wanted—and by mid-April Hawk had allowed himself to admit that he wanted Serena Millbanks—was not the kind of female a duke should choose to wed.

And now this disturbing letter from Norfolk.

"The devil take it," he repeated in suppressed fury. Cecily's account of Serena's suitor had thrown him against the ropes. He would have to leave at first light if he was to put a stop to this ridiculous affair, he thought, folding the letter and putting it in his pocket. But there was something he must do first.

"Sorry to disrupt your evening, Robert, but I am riding out to Winsor," he said abruptly, ringing for the butler.

"Winsor? At this time of night?" The marquess's expression was comical.

"Aunt Bess keeps late hours. And I must see her before I leave Town."

"Leave Town?" Monroyal repeated. "You have not been here a sennight and you must needs rush off? Cannot this wait until tomorrow, old chap? We are promised to the Carringtons' soirée tonight."

"John will send them our regrets," Hawk murmured, his mind already wrestling with the step he was about to take. "You *are* coming, I suppose? I shall be glad of the company when I get to Weybourne."

"Weybourne? Oh, the divine Miss Millbanks, I take it."

Hawk felt his friend's speculative gaze on him while he gave instructions to his butler to have their horses brought round, and to John Steele to cancel all his appointments in London.

"All of them, Your Grace?"

"Yes," Hawk replied shortly. "I am going into Norfolk, and I may go straight back to the Abbey when I have . . ." He paused, wondering how much he should confide in his secretary. "As soon as I have wrung a certain baronet's scrawny neck."

"Very well, Your Grace," Steele responded, quite as though his employer had not sounded ready for Bedlam.

Such was the efficiency of the ducal household that a quarter of an hour later, the two gentlemen were on their way, riding through the cool, moonlit night as though pursued by demons.

Lady Lexington received them close to midnight without so much as a raised eyebrow, and after reading Cecily's letter, gave Hawk her blessing.

"The Shelby chit may go hang, my dear Hawk," she remarked in her blunt fashion. "Sounds like a vaporish kind of female to me. Too much like your mother, dear. And one of those simpering milk and water misses in the family is quite enough, thank you."

She glared at the marquess, who had let out a crack of cynical laughter.

"Follow your heart, Hawk, and never look back," she advised. "Would you not agree, Monroyal?" she inquired pointedly of the amused marquess.

"I have no heart, my dear lady, so I would not hazard to go on a fool's errand."

"You will play the cynic once too often, Robert," she warned. "When your time comes, I wager you will change your tune, lad."

"That is one wager I would be sure to win, my lady," he drawled. "But I never wager on a sure thing. Takes all the fun out of it."

As he prepared for bed that night, Hawk wished he might be as sure about his own future. If he traveled all the way into Norfolk, he would not only burn his bridges behind him, but risk making a complete cake of himself. For an unpalatable thought came unbidden into his mind.

What would he do for the rest of his life if his Serena was already betrothed to her dull baronet by the time he arrived?

CHAPTER FIFTEEN

Facing the Truth

The ballroom at Clifftop Manor was neither large nor very grand, but the guests did not appear to notice. The orchestra engaged by Lady Babbington had proved to be a huge success, and the lively country dance presently in progress had seduced even plump Mrs. Caldwell into cavorting about the dance floor with blithe disregard for decorum.

Serena smiled. How unlike London, where any show of enthusiasm was frowned upon, and where aging matrons would never dream of exposing themselves to ridicule by daring to join in the fun.

"You have outdone yourself tonight, Miss Millbanks." The baronet's voice cut into Serena's ruminations, and she turned to smile up at him. "Allow me to congratulate you on the success of the ball."

"Such congratulations are sadly misplaced, sir," she murmured. "Lady Babbington and Miss Higgenbotham deserve all the credit, let me assure you."

"You are far too modest, my dear. But then, I admire modesty in a female," he added a little self-consciously.

Serena looked away, panic rising in her heart. He admired her modesty? Little did the poor man guess that Serena Millbanks was anything but modest. No modest female would have entertained a gentleman in her bedchamber in the middle of the night, would she? The picture of Hawk lying beside her on the bed came back with such force that Serena could almost feel the heat of his body pressing against hers, his lips warm between her breasts, his hands . . . Dear Lord, his hands! Serena closed her eyes and took a deep, steadying breath.

"Are you feeling unwell, Miss Millbanks?"

The solicitous note in Sir James's voice brought on a rush of guilt, and she opened her eyes. "Oh, not at all," she assured him, angry at her inability to keep the memory of Hawk out of her dealings with her cautious suitor.

Would it always be thus? she wondered. It was uncanny how thoughts of the duke had intruded at the very moment the orchestra was preparing to play a waltz. She had danced several waltzes with Hawk, and in a moment of intoxication he had declared that all her waltzes belonged to him. Well, tonight she would prove him wrong. She would dance this waltz with Sir James, and afterward, she must contrive—as the romantical Lady Babbington had suggested—to get the baronet alone on the terrace.

The rest would be up to him, she vowed.

The musicians settled into the sensuous sway of the waltz, and Serena placed her hand in the baronet's. The touch of his hand on her waist only increased her nervousness. Perhaps when he kissed her, all these silly doubts would vanish, she thought, forcing herself to listen to Sir James's monologue on the improvements he had introduced into his breeding program that spring.

And then, all too soon for Serena's peace of mind, the music came to a close, and she found herself cold with apprehension rather than overheated with the exertions of the dance. She would catch her death of cold if she ventured out on the terrace in that condition, she thought hysterically, and for a moment the silk lilac fan hung motionless on her wrist. From across the room, she caught Miss Higgenbotham's encouraging glance and with a faint smile on her lips, Serena deliberately raised the fan to her face.

Sir James never did kiss her on the terrace as Lady Babbington had predicted. They had barely reached the open glass doors, when a flustered footman darted across the room with the startling news that two gentlemen were asking for Miss Millbanks downstairs.

Serena gaped in surprise. "Two gentlemen? Why did Billings not show them up?"

"They have but this instant arrived from London, miss."

Serena's heart gave an uncomfortable lurch. "Did you get their names, Thomas?"

"One of them is the Duke of Wolverton, miss," the footman answered in an awed voice. "Mr. Billings has put them in the library."

Afraid to look at Sir James, Serena glanced about the dance floor, but her co-hostess was nowhere in sight.

"Have you informed her ladyship?" she demanded. After sending the footman to find Lady Babbington and apprise her of the unexpected arrival of the master of Clifftop Manor, Serena turned to the baronet.

She had not expected him to be overjoyed at Hawkhurst's sudden reappearance in Norfolk, but was unprepared for the flat hostility in Sir James's eyes.

"If you will excuse me, sir," she murmured, conscious of the breathlessness in her voice. Sir James bowed wordlessly, and as Serena made her way toward the door, she sensed his cool stare boring into her back.

Had Hawk deliberately set out to ruin her life again? she wondered, sweeping down the curving staircase to the hall below. Or was this the intervention of the Fates, determined to make an ape-leader out of her at all costs?

Hawk had vowed not to betray his eagerness to see her, but it was all he could do to remain staring into the crackling fire when he heard the library door open. It was the sharp intake of breath from the marquess that caused him to forget his resolution. He swung round and stared, and for a fleeting moment, he did not recognize the delicately beautiful creature standing in the threshold. Then he saw the violet eyes widen, and instinctively he knew that, in spite of her outward poise, Serena was apprehensive. And possibly angry.

He suppressed the urge to take her in his arms.

The marquess broke the awkward silence with his usual polish. "My dear Miss Millbanks—or may I call you Serena? Behold me quite prostrate with admiration. Here we are, tongue-tied like two grubby schoolboys at the sight of an angel."

"How absurd you are," she retorted, amusement replacing the alarm in her eyes. Her gaze flickered for a moment in his direction. "Welcome, Your Grace," she said coolly, and made a brief curtsy before returning her attention to the marquess.

Monroyal advanced and made an elaborate show of raising first one, then the other hand to his lips. Hawk wished he had half the rogue's address.

"We find you in astonishing looks, my dear," the marquess murmured, and Hawk winced at the seductive nuance in his friend's voice.

Serena laughed outright. "I astonish you, my lord? How quaint. Is that intended as a compliment I wonder?"

"A most heartfelt compliment, I assure you, my dear Serena. I have never seen you look quite so ravishing."

"I insist that you stop this silliness instantly, my lord, and tell me what brings you both into Norfolk."

"Merely one of Hawk's odd starts, my dear." The marquess flicked an imaginary speck of lint from his sleeve. When he raised his eyes, he was grinning wickedly. "We heard about your ball, Serena, and nothing would do for Hawk but to ride up here *vent-à-terre* to claim a dance with you. Preferably a waltz, of course. Unfortunately, our portmanteaux are at least an hour behind us, so I fear it was a fool's errand after all."

The ease with which Robert kept up this stream of idle chatter amazed Hawk, but he was grateful for the chance to gather his thoughts. The sight of this elegant, satin-clad creature had momentarily deprived him of speech. Her auburn hair, caught in an artful knot of curls high on her head, shimmered in the candlelight, and the fashionably revealing gown gave her slim figure an elegance Hawk had never noticed before.

Only when she smiled—as she was doing now, with a candid spontaneity that wrenched at his heart—did this extraordinary female resemble the Serena he remembered. But that glorious smile was directed at Monroyal, for she had barely greeted Hawk, and then with a formality that was as foreign to him as the gown she wore. As he listened to the light repartee the rakish marquess exchanged with Serena, Hawk suddenly wished he had not invited Robert to accompany him on his wild ride into Norfolk.

"Do you really take me for such a flat as to believe that Banbury tale?" she demanded, her violet eyes dark with amusement. "I do believe you are both foxed, my lord. How could you possibly have heard about the ball?"

"It appears that your sister is a correspondent of no small note, my dear. She has revealed all," the marquess murmured dryly.

Serena's smile slipped, and she glanced at him nervously. So, Hawk thought with a sinking feeling, his lady had a guilty conscience. Could it be that the obscure baronet had stolen a march on him after all?

"I distinctly forbade Cecily to plague you, my lord," she murmured, a delightful blush tingeing her cheeks. "But she appears to labor under the misapprehension that you would wish to know just how many kittens Tibatha had in January, and how Jollyboy got into the hen house and smashed all the eggs, and about the new trick Rufus has learned, and how the second upstairs maid fell and broke her leg during the Christmas sea-

son, and, well," the rush of words faltered briefly, "all the
other minor events that have occurred since you left. I shall
see that she does not—"

"Other minor events?" Hawk drawled, abruptly regaining
the power of speech. "Such as her sister's secret betrothal to
an ancient baronet, I suppose you mean?"

No sooner had he spoken than Hawk wanted to recall the
words. Serena's face abruptly lost its delightful color, and her
eyes became wary. Hawk was aware that the marquess was
observing him closely, an odd smile on his handsome face.

"Wrong on both counts, my lord," she replied quietly.
"There is nothing secret about it at all, and Sir James can
hardly be called ancient. I do not think that Cecily could have
said so."

"So, it is true, then?" Hawk growled, fully aware that he
was behaving boorishly. Robert would doubtless have some
scathing remarks to make after this painful scene was over, but
Hawk was too angry to care.

"Is *what* true, my lord?"

Hawk's lips thinned dangerously, and he felt suddenly
empty. The wicked minx was taunting him, he realized, watching the dark pupils dilate with what could only be amusement.

"Are you or are you not betrothed?"

Hawk writhed inwardly at the slow smile that softened her
face, and braced himself for the worst.

"Not exactly," she said at last, almost reluctantly, he
thought. Hawk drew a deep breath. All was not lost then. The
man must be a regular slow-top not to have made his move by
now.

"And what do you mean by that, Miss Millbanks? A yes or
a no?"

The marquess lifted a perfectly manicured hand in a lazy
gesture of protest, displaying a rich profusion of lace at his
wrist. "Hawk, old man," he drawled in his seductive voice,
"do not fly into a passion over something which should be perfectly obvious to the veriest dolt. No doubt Serena means exactly what she said. She is not yet betrothed to her mysterious
baronet." He turned to the lady with a dazzling smile. "When
may we expect the happy announcement, my dear?"

Hawk saw Serena go rigid. "Sir James is not at all mysterious, my lord, merely cautious," she snapped. "And furthermore, I resent being quizzed about my private—"

"Cautious?" Hawk was unable to suppress a crack of cynical laughter. "My God, woman, have you run mad? How can you possibly contemplate throwing yourself away on——?"

His protest was cut short by a rap on the door, followed immediately by the entrance of Billings, who looked woodenly at Hawk.

"Pardon me, Your Grace," he said stiffly, "but Sir James Lockhart is about to take his leave and is asking for Miss Millbanks."

"Oh, he is, is he?" Hawk exploded. "Tell the esteemed Sir James that he may go and soak his head——"

"My lord!" Serena interrupted sharply. "I shall be along directly, Billings," she added, glancing at the butler, whose eyes had started out of his head.

"And as for *you*, sir," she snapped, her face white with fury, "if you think to cause a vulgar brawl in my house, I shall have to insist that you leave."

"*Your* house? I was under the impression that it was *my* house, my dear Serena," Hawk remarked softly, watching with small satisfaction the confusion his words brought to her eyes.

"Then *I* shall leave, sir," she stormed at him, sounding more like the Serena he knew and loved every minute.

Hawk smiled. "Not until you make your Sir James known to us, I trust, my dear," he drawled, advancing toward the door. "Come, my love. Your cautious lover awaits you. I should not keep him waiting if I were you," he added with a black look that belied the lightness of his words. "The poor fellow might bolt for the hills."

Serena made an uncomplimentary sound somewhere between a snort and a sniff and swept out of the room.

"Easy lad," the marquess murmured as the two men followed the stiff little figure down the hall. "You have made the lass as mad as fire. And you know what Serena is, Hawk. She will marry the baronet just to spite you if you do not have a care. Is that what you wish?"

"Of course it is not what I wish, you lackwit," Hawk snarled, well aware that his friend was right but unable to control his caustic outbursts. "And you may be sure that she will not belong to anyone but *me*," he added in a vicious undertone.

"Ah!" The marquess raised one eyebrow in mock astonishment. "So that is how the wind lies, is it? You are courting disaster, lad. This is not a female to trifle with, let me tell you. A monkey says she will not accept a *carte blanche*, Hawk. What do you say?"

"I have no intention of insulting Serena with such an offer, Robert. And I find your wager in poor taste."

The marquess merely smiled. "After that interesting display of jealousy, I wager she will not have you under any conditions. A monkey perhaps?"

"Oh, yes she will," Hawk retorted, as much to convince himself as to contradict Monroyal. But the sight of the gentleman waiting in the front hall sent an ominous chill down his spine.

The well-dressed, ruggedly handsome gentleman who took Serena's hands in his and smiled down at her was nothing like the country rudesby Hawk had conjured up in his mind. Surely this was not the ancient suitor Cecily had described in her letter? he mused. Sir James was definitely not ancient, and Hawk winced at the sweetness of the smile his Serena lavished on the baronet. For who else could this be but the cautious suitor?

He should have known that Serena would not be tempted by any country bumpkin, and the ugly warning assailed him that in Sir James Lockhart, he had some serious competition for the lady's affections.

An even worse realization followed closely on the heels of the first. Knowing what he did of Serena, could he bring himself to deny that the baronet might well be the ideal husband for a female as unpretentious and wholesome as Miss Millbanks.

Far more suitable than the rakehell Duke of Wolverton could ever hope to be, Hawk told himself with a sinking sensation in the pit of his stomach.

Serena awoke listless and heavy-eyed the morning following the ball. She had spent many sleepless hours speculating on Hawk's unexpected presence in Norfolk, but no reasonable explanation had presented itself. Monroyal's glib explanation that Hawk had taken it into his head to claim a waltz with her could only be another of the marquess's absurd jests. Serena dismissed it immediately, although she had for the briefest moment basked in the highly unlikely probability that it just might be true. Hawk was certainly capable of irrational starts when the mood struck him. Or when he was seriously castaway, she mused, remembering several such instances. But neither gentlemen had shown signs of being disguised last night.

Whatever the major's reason for invading the tranquility of

her life at Clifftop Manor, Serena thought as she sipped her hot chocolate later that morning, Hawk had seemed seriously bent out of shape at the prospect of her impending nuptials to Sir James Lockhart. The reason why this event should concern him, Serena dared not dwell on at any length. Her heart was only too willing to believe that, in a secret part of his being, Hawk could not give her up to another man; but her practical side rejected this notion as maudlin sentimentality. Had the wretch not had his chance last December? she reminded herself prosaically. He might have had not only her heart, but her body and soul as well that night. And what had he done? He had run away, she reminded herself with painful honesty. Run away rather than face an entanglement with a country miss with no breeding to speak of.

The chocolate suddenly tasted bitter in her mouth, and she put it down. The memory of that precious yet disastrous night in Hawk's arms still caused her too much pain, and Serena resolutely pushed it aside. More to the point, she must face the future and undo the harm the major's sudden reappearance had provoked in her plans to become Lady Lockhart.

The thought of Sir James made her heart sink.

The baronet had come so close to making his declaration last night. Had the major arrived a mere fifteen minutes later, she might have been able to tell him that yes, she was betrothed to Sir James, and that the sooner he took himself back to London the happier she would be. She might have faced Hawk with Sir James's kiss still warm on her lips and informed him that he would have to find another steward for Clifftop Manor, for she would soon be removing to her own establishment with her new husband.

But Sir James had not made his declaration.

And her foolish heart had jumped with unmistakable joy at the sight of the duke, bringing back a flood of memories and impossible dreams she had tried so hard to bury under her practical plans for the future.

With her usual honesty, Serena forced herself to face the possibility that those plans might well be moot. If Sir James's expression of hostility when he learned of Hawk's arrival were any indication, he might well wash his hands of her altogether. He had left before the ball had ended last night, and his parting had been stiff and more than usually formal.

Perhaps she would get no declaration from the baronet after all.

This realization, which should have caused a female on the point of receiving an offer of marriage to dissolve into a fit of the vapors, left Serena strangely relieved. It was not as though she had actually set her sights on Sir James or even given him much encouragement. He had not been the choice of her heart, she reminded herself as she trod downstairs to the breakfast parlor. Her heart had wanted much, much more than the marriage of convenience Sir James would have offered her. It had wanted joy, and excitement, and laughter. And above all, it had longed for love.

Straightening her shoulders, Serena entered the breakfast parlor, determined to face the prospect of becoming an ape-leader after all. The sight of Hawk, conversing animatedly with Cecily under the doting eye of Miss Higgenbotham, caused her to falter briefly. How many times had she imagined such a familial scene? she wondered. And Hawk had always been the center of these impossible dreams, as he was now the dominating presence at the breakfast table.

Brushing these intrusive thoughts aside, Serena murmured her greetings and took the chair the duke had risen to offer her.

"My dear Serena," Miss Higgenbotham said brightly, "I have mentioned the need for a new roof to His Grace, and he has undertaken to see to it personally."

"And Hawk has promised to take us to see the gypsy camp on the other side of Weybourne," Cecily cried, her eyes shining with excitement.

Serena glanced at her sister with no little exasperation. "I thought I had already forbidden you to go anywhere near the gypsies, Cecily," she said reprovingly. "And as for the roof"—she turned her accusing gaze to Miss Higgenbotham—"I am quite capable of dealing with that. In fact, I have already spoken to Mr. Hopkins in Sheringham about it, so there is no need to—"

"Oh, *do* please let us go, Serena," Cecily wheedled. "Surely there can be nothing to fear if Hawk escorts us."

"I have already made my wishes clear in that regard, Cecily," Serena responded calmly, "so do not be tiresome, child, I beg of you." She motioned to Billings to serve her tea and reached for a slice of toast.

"I am not a child," Cecily muttered darkly.

Miss Higgenbotham cleared her throat, and Serena sensed she was about to receive one of her homilies. "I distinctly recall your complaining that you knew nothing of repairing roofs, my dear Serena," the governess remarked diffidently. "I considered it a fortunate stroke of Fate that the duke arrived in time to take that burden from your shoulders, dear."

"I have since learned a great deal about roofs from Mr. Hopkins," Serena said coolly. "More, I daresay, than was strictly necessary to know. So while it is kind of you to offer your assistance, sir,"—she met his gray stare across the table—"I assure you there is no need to put yourself out over a mere roof."

This time it was the duke who muttered something inaudible, which Serena chose to ignore. She took a large bite of toast and averted her gaze. Her appetite seemed to have all but disappeared.

After an awkward silence, Hawk excused himself. "I would beg the favor of a few words with you after you have breakfasted, Miss Millbanks. I shall be in the library."

The prospect of enduring a private interview with Hawk deprived Serena of the last remnants of her appetite, and it was with some trepidation that fifteen minutes later, she knocked on the library door.

Hawk rose as soon as she stepped over the threshold and came striding toward her. He startled Serena by clasping both her hands and raising them to his lips, gazing down at her enigmatically as his mouth lingered over the caress. Then he smiled his disarming, crooked smile, and Serena felt a familiar rush of affection at the laughter in his eyes.

"Actually, I wished to invite you to stroll in the garden with me, my dear," he said huskily. "I have something of importance to discuss with you, Serena."

Strolling among the roses and sweet-smelling lilac bushes was the last thing Serena wished to do with Hawk. It was difficult enough to maintain a semblance of polite indifference when the rogue held her hands and smiled at her just so. Out in that romantical, sunlit setting, she feared her inhibitions would dissolve, and she would make a complete cake of herself. Had she not already done so during that memorable night by confessing her love for him? No doubt he had paid no heed to those mindless ramblings, but Serena was all too conscious of having revealed more than was wise of her secret yearnings to a man who could never be hers.

Numbly, she shook her head. "If it is the accounts you wish

to examine, sir," she said quickly, "the books are all here in the library, and I can show you—"

"The devil fly away with the accounts," Hawk answered brusquely. "I do not care a fig for them, love." He paused abruptly, and his voice gentled. "Tell me that you are not going to wed that Lockhart fellow, Serena."

The blunt question took her by surprise. Serena withdrew her hands from his grasp and turned away, her mind in a whirl. What possible interest could Hawk have in her future plans to wed or not to wed? she wondered, vaguely uneasy at his evident dislike of the baronet.

She walked over to the open window and gazed at the terraced rose beds off to the left, near the dilapidated summer house. The duke's question hung in the air around her, and the invigorating sea breeze blowing off the cliff did nothing to clear her mind.

"Well," she murmured desperately as the silence lengthened, "the sea air certainly agrees with me, the neighbors are cordial, and Sir James is exactly the kind of gentleman my dear Papa would have wished for me."

She heard Hawk utter a sound alarmingly like a growl as he came to stand behind her. Serena tensed, but he did not touch her.

"You have not answered my question. Are you going to wed him?"

Serena shuddered. This persistent interference in her private affairs was beginning to make her angry. What could it possibly matter to the Duke of Wolverton whom the lowly Miss Millbanks chose to wed?

"Sir James has yet to ask me," she admitted reluctantly. "And after your rudeness to him last night, I would not be surprised if he had thought better of it. I may yet live to lead apes, thanks to you," she added impulsively.

There was a short silence, which Hawk broke with another abrupt and—to Serena's mind—impertinent question.

"Do you love him?"

Serena whirled about to face him, and found herself far too close to his broad chest for comfort. She stepped back hastily and glared up at him. Love Sir James? she thought. How could she love another man when the very sight of Hawk set her pulse racing? When the nearness of him made her bones turn to jelly and a strange lassitude invade her senses? How could she love Sir James when this maddening man had stolen her heart and awakened her senses to a desire so intense Serena could barely restrain herself from casting herself into his arm without thought of the consequences? How could Hawk be so foolish as to believe that she was free to give her heart to another man?

"I fail to see what concern that could possibly be of yours," she replied icily. "How dare you question me on such a private matter?" she stormed, her anger increasing. "Do you hear me demanding to know if you have given your heart to Lady Maria Shelby? I tremble to think of the monumental set-down you would give me if I were guilty of such impertinence, yet you have the temerity to quiz me—"

"What do you know of Lady Maria?"

Surprised at the impatience of his tone, Serena strove for composure. "The news of your imminent betrothal is in all the newspapers, sir," she said coldly. "What else is there to know, pray?"

"A good deal, if I may say so," he observed. "Did you not know, for instance, that the chit is a mere schoolgirl and unbearably insipid?"

"And a great Beauty, I hear."

"Oh, yes, a Beauty all right." Hawk laughed unpleasantly. "And eminently suitable, or so my mother insists. But unable to carry on the most rudimentary conversation, and cursed with the unnerving habit of tittering at everything I say. The weather, the state of the crops, the latest production at Drury Lane—everything is greeted with a titter, until one must conclude that the chit has nothing in her head but—"

Serena unexpectedly found herself feeling sorry for the young lady who had inspired this scathing criticism. "Like as not, you have scared her out of her wits, Hawk," she suggested.

"The lady has no wits to scare, love. And I have no intention of leg-shackling myself to such a pathetic creature."

"The *Gazette* tells a different story."

The major shrugged impatiently. "Have you any idea what it is like to attempt a conversation with a female who refuses to look you straight in the eye, my dear? And when I raise my voice, she cringes. One would think I am a veritable ogre."

Serena laughed at this. "You often are, sir. Besides being odiously overbearing, you have a tendency to scowl when anyone gainsays you. I have cringed myself at times."

"Now that is a bouncer if ever I heard one," Hawk remarked, his eyes roving hungrily over her face until Serena felt her cheeks grow warm. "I do not recall that you showed the slightest hint of cringing that night on Lady Berkford's terrace. Do you, my love?"

"You were disgustingly foxed, sir. I am surprised you remember anything at all of that unpleasant scene."

"Unpleasant?" His voice dropped to a husky whisper that set off a riot of emotions in her breast. "Are you trying to pretend that you did not enjoy drawing my cork for me, love?" His gray eyes mocked her.

"Of course, I did," Serena responded without thinking. "You deserved it, too. You behaved like a beast."

His eyes were laughing openly at her now. "I wonder why my memories of that night differ so fundamentally from yours, my dear. I distinctly recall a kiss so sweet it took my breath away."

"Your memory is faulty, sir," Serena stammered, unable to suppress a surge of pleasure at this unexpected revelation. "I do not wish to be reminded of that evening."

"I cannot forget it," the duke said, and Serena noted that he was no longer laughing. After a short pause, he continued in a low voice, "You have not answered my question, Serena."

Serena did not need to be reminded of that awkward question. One that had nothing whatsoever to do with Lady Maria or that fateful encounter on Lady Berkford's terrace. But how could she confess that she felt no tender emotion for the man she had made up her mind to wed? And it did not help matters that Hawk appeared bent on dragging the confession out of her.

"A simple yes or no will suffice, love."

"There is nothing simple about any of this." Serena heard the note of hysteria in her voice and took a deep breath, wishing quite irrationally that Hawk would take her in his arms again and tell her that everything would be all right.

"I am well aware of that, my dear. But as my Aunt Bess would say, you must follow your heart, Serena."

He raised a hand as though he would touch her, but Serena flinched, and he let it drop. She could not allow him to do that, she told herself, even though her whole body craved it beyond rational thought.

"Really?" she said with forced asperity. "How very romantical of Lady Lexington. Unfortunately, there are some of us who cannot afford to be quite so whimsical, sir. I have Cecily's future to think of, and . . . and . . . so many other things," she finished lamely.

Hawk had moved away, but now he came to repossess himself of her hands. For the life of her, Serena could not find the strength to draw back.

"Then it is just as well that I took my aunt's advice myself," he said in a low voice. "In her infinite wisdom, Aunt Bess made me see that I was sacrificing my life on the altars of convention, much as you would do if you insist on this mad alliance with your baronet, Serena. She assured me—with her usual bluntness—that I should follow my heart."

The major raised her fingers to his lips, and his eyes were so full of tenderness that Serena felt the tightness of tears in her throat.

"Call me whimsical if you will, love, but that is the long and short of it. I finally decided to follow my heart and do what I should have done months ago."

Serena swallowed a lump that seemed to obstruct her vocal cords. Her wildly racing heart was ready to attach the most irrational of meanings to Hawk's words, but her mind fought to bring order to her chaotic emotions. She had meant it when she said she could not afford to be whimsical about the future. A comfortable, convenient marriage to Sir James held no special appeal for her, but she was not such a flat as to deny that such an arrangement would be infinitely preferable to accepting a less respectable offer from the Duke of Wolverton. And Hawk appeared to be working up to making her such an offer. She must brace herself against the insidious sweetness of his voice, and arm herself against the warmth in his eyes.

"Your heart must have seriously misled you if it brought you to Weybourne, Your Grace," she said with a coolness she did not feel. "I understand that Lady Maria resides somewhere in Dorset."

"The devil fly away with that chit!"

Hawk had raised his voice, and it suddenly occurred to Serena that the duke was almost as agitated as she was herself. This struck her as odd indeed. How much poise did it take for a gentleman of rank and fortune to offer *carte blanche* to a female of little beauty and no consequence whatsoever? she wondered. She could not believe that Hawk was a novice in the art of setting up ladybirds for his exclusive pleasure. If she did not know better, Serena might almost have imagined that the duke's intent was of a more serious and lasting nature. But this was her heart's nonsensical murmurings again; her head knew better than to hope for miracles.

Serena gritted her teeth and returned the compelling gray stare. As quickly as it had come, Hawk's anger dissipated and his eyes softened until Serena felt herself ready to melt in their mesmerizing warmth.

He pressed her hands against his chest, and Serena distinctly felt the pounding of his heart beneath the sober waistcoat. She must be strong, she thought distractedly, if she were to escape the fate of those other unfortunate females who had shared his bed on a temporary basis. If she listened to her heart . . . Serena took a deep breath. If she listened to her heart . . . She refused to consider what delights might be in store for her if she listened to her heart. Abruptly, she closed her eyes to shut out the temptation that was staring her so flagrantly in the face.

"Serena, my love," she heard him say in a husky, caressing voice, "I really do not know how to say this to you." He paused to clear his throat, and Serena braced herself for the worst. "You must know that I cannot live without you, my dear."

No, she thought miserably, she did not know any such thing. Serena wished she had the strength of mind to disengage her hands from his grasp, but the wild rhythm of his heart held her in thrall.

"Look at me, sweetheart."

She felt a tremor of panic run through her body. If she looked once more into the enticing warmth of Hawk's eyes, she would succumb to madness. She was sure of it. With her eyes closed, she might find the strength, somewhere in the rational corner of her mind, to deny him what he was about to ask of her. But if she opened them . . .

An insistent rapping of the door jerked Serena out of her trance, and she glanced round quickly as Hawk released her hands and strode over to the window, his back rigid with impatience.

The impassive face of Billings peered round the door. "Pardon me, miss. Sir James has arrived and is asking for you, miss. I have put him in the Blue Parlor."

The butler withdrew, leaving an uncomfortable silence behind him.

"It appears you are in high demand this morning, my dear," the duke remarked in a tightly controlled voice. "Do not let me keep you, Serena," he added, an edge of bitterness in his tone.

She should have been relieved, Serena told herself as she shut the library door behind her and drew a deep breath, to have avoided the impossible offer Hawk had been about to make. An offer Serena knew she could not—*should* not—accept.

Instead, she felt that her heart was breaking.

CHAPTER SIXTEEN

An Unsuitable Match

The sound of the library door closing behind Serena felt like a rifle report to Hawk's heightened senses. That dratted baronet had stolen a march on him after all, he thought, striding furiously about the room before flinging himself to the window to stare sightlessly out upon the sunlit garden.

His thoughts churned chaotically. Whatever had possessed him to waste time talking about his rival and the tittering chit his mother had chosen for him, when he should have seized the opportunity to fix his own interest with Serena? Why had his wretched tongue tied itself in knots when he needed so desperately to tell her how much he loved her? He had pictured the scene dozens of times during that long, cold ride up from London. But all he had been able to admit was that he could not live without her. This was true, of course, but he had planned to say so much more.

Hawk had planned to kiss her, too. He had needed quite desperately to kiss her, but inexplicably she had flinched, and he was suddenly unsure of himself. And of her. She had neither admitted nor denied loving the baronet. Could it be, Hawk wondered dully, that he had truly lost his Serena to another?

That prospect did not bear thinking of.

He heard the door open behind him and turned eagerly from the window. It was not Serena but Monroyal who sauntered in, a knowing smirk on his handsome face.

"Well, old chap, am I to wish you happy?"

Hawk grimaced and turned his back on the marquess. He had no stomach for his friend's caustic sense of humor this morning. Particularly since he had made such a mull of what had seemed a perfectly simple task. He had discovered that making an offer of marriage was not nearly as simple as he had, in his innocence, imagined.

"Ah!" the marquess murmured, strolling to the sideboard and serving himself a small sherry. "I see that you are still a free man, Hawk. An event to celebrate, my dear boy." He came to stand beside the duke at the window.

"Did she turn you down, lad?" His voice was unexpectedly gentle.

Surprised at his friend's lack of sarcasm, Hawk shook his head. "I have not yet had a chance to—"

"Never say you have failed to lay your cards on the table, Hawk. What kind of a sapskull are you? Billings tells me you have been closeted in here together for a good half hour. At the very least I expected you to make a push to win her when I made that wager, old man. Hardly sporting otherwise."

"Damn you and your bloody wager, Robert. Getting riveted is no sporting event, let me tell you."

The marquess raised an exquisite eyebrow and smiled gently. "Getting cold feet, are we? Well, I warned you not to entangle yourself with virgins, Hawk. Dashed skittish creatures. Never know what they will do next." He paused to glance out into the sunny garden. "Hey, I say, old man," he exclaimed suddenly, raising a jeweled quizzing glass to his eyes. "What have we here? Seems that our cautious suitor is about to hedge you out of the running."

Hawk swiveled around to follow the marquess's stare, and he swore under his breath at the sight of Sir James Lockhart escorting Miss Millbanks across the lawn toward the rose arbor. Serena's hand was tucked rather intimately in the crook of the baronet's arm, and she appeared to be hanging on his every word.

"Damn the bastard," he growled, watching with simmering fury as his rival clasped both Serena's hands and inclined his head, apparently engaged in serious conversation. And then Serena smiled up at the baronet, a sweet, spontaneous smile that twisted a knife in Hawk's heart. She was accepting him, he thought, unable to drag his eyes away from the scene unfolding before him.

"Lord, but the man is long-winded about it," the marquess murmured beside him. Hawk winced, but he had to admit that his friend only voiced his own hostile thoughts.

"I shall tear him limb from limb," he muttered viciously as the baronet suddenly placed both hands on Serena's shoulders and bent to kiss her. Although the embrace was admittedly brief and lacking in passion, Hawk felt as though his heart had been pierced by a French bayonet. Serena made no move to resist; in fact, Hawk could have sworn that she lifted her face to receive the baronet's kiss.

With a violent oath, Hawk swung away from the window and made directly for the sideboard. He grabbed a decanter and sloshed a generous amount of brandy into a glass, but before he could raise it to his lips, he heard Monroyal chuckle.

"The country suitor appears to have been routed, Hawk," he drawled in his lazy voice. "If my eyes do not mislead me, Sir James is quitting the field."

"Nonsense," Hawk responded savagely. "You saw him kiss her."

"Hardly a lover-like embrace, I would say."

"Damn you, Robert," Hawk repeated, and raised the glass, abruptly thought better of it, set it down again, and stalked out of the library.

Two minutes later, having taken the stairs two at a time, Hawk found himself in the formal drawing room in the East Wing, staring up at the portrait of his brother that still hung over the mantel there.

"Damned if I know what to do now, Derek," he muttered harshly. "I seemed to have been outflanked by a bloody no-body."

For several interminable minutes, Serena stood on the rose terrace staring at the broad shoulders of Sir James Lockhart retreating across the lawn. Then she took a deep breath and let it out slowly, relishing the illusion of weightlessness that spread through her limbs. One less uncomfortable scene to live through, she thought; one less painful decision to make. Sir James, bless his heart, had made it easy for her—perhaps for both of them—by his sudden decision to accompany his nephew Christopher to London. To make sure that the youngster got into no serious trouble, he had told her, although it did not take much wit to guess at the real reason for his departure.

Serena admired his tact and appreciated his thoughtfulness in bearing the news himself. After all, as yet nothing had been established between them, no promises made, and—Serena sincerely trusted—no hearts wounded. Of this latter point she was less sure, particularly when the baronet had startled her with that chaste kiss. But she did not begrudge it. There had been nothing lover-like about it, nothing at all like Hawk's bear hugs that left her breathless, trembling, and wanting more. Sir James had not even put his arms about her, and it was only at the last moment that Serena had realized what he was about. Impulsive as always, she had raised her face to him, mindless of prying eyes.

"I have wanted to do that for some time, my dear," he had said, in that serious way of his. And before she could recover her wits, he was gone, wishing her every possible happiness in her marriage. *Marriage?* she mused, her eyes following the tall figure disappearing round the corner of the house. The man must have lost his wits. What marriage could there be for Miss Millbanks if her cautious suitor took himself off to London?

Serena shook her head in puzzlement as she walked slowly back to the house. She shrugged off all thoughts of the baronet as she made her way to the library. A far more troubling scene awaited her there, she knew. And unlike the chivalrous Sir James, Hawk was not likely to take kindly to having his plans upset by a reluctant female. Steeling herself to resist temptation, Serena pushed open the door and stepped into the library.

"Oh! I beg your pardon, my lord," she gasped.

The Marquess of Monroyal turned from the window and met her startled gaze. His eyes, so like Hawk's in color, yet so different in every other way, regarded her with amusement.

"Do you make a practice of kissing gentlemen callers in the rose garden, my dear?" he drawled, sauntering over to raise her hand flirtatiously to his smiling lips. "I wonder if I might interest you in accompanying me for a stroll there?" he added, his voice dropping suggestively.

Serena jerked her hand away and wiped it on her skirt. "You are a heartless rogue, my lord," she chided. "Can you never be serious?"

"Serious? Now why would I wish to do anything so fatiguing?"

"Where is Hawk?" she asked bluntly, ignoring this facetious question. "I left him here a moment ago."

The marquess shook his dark head, his eyes mocking. "I imagine that after witnessing the shameless spectacle in the garden just now, Hawk rushed upstairs, presumably to put a bullet through his head."

Serena started at these words, then shook her head. "Rubbish! Hawk would not do anything so foolish."

Monroyal laughed shortly. "Heaven alone knows what he would do, Miss Millbanks," he murmured, moving to refill his glass at the sideboard. "Hawk is a changed man, my dear.

Crops and the weather have become his chief concerns of late, would you believe it? And *sheep*." The marquess's lips curled disdainfully. "He has never been the same since that memorable evening you stumbled into his life."

"He stumbled into *mine*, sir," she corrected him shortly. "I was leading a perfectly respectable and uneventful life before he chose to draw the censure of London down on my head with his reprehensible attentions."

"Then you had best go up and tell the poor devil you will not have him at any price, love," the marquess suggested with deplorable nonchalance. "I have a monkey riding on it, I should warn you."

Serena stared at him in horror. "You are a thoroughly callous and odious beast," she said in a quivering voice. "How can you wager on such things? Is nothing sacred to you?"

"Nothing that I can think of." He smiled—a little sadly, Serena thought—and winked at her. "But I do have a suggestion to offer, Serena. Listen to what Hawk has to say, my dear. The poor bastard is besotted. You have addled his wits, so be kind to him, love."

Serena felt her heart swell with anguish. "I cannot do so, my lord," she whispered, trying in vain to control her trembling lips. "He must know that I could never—"

"I fail to see why not," the marquess cut in impatiently. "He will not beat you, you know, and he has enough of the ready to satisfy the most extravagant kind of harpy. And in all fairness, I cannot accuse you of that, my dear," he murmured, casting a pained glance at her plain round morning gown in well-worn muslin.

Serena found herself deprived of speech by this artless recital. But what could she have expected from a man like the marquess? she told herself, a man notorious for his immoral liaisons with opera dancers and society matrons alike.

"You are thoroughly depraved even to suggest such a thing," she said icily, turning away abruptly. As she swept hastily out of the room, she heard Lord Monroyal's startled voice call out to her.

But Serena was past caring for the marquess's spurious advice. It would be difficult enough to resist Hawk's offer without listening to that devil expound on the advantages of illicit arrangements.

She fled up the stairs, knowing exactly where she would find the man who had turned her life upside-down.

*   *   *

Major Guy Hawkhurst stood before the empty hearth of the formal drawing room, staring up at the portrait of his brother.

Serena paused on the threshold, suddenly shy. His broad shoulders, rigid in the comfortable twilled woollen jacket, and his booted feet, set apart on the green figured rug, radiated aloofness. On the whole, Serena thought, regarding him nervously, Hawk had never seemed so remote and beyond her reach.

Gathering her courage, Serena moved across the carpet toward him, not quite sure how to flush out the man behind this cold facade. She opted for an apology.

"I must beg your forgiveness, my lord," she murmured, coming to a stop beside him and glancing up at the face she had once taken for his. "I should have removed the portrait months ago as you requested, but—"

"But you chose to defy me. Confess it, Miss Millbanks."

His voice was harsh, and he did not look at her. Serena regarded his profile wistfully, committing it to memory for the long years that lay ahead. Then she sighed.

"What a harridan you must think me. The truth is, I like to have Derek here. I come to talk to him occasionally. Unlike you, sir, he is never rude to me." And he reminds me of you, she added to herself. Small consolation of course, but better than nothing.

He looked at her then, and Serena had to turn away from the desolation in his gray eyes.

After an awkward pause, Hawk said in a dull voice, "I suppose I must wish you happy, Serena? I would much rather tear that rudesby of yours into little pieces and feed him to the dogs."

Serena could not repress a smile. "Luckily, Sir James is leaving for London this afternoon, so he will be quite beyond your reach."

"London?"

"Oh, yes," she said airily. "It appears that his nephew is in need of supervision during his stay there." She smiled at the puzzled expression on the duke's face.

"Are you telling me that the jackass has jilted you?"

This time Serena chuckled audibly. "Hardly that, sir. There was nothing official between us, you see."

Hawk swung round to face her then, his eyes wary. "And unofficial?"

Serena shook her head. "Not really. There might have been before . . ." She let the words falter and die. Marriage to Sir James no longer seemed possible. For the life of her, Serena could not understand why she had ever believed it might be.

Unfortunately, marriage to Hawk seemed even further removed from the realms of possibility. And any moment now, he would make her that other offer, the one she had sworn to refuse.

"Before I came back, love?" he said softly. "Is that what you were going to say?"

The sound of the endearment washed over her like a warm breeze, threatening her poise and seriously undermining her resolution to send Hawk on his way with a bug in his ear. She took a deep breath and let it out slowly.

"No," she replied, stretching the truth slightly. "I was about to say before I came to my senses. Sir James is a kind, decent man who deserves better than a female who cannot give him the comfort and affection he would expect in a wife."

"And how would you know what Lockhart expects in a wife, Serena? Did he provide you with a list of such requirements, by chance?"

Serena smiled at this notion. "Sir James is a country gentleman," she explained patiently. "And I understand country gentlemen very well, sir. I am the daughter of one, in case you had forgotten."

"I have forgotten nothing about you, Serena. *Nothing* at all," he repeated, his gray eyes fixed with fierce intensity on her face. "And let me remind you, my dear, that you understand me, too. You know *everything* about me. More than any other woman, I might add, including my mother." He paused for a moment, then continued in a husky voice that played havoc with Serena's resolution to reject him.

"I had hoped you would remember the night I shared my brother with you, Serena," he continued softly. "That night changed my life. I did not realize it at the time, but when I got back to Wolverton Abbey I saw things with different eyes. With Derek's eyes, perhaps, but most certainly with yours, Miss Millbanks."

The duke smiled down at her, and Serena felt her bones begin to melt and her knees grow weak. This interview was not going at all as she had imagined. Hawk had still not mentioned the purpose of his visit, and her resolve to stand firm against him was showing alarming signs of crumbling around her. Was she to be a fallen woman after all? she wondered, quite unable to drag her gaze from the warmth in Hawk's eyes.

"I am glad to hear that you have reformed your rakehell ways, sir," she managed to say in a stiff voice, determined to deflect the conversation from the subject of that night he had lain beside her on her bed upstairs.

"Reformed?" he exclaimed with a crack of laughter. "That is rather an understatement, love. I am much more than reformed, Serena. I am a new man. I have become—and I know you will find this hard to credit—as much a country gentleman as your cautious suitor, love. A man who is beginning to see why Derek spent so much time at the family seat, and what he meant when he told me I was not cut out to be a soldier." He paused again, and Serena saw the flash of pain in his eyes. "Derek was not a soldier either, of course, but it took his death to show me that he was right. My place was at the Abbey with him. Running away to the Army brought disaster on all of us."

Instinctively, Serena reached out to him, and he clasped her hands convulsively, drawing her closer. His gaze moved to the portrait of the late duke, and she knew by the grimace on his face that he was reliving the guilt and tragedy of that day at Vittoria. She searched her mind for the words to bring him back to her.

"If what you say is true, Derek would approve of you now, Hawk," she whispered gently, squeezing his hands, and was gratified when he looked down at her, his eyes strangely tender.

"It is true, Serena, and I have you to thank for that, my sweet," he murmured, raising her hands to his lips and pressing them there, the warmth of his mouth seeping through her senses like sweet wine.

Serena gulped. "You mean Derek do you not?"

"No, I mean *you,* love. Derek may have saved the Hawkhurst name from dishonor, but it was *you* who saved it from dissipation, Miss Millbanks. Saved the whole line of Hawkhursts from extinction, like as not." He paused, and his expression became serious. "And speaking of the Hawkhurst line, my dear, I am counting on you to help me preserve the family name at Wolverton for generations to come."

He grinned crookedly at her, and Serena felt her heart flip-flop at the implications of his words. He must be teasing, she told herself firmly. He had ever been a sad tease, and she had always relished that rapport between them. But what he spoke of now was no teasing matter. She tried to pull away, but her hands were caught fast.

"Perhaps you had best apply to Lady Maria Shelby for that onerous task," she suggested, attempting to match his light tone, while choking down the sob that rose in her throat.

"Impossible," he murmured, his breath warm on her fingers. "My Aunt Bess will not hear of it. Two simpering milk and water misses in one family goes beyond the pale, she says. And I agree with her, Serena."

The expression in his gray eyes suggested alternatives Serena would not allow herself to dwell upon. "Then, I am certain the duchess will be only too happy to chose a more suitable candidate—"

"I have already found a more suitable candidate," he interrupted, slipping an arm about her waist and drawing her against him. "It remains to be seen if she will have me, of course."

Serena drank in the heady masculine scent of him, her nose pressed deeply into the crisp folds of his cravat. Her nose had been there several times before, she recalled, closing her eyes to keep the happiness of the moment locked inside. And his arms had held her before, too. In just this comforting way, his hand traveling confidently up her spine to cradle her head, pressing her nose more deeply into the ruined cravat. Greedily, she drew the scent of him deep into her very being. Now if only he would kiss her, she thought dreamily, as he had so often in the past, her happiness would be complete.

No, it would not. She was daydreaming again.

Serena's eyes flew open, and she raised her gaze to Hawk's. There was something still unresolved here, she thought, straining to recall what it was he had just said.

"H-have you asked her?" she said, suddenly remembering.

Obviously taking her upturned face as an invitation, Hawk settled his lips firmly on hers. Serena knew that she should protest this intimacy, but the need to taste him overcame her modesty, and she opened her mouth. There would be plenty of time for regrets after he had gone off to marry this new candidate he spoke of, but for this precious moment he was all hers. She reached her arms up to pull him more firmly against her and heard him moan softly against her mouth. The way he responded to her eagerness reminded Serena of the night they had spent together on her bed. His mouth went wild, caressing, probing, demanding, and promising the sweet ecstasy she had yearned for and been so willing to give that unforgettable night.

Suddenly he lifted his head, his eyes twin gray pools of banked fire.

"No," he whispered huskily. "I am terrified she will not have me."

This appeared to Serena so patently absurd that she giggled nervously. "How silly you are, Guy," she said tenderly. "You have only to kiss the lady like this, and she will deny you nothing."

He grinned, a sly, satisfied gesture of triumph that set Serena's heart dancing chaotically. "So?" he murmured. "That is the secret, is it?"

His mouth came down again before Serena could gather her thoughts. And then there was nothing in her mind or heart except the man who held her and the hot kisses he pressed upon all parts of her within immediate range of his mouth.

Serena closed her eyes and gave herself up to pleasure, banishing all thoughts of the future from her mind. She could not have said how much time elapsed, five minutes? ten? an hour? perhaps an entire day? Eventually she became aware that the storm of passion had ceased and that Hawk was whispering in her ear.

"And will you deny me anything, my sweet Serena?"

The words were spoken so softly that Serena had to strain to catch them. The answer came unhesitatingly to her lips before she had time to consider the consequences.

"Oh, no," she breathed, her entire body tingling with desire.

He grinned and kissed her briskly on the mouth. "Then it is all settled, my pet. You will come with me to Wolverton?"

Serena stared at him blankly, wondering if she had heard aright.

"Wolverton?" she echoed, uncertain whether to laugh or cry. "Wolverton Abbey? Do not tease me, Guy."

"Yes, love, Wolverton Abbey. I want to take you home with me, Serena. Aunt Bess told me to follow my heart, remember? Well, I finally took her advice, and it led me here to you. Aunt Bess approves of you, sweetheart, and Derek would have approved of you, too. You would have liked him, Serena. You are two of a kind. And I shall need you with me if I am to make a go at running Wolverton."

Serena shook her head to clear her muddled thoughts. "You are not making any sense, Guy," she pointed out weakly.

"There is no way I can accompany you to Wolverton. Your mother would have a fit of the vapors."

"We shall move her into the Dower House, love," he replied briskly. "I have already had the forethought to refurbish it."

The floor seemed to sway alarmingly beneath her feet, but Serena was determined to make some sense out of this Banbury tale Hawk was spinning.

"You wish me to remove to Wolverton?"

The major looked at her as though she were exceptionally dull-witted and tweaked her nose playfully. "I had hoped you would wish to, Serena," he said with a smile. "After all, you have just accepted my offer of marriage, you know, and it is customary for husband and wife to—"

"Offer of marriage?" Her voice rose in alarm. "I did not hear any such thing, sir."

"Then you could not have been listening very carefully," he remarked with maddening assurance. "I distinctly heard you promise not to deny me anything, love."

Serena glared at him. "There was no mention of marriage," she said stubbornly.

His grin was devilish, and Serena felt herself blush as she anticipated his next words. "Then perhaps you will explain to me exactly what it was you promised not to deny me, love."

Serena tried to wrest herself out of his grasp, but he only held her more tightly against him. "Ah, I see," he murmured, his voice full of amusement and a tenderness she had only dreamed of hearing in it. "You are a naughty minx, love, but you may be sure I shall do my best to accommodate you as soon as possible."

"But this will never *work,* Hawk," Serena wailed, her nose once again buried in his much-abused cravat.

He chuckled deep in his throat. "I think it will, dearest. I have a pretty good grasp of the fundamentals, you know."

Serena's head shot up and she glared at him, her cheeks pink. "That is not what I meant, and you know it, you wicked rogue."

He laughed at her, his eyes dancing with genuine amusement. "Then tell me you will come to Wolverton with me and hold my hand when things go wrong, as I fear they will, for my knowledge of crops and sheep is pitifully meager. Did you know that I have over two thousand of the woolly monsters, love? And you would not credit how stupid they can be. They are overrunning the place."

Serena smiled, her heart suddenly full beyond bearing.

"Oh, I know all about sheep. They require a firm hand and a couple of good dogs. We shall take Jollyboy with us, Guy. He used to take care of Papa's flock before it was sold off."

"Then you will come?"

Of course she would come, Serena thought, watching the shadow of doubt lingering in the duke's eyes. Wild horses could not keep her from going with Hawk to the ends of the earth. But she must try to curb this mad enthusiasm and behave like a lady.

"As a sheep herder, sir?" she inquired with a moue of disapproval.

Hawk reached for her again, and Serena thought her ribs would crack.

"As my wife, you silly goose," he murmured in her ear.

"Wife?" she managed to mumble through the folds of his cravat. "I have yet to hear that offer, sir."

"Miss Millbanks," Hawk said, holding her at arm's length and laughing into her eyes, "will you marry a poor country gentleman who knows very little about sheep, but who is willing to learn? With your assistance, sweetheart, and Jollyboy's, too, of course."

Serena gazed in wonder at the face of the man who had stumbled into her orbit on a dimly lit terrace a few short months ago, who had accompanied her across half of England, opened his heart to her and stolen hers, and then abandoned her life as abruptly as he had come into it.

"Why did you leave me that night, Guy?" she whispered, quite ignoring his proposal.

His expression became serious, and he leaned forward to kiss the tip of her nose. "Because I realized that you meant more to me than that, Serena. I think it frightened me to hear you say you loved me. It seemed such an enormous responsibility—the love of a woman like you. So I did what I do best, love. I ran away rather than face the truth."

His grin was crooked and brought tears to her eyes.

"But you came back."

"The thought of losing you was even more frightening. I had already lost Derek through my own stupidity; I could not bear to lose you, too, love."

Serena heard him draw a deep, shuddering breath and reached up to cradle his face with her hands.

"You have not lost me, Guy," she whispered, touched beyond words at this confession. "And I will go with you to Wolverton." She smiled shyly up at him. "As your wife, my love. And you will help me find a decent husband for Cecily when the time comes. We will take Jollyboy to help us with the sheep, and Miss Higgenbotham to help us with . . ." She hesitated, suddenly unable to mention that Higgy would be wonderful for their children. "Well, she is bound to be handy for any number of things," she concluded hastily, well aware, from his wicked grin, that Hawk had guessed at the tasks in store for Miss Higgenbotham.

She blushed vividly and was about to pull Hawk's head down for another kiss when she heard a knock on the door.

The Marquess of Monroyal put his head into the room and glanced around curiously. "From that silly grin on your face, Hawk, and Serena's blushes, I gather I have lost another wager." He sauntered toward them, quizzing glass at the ready. "Congratulations are in order, I presume?"

"Indeed they are," Hawk murmured, his arm tightening around Serena's waist, his eyes overflowing with love. "And do close the door on your way out, there's a good fellow."

Serena never did hear the door close behind the marquess. She was completely absorbed in kissing the besotted grin from the Duke of Wolverton's face.